EVERY
HAPPY FAMILY

EVERY
HAPPY FAMILY

DEDE CRANE

COTEAU BOOKS

Edited by Sandra Birdsell
Designed by Tania Craan
Typeset by Susan Buck
Printed and bound in Canada at Imprimerie Gauvin

Library and Archives Canada Cataloguing in Publication

Crane, Dede
     Every happy family / Dede Crane.

Issued also in electronic formats.

ISBN 978-1-55050-548-1
     I. Title.
PS8605.R35E94 2013   C813'.6   C2012-908203-1

     Every happy family [electronic resource] / Dede Crane.

Electronic monograph.

Issued also in print format.

ISBN 978-1-55050-738-6 (EPUB).--ISBN 978-1-55050-549-8 (PDF).--ISBN 978-1-55050-739-3 (MOBI)
     I. Title.
PS8605.R35E94 2013   C813'.6   C2012-908204-X

COTEAU
BOOKS

2517 Victoria Avenue
Regina, Saskatchewan
Canada   S4P 0T2
www.coteaubooks.com

Available in Canada from:
Publishers Group Canada
2440 Viking Way
Richmond, British Columbia
Canada   V6V 1N2

10 9 8 7 6 5 4 3 2 1

Coteau Books gratefully acknowledges the financial support of its publishing program by: The Saskatchewan Arts Board, including the Creative Industry Growth and Sustainability Program of the Government of Saskatchewan via the Ministry of Parks, Culture and Sport; the Canada Council for the Arts; the Government of Canada through the Canada Book Fund; and the City of Regina Arts Commission.

PARTS

· · · · · · · ·

It took place over the course of five years...
a slow unraveling of life in the weave she recognized
and at times believed she herself had woven.
It began in early April, 2006, with young and old alike.

•••••••••••••••••••••

JILL

·······

The smallest construction of sound is helplessly built around silence. One cannot exist without the other. She likes his use of the word helplessly. *Similarly every sound can only exist if heard, and hearing only exists when there's sound. Because every experience must occur within relationship, if a tree falls in a forest and no ears are there to hear it, it has not made any sound.*

It's Sunday morning and, the only one up on at this hour, she has made coffee, wandered to the kitchen table and scanned the opening line of the student essay on top of the pile. Now she steps up to the French doors looking out on the back patio and yard beyond to search for the two ducks that have recently taken up residence. Their woody colours blend in so well it's like hunting objects hidden in a drawing. There. Sleeping a foot apart among the brittle fountains of last year's annuals, beaks buried under wings, the two smooth oval presences bring the yard into focus, give it new purpose, as the kids are past playing within its confines. She sips her coffee, traces its thread of warmth down her throat. The morning's quiet is intoxicating, and for a suspended moment she is nobody's wife, daughter, mother, sister, teacher, colleague, and the tension that by the end of each day girds the muscles of her neck doesn't exist. She imagines a sleeping duck tucked into the crook of her neck like a downy headrest, warm as a hot water bottle, the soothing vibration of a live creature. Make that one fat duck on either side.

She steps sideways to get a better view of them and something crunches under her slipper. Popcorn like a game of jacks is scattered on the floor behind the couch that separates the kitchen from the family room. Jill's focus shrinks to the kids' dirty mugs of hot chocolate on the coffee table, the smudged water glasses, greasy bowl, the bag of marshmallows left open and growing stale. Les's precious cooking knives laid out on the island — including an expensive new cleaver, though she didn't know what was wrong with the old one — all waiting to be sharpened and transferred to their leather holder that his sister, Annie, made out of repurposed bomber jackets. The empty milk carton on the counter, a trail of chocolate powder, greasy saucepan. The kitchen is spotless when she goes to bed and, as if she's only dreamed it, messy the next morning.

It's her fault, she spoils the kids, wants them to believe that the goodness in their lives — cleanliness, meals, paid electric bills, hot water — happens effortlessly, magically, so they can be carefree as long as possible. But that sort of love has its breaking point, she thinks, hit by a swell of weariness as the day's tasks unfurl before her: wash towels and sheets, return Pema's backpack with the broken zipper for a new one, mark a half-dozen essays, nail down the title for her paper. And Les works this afternoon, which means she has to drive to and from Beau's rugby game and somehow figure out dinner. Reduced to a checklist, the day is now something to conquer, and because she never does anything halfway, conquer well.

Jill takes a bracing sip of coffee and glances at the stove clock. Two minutes past eight. Every Sunday morning she is someone's daughter, and she pictures her mother planted beside her phone growing a shade desperate. She sweeps up the popcorn and piles the dirty dishes into the sink so at least the counters are clear. Presses number one on her speed-dial, looking forward to today's conversation because she can use some motherly advice about the letter which is right now burning a hole in her underwear drawer. She hasn't told Les about it, not yet, because she knows just how he'll react. The phone on the other end rings only once.

"Hello?" Her mother sounds wide-eyed, as if she can't imagine who's calling.

"Hi, Mom. It's me."

Jill's mother, Nancy, seventy-nine, lives across the strait in North Vancouver in the family home still, despite Jill's gentle suggestions it might be time for a change — a condo near the seniors' centre and with no garden to maintain.

"Jillian. How's your weather on the Island? It's been overcast here all week. It's like living one's life behind a veil."

Jill sees the drake lift his head, its rainbow-slick feathers catching and bending the light.

"The fog fills the inlet and rises up and up…"

His neck does a one-eighty as he aims his beak at his sleeping mate and looks miffed she's not awake.

"Even with your dad's binoculars the mountains are difficult to…"

With a shudder — of annoyance? — he burrows his head back under a wing.

"…but it's supposed to lift by this afternoon," finishes Nancy, punching the word noon just like that irritating weatherwoman on the late news.

As Jill understands there's been a pause she failed to fill, her mother asks, "And how's your work, dear?"

An itinerant linguistics scholar, Jill lives on Vancouver Island, in Victoria. Her mother used to ferry over once a month and stay for the weekend but had to give up her driver's license as a result of floaters and bicycles, among other distractions.

"Great. Fine." In bygone times she would have included her mother in choosing the title of her paper.

"So all's well with the family?"

"We're hanging in there," says Jill on a sigh, having never gotten past wanting a little sympathy from her mother. "Beau broke his thumb in a game. I was in the middle of a class when I got the call. Had to drop everything and drive him to the hospital."

"Beau?"

"Playing his rugby. They set the bone in a splint. They don't cast thumbs, and it should be fine if he doesn't re-injure it. The doctor said he'd have to sit out the rest of the season."

"I remember your brother chasing you around the backyard," says Nancy, and Jill, all too familiar with the story, chimes along in her head, "*with the wicker basket*, which he put over your face and you fell and *broke your arm*. You were —"

"Twelve. I was twelve," Jill says to hurry things along, "Kenneth, ten and he —"

"Was *big for his age* and didn't understand *his own strength*."

What is it with older people and their repetition? As Nancy keeps talking, Jill checks her impatience, focuses instead on the quality of her mother's voice. She always tells her first-years that it was her mother who inspired her love of language because of the way she told bedtime stories, with a hushed deliberation, the kind of shy song that forced a child to quiet her thoughts in order to listen. It was a technique Nancy had learned as a grade three teacher, and Jill used to have to punch up the volume on the phone to hear her properly. Now, sadly, she doesn't bother.

"…broke my collarbone twice, once as a child falling out of the grand oak in our backyard, *the finest climbing tree in the neighbourhood*. And again when you and Kenneth were in high school, *catching your clumsy father* when he stumbled down the front steps."

"He was clumsy all right," says Jill, aware of repeating herself now. Her mother's memories of Dad, seven years dead, have airbrushed out his drinking, his passive violence.

"And how are the boys?" says Nancy.

"Les managed to find Quinn a job at his new restaurant. As a line cook."

"In that nice restaurant with the water running down the walls?"

"No, that place didn't make it. Closed in November. Did I not tell you?" She might have been too upset about it at the time, because as second chef Les was finally making a decent wage. They had almost paid off their line of credit.

"I worry that you work too hard."

"I'm okay, Mom," says Jill, smiling to hear her say it. "It took a while but he's found another job. And hey, one of the profs is retiring next year. If I get one more paper published I should have a shot." She's been a long-term sessional in the department for ten years now, but knows that having received her doctorate from this same university is a count against her.

"Should have a shot," echoes Nancy.

"We'll see. Hey, I persuaded Quinn to apply to the university's new architecture program. He's too arty to settle for engineering. And with his math grades, he won't have any problems getting accepted or," – she lowers her voice – "winning the entrance scholarship I applied for on his behalf. With his kind of focus, that kid will be exceptional at anything he does. By the way, the scholarship is between you and me. He's not good with rejection."

"Between you and me."

"Were you able to open those pictures I sent? Of his New Year's grad?" It was the first high-school dance their shy son had attended. Jill and Les figured it was because he finally had a girlfriend to go with.

"Pictures?"

"That I sent to your email?" To make up for Jill not visiting as often as Nancy would like, Jill had given Nancy her old laptop with the notion of Skyping together and emailing family photos.

"Why don't you put them in the mail. I can't get that machine to work. I may be getting interference from my tenants."

With some persuading, Nancy converted her downstairs into an apartment, then Jill found a gay couple to move in, knowing men downstairs would make Nancy feel safer. She'd bargained the cost of utilities in exchange for taking responsibility of the garden.

"I told you it doesn't work that way, Mom. Your tenants are both computer programmers you know. You might ask them to help you."

"I don't like to bother them," says Nancy, and Jill knows what's coming. *"It's not like they're family."*

She refuses to feel guilty. "Do you want me to ask them?"

"No, no. I'll wait for you. When are you coming?"

"Mom, I can't possibly visit until end of term and after my marks are in and my paper's thesis nailed down. So, first of June hopefully."

"Oh." Nancy sounds hurt.

Please don't do that, thinks Jill.

"The doctor has changed my thyroid prescription," says Nancy. "Those are the little blue pills."

She hates her working title, "Occitan's Morphemic Influence on the Romance Languages." It lacks the rhythmic accents she's looking for, though it's better than the childish beats of her first one, "The Fall of Langue D'Occ and Rise of Langue D'Oui."

"And now my legs are less crampy in the morning."

She could mix affirmative and negative, "Langue d' Occ, The Dying Language of Yes." She grabs a pen to write that down.

"Do you remember John Early?" asks Nancy, suddenly animated.

"John Early?" Jill prints the title, holds the page up to see how it looks.

"His wife, who died some time ago, worked for your father, and we used to have dinners together."

"I'm sorry?"

"John and Katie Early used to have us over for dinner. Their home was over on, what was the name of that street..."

There's a flurry of activity in the yard; the drake is chasing after the female. He looks furious. A mating ritual, or something Mrs. Duck said?

"Anyway, John's undergone an operation," Nancy says. "Today. Yes, today. Nothing major. His gallbladder."

"Dad had his gallbladder out."

"Yes, and remember how he couldn't lift anything and we waited on him hand and foot?"

"You waited on him hand and foot." The drake flaps and bounces on the female's back, his beak stabbing at her neck. The brutality lasts about four seconds before he hops off, takes a few drunken steps and then straightens out.

"John's house has stairs, which make things difficult, and he shouldn't be home alone after his operation."

"Sooo..." The female duck waddles towards the pan of water Jill put out yesterday. Fucked duck, she thinks and covers the mouthpiece of the phone. "Fucked duck," she says aloud, enjoying the back-to-back bump of the letters D and the see-saw play of the tongue. "Fucked duck."

"So I've invited him to stay here."

"What's that?"

"I've invited him to stay here."

Jill eases up the volume on the phone. "John?"

"Early."

"Mom, are you serious?"

There's a pause and then Nancy says, "Yes."

"You can't be taking care of him. You're not up to being someone's —"

"I can make him toast when I make mine," she says. "Two cups of tea instead of one, talk to him, play a game of cards. He'll have a nurse come check on him. He's on the Meals on Wheels plan like me, and I've arranged for his meals to be delivered here with mine."

When did she arrange all this? "Are you still afraid of being alone?" Last fall there'd been a robbery in the neighbourhood, that, at the time, was all her mother could talk about.

"I did tell you there was a break-in. That ghastly purple house around the corner. With the beige deck."

"Don't you think it's time to sell, Mom? You could get a condo over here on the Island."

"I want to *die with my view* and my garden. Condos don't have any *cross-ventilation*."

"How long is this John fellow planning to stay?"

"John Early? We're going to take it day by day."

"Whose idea was this?" She knows what a pushover her mother can be.

"Mine. In fact, I insisted."

She only hopes it's true. "So it's a temporary arrangement?"

"Yes."

"Good. But really, Mom, having a sick person around?"

"It'll be nice having company."

Jill holds her tongue and sips her coffee.

"John has a computer too and can help me out with my problem."

Out of curiosity she has to ask, "Have you, or does he, I mean are you interested in each other in any romantic sort of way?"

Nancy lets go a flutter of a laugh. "Oh, not any more, Jilli. I'm too old for that nonsense."

Any more? She imagines her young, fine-boned mother flirting across the table over Mrs. Early's roast chicken and Hawaiian salad, Dad too drunk to notice. "So when's he coming?"

"He's spending tonight in the hospital, for good measure, and will be dropped off here tomorrow."

"Dropped off by?"

"Taxicab. His children are spread out across the globe. One lives in Kalamazoo, one in Timbuktu."

Jill laughs. "That was funny, Mom." Nancy isn't laughing. "Where do they really live?"

"I'm going to put him in your room downstairs, if you don't mind terribly."

"My room's upstairs."

"I mean upstairs."

Kenneth's former bedroom, testament to his baseball glories, was downstairs. Most of it is in boxes in Jill's garage.

"I have trouble envisioning an older man sleeping in my room," she says, picturing the white-painted furniture and eyelet sheets, Nancy's sentimental arrangement of dolls and favourite books. "But go ahead, it's *your* house." She emphasizes the *your* because she knows what's coming.

"It's your house too."

Kenneth hasn't been home since their father's funeral. Calls Nancy on her birthday and at Christmas. "Men," the department secretary said after Jill vented about her brother's lack of help. "They get looked after. Women do the looking." Her cheerful resignation pissed Jill off. Will Pema stick around when she needs looking after? The letter came in a brown, wrinkled envelope, the address painstakingly printed and the ink smudged on one side. An exotic mess of stamps fills one corner. She feels the base of her neck tighten. It's not like Pema even remembers her birth mother.

"I'm glad you'll have company, Mom, but please, don't wear yourself out."

"I sure miss Lucy. It must have been terrible for her."

"Look, I need to go but I'll call you next Sunday." Jill's sorry but she can't hear again how her mother's best friend collapsed in the bathroom, no one finding her until the following evening.

"Okay, Jillian dear. Goodbye till then."

"But do call, Mom, if you need to," Jill adds, though she knows Nancy never would, for fear of *interrupting*. "I'll call you next week."

"I'm pleased about John Early coming," Nancy says as if to herself.

Jill hangs up. Something else to worry about. Didn't even get a chance to bring up the letter. She hears the creak of a door upstairs and thinks she should make Pema and Beau do their own dishes for a change. Then imagines the excuses, the procrastination over whose turn it is, their need to eat breakfast first, which'll mean more dirty dishes. She pulls on her rubber gloves.

•••

Sunday morning and heavy rain blurs the backyard. Jill didn't sleep well last night and arranges the pillows on the couch in the family room in order to lie down before calling her mom. Her hand hits something hard wedged between the seat cushions and she draws up an empty mickey of vodka. For a moment, she's sixteen, on a bottle hunt, out to prove her mother's ignorance. She'd found three: one in his workshop, one in the hall closet, one in the trunk of the car.

Quinn had Lauren over last night, and when she and Les came home from the movie, she thought he was unusually talkative and looked a little...stupid. All teens experiment with booze, she tells herself; it's the sneaking around she can't, won't, tolerate. She gets up and places the bottle on the mantel where he'll see it. So they can talk about it.

"Vodka," she says into the quiet. "Vodka." Two hard double consonants followed by the open, feminine *ah*, like a cough of frozen air. The name sounds like a toast to Slavic health. "Wodka!" She'd like to know who bought it for him. Remind him he's an example to his brother and sister. And that, while his brain's still developing, it's just not smart to drink too much.

She stands at the picture window in the family room, dials her mother's number. The line rings twice before Nancy picks up.

"Mom, hi."

"Jillian, dear. Hello."

"How's your week been? You taking your pills?" Besides her thyroid issue and an arthritic hip, Nancy is borderline diabetic.

"I fill up my days-of-the-week container each Sunday after your call."

What happens if I don't call? "So how's it going with John?" she asks, though she wants to skip right to the letter and get Nancy's advice on how to respond. She pushes up the volume on the phone.

"Jillian, it couldn't be more pleasant having him around. He was up and moving after two days. But then he's still nice and trim. Your father had that stomach of his. I never understood how *something made of fat* could be *hard as a clenched fist*."

"I know."

"He built a little cage for my planters, out of chicken wire and black plastic bags." Four flower boxes on benches are the extent of her mother's gardening now.

"Like you saw on that show," Jill says, feeling sheepish because last spring Nancy asked if Les might be able to devise such a thing, and she'd forgotten to mention it to him.

"We planted kale seeds in one planter. He has this wonderful recipe for winter kale apple soup."

"But you used to make that."

"Oh? It was John's recipe. His wife's."

"It was good soup."

"Extremely good, yes. Very good soup. And nutritious."

"So, if John's building things, it sounds like he's recovered then?"

"But his house has stairs and he uses a cane. Though he says, and I agree, that moving to a walker is a slippery slope to a scooter."

Jill heard that very remark on *The Daily Show* the other night. The scoundrel is stealing Stewart's jokes.

"This morning my throat's sore from singing."

"Singing?" Jill looks at the phone in her hand.

"John plays the piano. Gershwin, Rogers and Hammerstein, all the old show tunes."

Her mother had a quiet but pretty singing voice from what Jill can remember. She gets a small thrill thinking of her singing. "Sounds like a regular party over there."

"We did have a little wine with our dinner."

"Mom, since when do you drink wine?" She's surprised by her scolding tone. Her mother usually celebrates with an extra cup or two of coffee.

"Never too late to start."

"John's a drinker then?" she has to ask.

"No. No. Just one glass. Helps the aches and pains."

Jill waits for the usual questions about the kids, but they don't come. "Mom, I need to talk about some —"

"We began the day with a game of rummy. We've been playing all week, a penny a point."

"You and Dad used to do that."

"Yes. And then we took a hobble up and down the block. I enjoy going to visit Dixie, that cat I told you about, in the Bergman's old house?"

"The white cat?"

"Dixie. Long hair. A handsome thing but he's been in for a shave. His skin under all that white fur is a lovely pink. Looks like a pink and white poodle. I had such a laugh. John too."

"Where's John now?"

"He's where... out on the patio, putting a clever handle on those cages to make them easy to lift."

"A regular handyman."

"So how are things there?" Nancy asks, sounding almost smug.

"We're all fighting some stomach bug." It's been a wretched week. Rainy and cold, everyone off their food, her classes flat, Quinn almost getting himself fired after singeing off his eyebrows — too much rum on a flaming goat cheese appetizer. He looks like a startled baby.

"Drink ginger tea," says Nancy.

"Yes, we will. But I wanted to talk to you about Pema who, by the way, has decided to go with Katie and family to their place in the interior this summer."

"That sounds good."

"Her first time away. Nearly six weeks. I was going to get her a summer tutor — she still struggles with basic math concepts — but I think the independence will be good for her. Beau'll miss her. Like twins, those two. Anyway, I got this crazy letter in the mail."

"You've had lots of rain," says Nancy.

"We have." Why is she changing the subject?

"We had a thunderstorm," Nancy adds, quietly.

"You hate thunderstorms."

"This one she didn't hate."

Jill laughs.

"John took her by the hand and made her sit with him on the deck."

"Mom, you're speaking in third person."

"He told her that lightning opens the sky to give us a glimpse of heaven."

"He held your hand?" says Jill.

"He did."

"He sounds too good to be true."

"He is a good man, Jilli."

Jill stops. That's the line she used whenever Jill was angry at her failure of a father and feeling, somehow, that her mother was to blame.

"And I need to go, it's tea time."

Nancy has never been the one to terminate their Sunday call. "At eight in the morning?"

Nancy doesn't respond.

"Okay, Mom."

"Bye, Jillian." Nancy hangs up with a noisy clatter and Jill can't help feeling jealous. Who is this guy stealing her mother's attention?

She hears Beau's lead-footed trek from bedroom to bathroom and recalls the word he came up with at last night's dinner when she brought up Grammy's new housemate: "Geriaction."

•••

Jill sits at the kitchen table with her coffee and computer determined, after she calls her mom, to buckle down and work on her paper. Movement in the yard makes her look up to see the ducks pecking at the grass, as if drinking the previous night's rain. This morning feels like peace, she thinks, after last night's loud, giddy sleepover. Four grade nine girls, glitter in their teased-up hair, trying to master the choreography off some misogynist rap video. Clumsy and innocent on the one hand, on the other, their sexy moves to words like 'bitch slap' were disturbing. At one point Pema dragged Beau in to watch. It's like feminism never happened. She gave them a quick lecture on the power of language, which effectively shut it down, though that wasn't her objective. Awareness was her objective.

She calls her mother's number.

"Hello?"

"Mom, hi. How are you?"

"Oh, it's you Jillian."

And she was expecting? "What's new?"

"Well, lots, if you must know."

What, is she prying now?

"But first, how are you and everyone there?"

"That stomach flu's gone."

"Ginger tea."

"Yes. That helped," she lies.

"And?"

"Your contrary grandson, Beau, is playing rugby despite

the doctor's orders and won't listen to me. Has a lot of pride, that kid."

"A lot of pride."

"Oh and Pema" — she lowers her voice — "had her period."

"Had what?"

"Her period. Finally." The oldest in her group of friends because she refused to start school without Beau, Pema was, nevertheless, the last to have her period. "I think she's happy. Played it cool though. I tried to research Tibetan traditions around first menstruation but came up empty and took her out for high tea at the Empress, invited Auntie Annie along." Annie was invited because Jill finds herself uneasy when alone with Pema, their conversation a little forced. "So it was just us girls. We even got dressed up. That was Annie's idea. The tea is something Pema always wanted to do and, though it's overpriced, I wanted things to be celebratory. Undermine any notions of it being a curse." Afterwards, Jill had considered telling Pema about the letter, had even brought it with her in the car, but then decided it would be mixing messages. "We had a good time."

"That's nice, dear," says Nancy flatly, and Jill wonders if she's offended her. Nancy had been morose when Jill hit puberty. It was just a matter of time, she'd said, and then she gave instructions on how to hide all evidence from her father and brother.

"So was John able to open those pictures I emailed?"

"Pictures?"

"Of Quinn and his girlfriend? New Year's grad."

"Yes, yes. Very nice. Quinn looks very handsome and also his girl."

"Lauren."

"Lauren."

"I've always liked that name. It has a tough elegance. You

liked his pink tie?"

"I liked his pink tie."

"A little gangster-looking against the black shirt, but that's what's in. Speaking of Quinn, I don't think I told you how he almost got fired."

"Do you remember Lyle Jarvis?" says Nancy. "He lived in the powder-blue house beside Cates Park. He had a daughter, you know her, Meredith or Marilyn, she went to your school in Deep —"

"Yes," Jill says just to stop her. It's her turn to be offended.

"Well, his wife died and he didn't want the upkeep of a house and garden and he moved into an associated living complex."

"Assisted living."

"That's right. It's up on the hill beside Parkland."

"Parkgate."

"Where he had his meals taken care of. They also provided a hot tub and jazzuci that he appreciated for his back."

"It's Jacuzzi, Mom," says Jill, laughing. "Have you had your morning coffee?"

"So I've suggested he move in here."

"Come again?"

"Lyle. I've suggested he move in here."

"Move in?"

"It's been such a pleasure having John, so I thought why not."

"What, is John still there?"

"John's still here."

"I thought you said it was temporary."

"Lyle lost half his pension in the economic downgrade. Just poof, gone."

"Downturn. You said it was a tempor —"

"He can no longer afford all that pampering."

It's as though Nancy can't hear her.

"John can take over your room and Lyle can have Kenneth's."

"Kenneth no longer has a room."

"I mean the den."

"This is happening way too fast, Mom."

"What's too fast about it?"

"Well, where do I stay when I come over?" As soon as Jill says it she's ashamed. She's there maybe ten days a year, nine, some of those a mere sleepover convenience after a conference.

"You can sleep in with me."

She hears a quack, sees the ducks flutter then waddle off under the rhododendron. A squirrel, tail twitching, is perched on the compost bin.

"We'll pool our money," her mother continues.

"Money?"

"For groceries, the maid and a nurse when we need one. We will need help some day. Three oldies are better than one. Though if we had a fourth we could have our own bridge club."

"You're turning the house into an old folks' home."

"I am?" She sounds happily defiant. Jill's not used to her mother sounding defiant.

She'll ask Les what he thinks. Though he was all for John being there. What's wrong, he said, with two old lonelies shacking up? Said it would take the pressure off her.

"I'm coming over. Next weekend. No, wait, Beau has a tournament."

"You're busy."

"I want to meet these new men in your life."

"Men in my life," says Nancy with a giggle. "I should go, Jillian. John wants me."

"Okay, bye then," says Jill, and Nancy just hangs up.

Jill turns off the phone, stares at the squirrel digging in her neglected garden. It can't be sexual, can it?

She pulls out a bowl to make pancakes for the gaggle of girls when they wake. Two frying pans or one? Her Tibetan daughter will put away three big ones easily. Her friend Bess at least four.

•••

It's Sunday morning and Jill calls her mother's number, scans the backyard without thinking and then remembers that the ducks are gone. Thursday morning was the last sighting, and she misses their effortless company. Four rings. Six. Where the hell could she be? Jill hangs up and tries again. Nancy answers on the fourth ring.

"Hi Mom, what took you so long?"

"Oh, Jillian, I was in the bathroom and didn't hear the phone."

"And your housemate? A little deaf?"

"I think they still think of it as my house."

"They?"

"Yes. John and Kyle, dear."

"You mean Lyle?"

"Yes, Lyle's here. With John. How's everything where you are?"

"Fine. We're fine." Jill's given up on trying to talk to her mom about the letter from Nepal or telling her the story of Quinn's flaming cheese incident. "What did they do with their belongings? John owns a house, right?"

"He put it on the market and it sold in a day."

"And his furniture."

"Auction. I told him 'Everything you need is right here.'"

"Tell me honestly, Mom. You're happy with this arrangement?"

"It's just grand. And Mary Ketchum is thinking of moving in."

Jill's surprised at her loud, "Ha!"

"We need a fourth for bridge. It would be lovely to have another woman around."

"Mom. I know it's your life, but I just don't think you should be making these kinds of decisions on your own. I'd like to —"

"She's very mobile."

"Meaning?"

"She can manage the fetching."

"Are you waiting on those men, Mom?" Jill glances at the coffee table's dirty glasses, opened chip bag and bowl of salsa dregs. The beer glass on the table beside Les's chair.

"John's been very good, I must say. Very helpful. Kyle's another story —"

"Isn't it Lyle?"

"He's a little lazy, I'm afraid, but a good conversationalist. Is up on all the latest in politics. Worried sick what Harper's going to do with our pensions."

"Like you."

"You do remember Mary, my bridge partner?"

"Yes, but where would Mary sleep? In with you?"

"No, I'll have John in with me because I've got the electric bed and he has back trouble."

"In with you?" She thought Lyle had the back trouble.

"The beds are pushed together to look like one, but they're actually two three-quarter sized —"

"You don't have to tell *me* that. But isn't that a little intimate?"

"What?"

"John and you sharing a room?"

"After my thyroid operation, there were three other women in the room. One snored, dear, but you make do. One had flatulence."

"Okay, but I'm beginning to have a hard time believing you and John aren't more than just roommates."

Nancy starts to laugh, and laughs some more until she's snorting and then gagging and Jill's worried she's having some sort of attack.

"Mom?"

There's muffled coughing, as if Nancy's holding her hand over the phone. A minute later, she's back, breathing hard into the receiver. "Sorry, Jillian dear. John's dancing out on the deck. It's very humourful."

Is that a word, humourful? "Would you like to go, then?" she says, not bothering to hide her frustration.

"No, no. Stop that, John," she calls out. "Okay, Jillian, you go ahead."

"I'd like to come over next weekend." Jill can't deal with not knowing just what's going on over there. "I'll have to check my schedule. And Les's."

"It's the Masters' tourney next weekend. We plan to wear green and place bets. I'll make my mini-quiches."

The old have a small repertoire, she thinks, recalling her parents' Masters' parties, her father's green corduroy jacket, Nancy's olive-green sweater with the white seersucker patches on the elbows, circular to resemble golf balls, the same mini-quiche appetizers Nancy made for every event. "I'll let you know if I'm coming. I should go empty the dishwasher," says Jill, feeling dismissed.

"That's fine. We'll talk soon."

This time Jill hangs up first and for no good reason wants to have sex. She takes a swig of coffee, dismisses the thought that her desire came out of anything to do with the conversation with her mother and heads upstairs knowing that Les, no matter how sleepy, can be counted on to rise to the occasion, so to speak.

•••

Jill crosses the Second Narrows Bridge into North Vancouver. Beside her on the passenger seat is a boxed coconut créme pie — easy on the dentures — and a half-decent bottle of Chardonnay. She doesn't like the palpable distance that's grown between her mother and her these last few weeks and has made a decision to be positive and supportive. Even put on a green shirt to get into the golfing spirit. She meant to bring exams to mark on the ferry but, in her eagerness to see the underside of this new leaf her mother has turned over, forgot them on the hall table. Will have to mark like a madwoman tomorrow. Maybe she marks too hard and should be more chummy with students. Hiring committees put a lot of stock in student evaluations.

She takes the exit ramp onto the low road into Deep Cove. What to expect, she wonders, besides the golf tourney on TV, party hats maybe. They'll probably insist she make a wager. She hears their quiet boisterousness, the mumbles from the men, the well-meaning laughter from the women as they pass the mini-quiches. She just hopes the house doesn't smell.

She didn't tell Nancy she's coming, didn't want anyone to go to any fuss, and brought a pillow and a sleeping bag in case she stays the night. Which will have to be on the couch by the sounds of it. All she really wants is to know that her mother's not being overrun in her own house. Or overworked or made anxious. She's nearly eighty for god sakes. Jill would also like to know just how much rent people are paying, if any, and how they're handling the expenses. Nancy may not have a mortgage, but there's still the property tax, house insurance, utility bills.

Passing through the reserve with its waterfront property, Jill finds it oddly comforting how, unlike the explosion of monster homes around her mom's place, here each house and yard looks the same as it did thirty years ago, as does the old Shell refinery across the inlet — the one whose sign dropped its S and was made famous in writings by Lowry.

She passes by Cates Park, the site of too many firsts, she thinks, her head growing light with nostalgia. She *was* a bit wild, but then it was the era too. Her kids would never believe it, and she wouldn't want to encourage them with stories of her own stoned, drunken teenage exploits. By its very profundity, having children changes you, sobers you. You're dropped into this chasm of dire love, willing to sacrifice anything for their safety and comfort. If she'd been willing to uproot Quinn from school and move the family, she'd have a tenure-track job by now. But she couldn't imagine him starting over at another school with unfamiliar faces.

The other day, putting laundry away in Quinn's room, she discovered a box of condoms right there in his sock drawer. Was tempted to check if any had been used but controlled herself. Shy kid that he is, she thought such a milestone might have taken longer to reach. Probably his girl's idea, Lauren clearly calling the shots in that relationship. On her trendy whims, she gets him out of the house at least, and away from the computer. Wasn't a bit surprised to hear that she was the booze connection.

Jill can't imagine, won't imagine, anything sexual going on between her mother and John. She can assume them holding hands, snuggling even, but tries not to picture them spooning under the sheets in their apnea-riddled sleep. She pulls up to the stop sign. No — it's good Mom has people around her. To spoon with. Les thinks it's great. "Why the hell not?" he said. "How much more time has Nance got? Might as well go out with a bang." He got her laughing, anyway.

She pulls up to an intersection where she waits for two young mothers with strollers to cross the street. One baby cries at a violent pitch, its mother doing her best to talk over the piercing note. The most primal unit of sound, Jill thinks, hearing the terror in it, and remembering her nursing days and how her milk would come in whenever she heard an infant, any infant, cry. Soon dribbling down her shirt like Pavlov's ridiculous fountain. Pick up your child, she silently begs, listen to that pure need. How she wished she could have nursed Pema, soothed her in that most intimate of ways, *filled her with my own blood*. Nursing, no doubt, was something Pema shared with her birth mother. All Jill could do when they arrived home with Pema, who was three and some, was to try and distract her, entertain her. Inject the milk of happiness through her pores. What romantic nonsense. Besides, Les was better than she was at that kind of feeding. And Beau was better than both of them. He had his sister laughing and starry-eyed from day one. Jill made it her job to ensure Pema would be able to succeed in this culture and fulfill that unspoken promise of a better life.

"Adoption is about loss," the woman at the agency had said, which Jill, in her naive excitement, had glossed over at the time. She had been embarrassed at how badly she'd wanted a daughter. There was no logic to her feelings. A third child didn't make financial sense. But when Annie came to them with pictures of this undernourished child living in abject squalor, her logic had been seriously depleted. She had, only days before, aced her doctoral defense. Her exhausted left brain on holiday, it was all right brain that registered that eager little face and set her hormones firing. And she'd failed to take the agency woman's statement as a warning, if indeed it was one, that the loss could come years later.

A right, then left onto Beachview. Les had been adopted. He was fine and he never got a letter from *his* birth mother. Part of Pema's arrangement was that there wasn't supposed to be contact, she thinks angrily. Legally she had every right to rip up the letter, pretend it never arrived.

The family home is up ahead, the driveway obscured by the laurel hedge that's in eternal need of clipping. Shame on her for stereotyping, but she had expected the downstairs tenants to be more fastidious. She drives down her mother's short, steep driveway to park beside the tenants' car. Wonders how they feel about all the *geriaction* upstairs. She should probably ask if the TV is being played at too obnoxious a volume.

"Reserve judgment," she tells herself, checking her face in the visor mirror. As long as her mother's happy and the house is functioning all right, that's what matters. "A trendsetter," Les called Nancy, and said it was sensible to pool resources when living on a pension. Suggested they might start thinking of their own future roomies.

She gets out of the car, centres the belt buckle of her skirt and grabs her gifts. She wore a skirt and nylons, earrings, because her mother would expect her to dress for company.

She'll have to check out the new greenhouse covers this John fellow rigged up on the deck planters. Les might want to make some for their patio, get a head start on his basil and tomatoes. She rings the doorbell and waits.

Through the smoked glass window alongside the door, she sees her mother's blurred figure grow bigger, bluer as she shuffles down the hall. Is she in her robe? At one o'clock?

"Who is it?" she calls.

"It's me, Jill."

"Jill?"

"Surprise."

"Coming," Nancy calls again, yet it's apparent she's standing still.

Oh, shit, thinks Jill. What has she interrupted? Not going to think about it. We're both adults here. "You going to let me in?" she tries with humour.

The fumble with the deadbolt followed by the chain sounds like effort. The door opens slowly and there's Nancy in her robe, pearl button earrings and lipstick the colour of pink peonies. It's been years since Jill's seen her wear lipstick. Nancy's hair, which is usually a soft helmet of grey curls, is squashed flat on the right side, making her head appear lopsided.

"Jillian, you came," she says in her demure musical voice. She grabs Jill's face in both hands and kisses her one, two, three times on alternate cheeks.

"Hi," says Jill with a laugh. Her mother is not usually this demonstrative.

"I was just going to get something on." Nancy's eyes dart downward at her bathrobe. "Yes, I was."

Jill glances past her towards the living room. Awful quiet. She tries not to picture them all in bed, listening. "I know you weren't expecting me."

"Nonsense, you're always expected," she says, eyes suddenly shiny wet, which makes Jill melt a little. "Let me take your coat."

Jill puts her gifts on the table and removes her jacket. Maybe they can go for a drive, just the two of them. Down to the Cove for ice cream and talk about the situation with Pema after all. She's relieved to see the house looks exactly the same, clean and spare, everything in its place. But is that a sourness in the air?

"You've brought things," says Nancy. "A pie? And a bottle? Am I forgetting some occasion?" She hangs Jill's jacket on a hanger, making it look complicated.

"No, no. Just thought I'd bring something to share. It's the Masters, isn't it?"

"Yes. The Masters."

"I wore my green." Jill plucks at her shirt.

Nancy smiles so wide her mouth looks misshapen. "How wonderful this is. You came."

Jill shrugs, feeling sheepish now. "I came."

"Take those to the kitchen. I'll go put on some clothes."

"Your olive-green sweater?"

"What?"

"You're going to put on your olive-green sweater?"

"Olive-green sweater. Yes. This is so nice."

Carrying bottle and pie, Jill walks behind Nancy towards the living room. There are no people sounds. Nancy pauses to turn and beam over her shoulder at Jill. "Just give us a few minutes," she says and turns down the hall towards the bedrooms.

Us? Make sure everyone's decent, please.

She goes straight to the kitchen where the stink is strongest, puts down the bottle and opens the fridge to put in the pie.

"Ugh." Behind a stack of plastic containers full of Danish is a reeking pack of partially eaten shrimp. Has everyone lost their sense of smell? She wraps the rotten seafood in two plastic bags and dumps it in the garbage. Notices boxes of Kleenex on the counter, a dozen or more, all with their box tops cut away. Whatever that's about.

Jill steps into the living room with its wonderful view of Burrard Inlet and the Northshore Mountains. Deep Cove really was a great place to grow up. She can thank her father for that much. The TV is on but muted, and captions run along the bottom in what looks like Spanish as a godlike camera pans down the tree-lined avenue of an immaculate golf green below. There is a single wineglass on the coffee table, one-third full, pink lipstick smearing the edge. She peers outside to the deck and its row of raised planters. There are no cages, no clever handles. Her neck muscles stiffen.

"You make yourself at home," Nancy sings out. "It's *your home too*."

Jill can't answer, can't make the simplest of sounds.

Mothers

. . . .

Les and Jill sit on the edge of their bed, the bedroom door locked. She can feel the faint backbeat of Quinn's woofer through the floor and tries to recall if she heard Quinn's girlfriend leave. She hands Les the unfolded letter but holds onto the envelope.

> *Dear Mr. and Mrs. Wright:*
>
> *I am write to tell you that I thankful for you care for my daughter, Pema. I know she is take good care of and happy to be at Canada. I was very bad situation when I gave Pema away for you. Now I am good situation. I have new husband, also two sister for Pema. Kitsi is eleven, Maitri is four. Refuge village Jampaling very nice. Good job for my husband and I make money with sewing chuba. I miss my first daughter very much. I like to see her and ask that she come Nepal for visit to Jampaling. I will take very good care. I hope hear from you. Picture of Pema would make me very very happy.*
>
> *Thank you. Datso Tsering*

"When did you get this?" he asks, looking at the envelope in her hands.

There was to be no contact. It was right there in the contract. Jill reaches for the letter but Les pulls it closer to his chest, rereading it.

"Maybe she couldn't make out the fine print," he says, ignoring her extended hand. "I know I would have been pretty stoked if my birth mother wrote me a letter like that."

She knew he'd say that. Just knew it. Finally he hands over the letter and, mouth set, she folds it, gets up and walks across the room to the dresser.

"Must have taken a lot of courage to write this," he continues.

Courage? She's never wanted to think of Pema's birth mother as possessing any qualities whatsoever. In those early years, it perversely comforted Jill to imagine the woman being desperately poor and uneducated, if not mute and thought-free, but never did she dare think courageous.

"Imagine giving away your three-year-old."

She couldn't imagine it then and still can't. She can't even try.

"And not burying that memory in the deepest of holes. I think that takes a lot of courage."

It's love, thinks Jill. Love that made Datso give Pema up in hopes of a better life, and love that makes her want her back. But I love her too.

"Pema's too young," she says, and from this safer distance turns to face him. "It would be utterly confusing. When she's eighteen and an adult, she can go to Nepal or Tibet or wherever she wants. It'll be hard enough then." She slips the letter back into the envelope, imagines taking a lighter to it. "To show this to her now" — she scoffs and waves it in the air — "would confuse the hell out of her."

Les remains his imperturbable self. An annoying trait she's always attributed to his being raised an only child by two staid older parents. They would discuss the purchase of a new pair of shoes for days.

Jill needs to explain further. "She's fourteen, a hormone soup. She dyes her hair every other week, because she doesn't know who or what she is."

"I didn't say we should show it to her right away," he says, treading lightly. "But I'm also not sure about waiting four years."

"You've waited forty-seven."

In his infinite patience, Les lets the comment slide and her harshness bounce back on her. It was a low blow and she hates herself for it, but can't apologize.

"Annie thinks they found her by the way."

She resents the weightless optimism in his tone.

"Annie always thinks they found her," she says. "Don't tell Annie about this, please, whatever you do. It would take about ten seconds before Pema got wind."

Behind her, Les sighs. "I love Pema too, you know."

Jill grits her teeth.

"Let's at least send the poor woman a picture of her daughter," he says.

Jill opens the drawer and tucks the letter inside. With her back turned, she closes her eyes and evens her tone to match his. "I've just lost the person I knew as my mother. I can't lose my daughter too." She wants him to say he completely understands, to come hold her, to be with her on this.

"So many mothers," he says in a far-off voice. "Like brush fires."

It hits Jill that, since last weekend, her own chances of losing her mind some day have increased exponentially. Perhaps the dementia is starting right here, right now. A slow unravelling, an involuntary loosening of her grip on life. And any control she believes she has over her life is part of the delusion.

A frantic-sounding laugh is heard from Quinn's room below.

Quinn's hands shake as, naked beside his bed, he touches the cool, clean skin of Lauren's waist, his stomach on fire from the three rum shots he downed in the bathroom before brushing his teeth a second time. He wishes to God the lights were off, but she wanted them on and he glances at the window blinds for any gaps. Hears voices from the family room on the far side of the wall and stops breathing, anticipates his mother's mortifying knock on his bedroom door. He can't shake the feeling that Jill somehow knows what he's up to. And the even weirder feeling that he wants her to know.

"What's wrong?" asks Lauren.

"Nothing."

Pressed up against him, Lauren runs the points of her fingernails through his hair and he is temporarily paralyzed with pleasure. She kisses him with intention and he knows it's his turn to kiss back with the same. He keeps his eyes firmly closed and is embarrassed how his growing penis pushes at her. As the rum blurs the edges of his self-consciousness, he tells himself he's going to be able to keep it up this time. Maybe Lauren will try something new. There's still that residual sense coming off her, though he fears it's fading, that the fault had been hers.

EIGHT MONTHS LATER

QUINN

······················

After the party, there's a cab. Jewish guy calls the front seat.

Dreading making his one phone call, Quinn sits on the bench in the jail cell and works a grass stain on his new grey boat shoes. With each heartbeat, blood pounds past his ears hammering home how much he drank last night, his mouth so dry it hurts to swallow.

"Can I get some water in here?" he croaks at the sound-proof door at the end of the hall where a muted conversation between receptionist and cop is visible through the door's long rectangular window. There's got to be a camera and mic in here somewhere and he's being heard over the phlegm-rattled snores of the guy in the cell across from his.

"Please?" A fresh thorn of pain momentarily blinds his right eye. How much did he drink?

Beside him, in the back seat is?

He flashes on being ten when neighbourhood kids, a year older and meaner, held him down, stripped him naked and hid his clothes. A nightmare come true, he had to run the long block home, using bushes and speed as cover. When his mom found out she went straight to the kids' homes and confronted their parents. He's not sure which was more humiliating, but the kids never bothered him again.

I didn't do it, he'll tell her and closes his eyes to shake down his dehydrated brain for whatever the hell he did do last night.

The cabbie wears a purple turban, his profile the spitting image of Auntie Annie's bust of Nefertiti.

What he does remember is the promise to help Mom move offices this morning. She probably tried to call his cellphone, which hopefully is still in his jacket, wherever that is — he pats the inside pocket of his vest — along with his wallet. Did the cops really empty the contents of his pockets into a Baggie, or is he imagining it?

God he's tired, though he did sleep or pass out at some point, because he remembers waking up. His neighbour's snoring stops cold, causing Quinn's shoulders to drop an inch, though he wasn't aware they were tensed. If he can only get a glass of — the man gasps, draws in a long rippled breath and resumes his stuttering blats. Sleep apnea. His girlfriend Lauren has a sweeter version of the same. His ex-girlfriend.

As she leans forward to direct turban guy, the top of Vanessa's thong makes a hot pink T — for touch — above the waist of her jeans. He bends to kiss Vanessa's blinding white skin but Todd stops him.

Vanessa and Todd were in the back seat with him.

He unties his laces and ties them again, redoes the left one to match the degree of tightness of the right. Pictures his bed and imagines lying in it and staring up at the Lego projects suspended from the ceiling. Star Wars ships, space stations, lunar vehicles. It was the only toy he ever asked for as a kid, and he had accumulated enough pieces, he once figured out, to build a human-sized single-car garage. He used to hide his creations from his brother, Beau, the human cruise missile, as Dad called him. There was nothing Beau got more pleasure from than destroying things Quinn felt protective of.

He follows Vanessa out of the cab. Todd grabs his arm. "Not yours."

Who even laid the charge against him? Vanessa?

"You tell us, Lothario," he remembers one of cops saying. A female cop?

He lies down on the cot's starchy pillow, fingers the scab forming between his nose and lip. A second scratch, along his neck, is also a mystery. Hit with the whirlies, he sits up again.

Shrugs off Todd with an elbow to the face.

Like splinters working their way to the surface, his lost memories appear in bits and shards to be nervously pieced together. Like last weekend when he'd woken up on top of Mount Doug to a strange dog licking his face. He gradually remembered the bottle of whiskey and the fire he'd made in the woods to burn the epic poem he'd written to Lauren, though the night climb up the mountain is still patchy. Two weeks before that incident, he'd woken up in a stranger's car. He'd been walking home from downtown, late, it had been raining and he must have wisely sought dry shelter. Luckily he woke up early and got out of there before the owner found him and called the police. He looks around the cinder-block walls. Not so lucky this time.

It scares him that he can get so drunk he's basically unconscious yet still moving around doing things. Because at that point, who exactly is making the decisions?

•••

Quinn hands in his final exam of the term: history of structures. Feels light-headed, empty, as if all that crammed information had actual weight and substance. Is pretty sure he aced it. Since Lauren dumped him, three weeks and five days ago in the room in which they first made love, he's had nothing to do but study.

Out in the hall, a group of fellow architecture students are coaxing people to go celebrate.

"Quinn, come to Mandy's and my place," says a sad-faced girl named Rebecca, the corners of her eyes and mouth listing downward as though plagued by gravity. "You can't study any more so you have no excuse this time."

"You *have* to come," booms Ritchie. He drapes a sloppy hand on Quinn's shoulder and yells, "It's time we brought you down to our level." Twenty years old and already sporting a paunch, Ritchie's the type of guy for whom loud is funny.

All term, Quinn has refused these kinds of offers because he's not comfortable in groups. Groups have too many variables, which therefore make it impossible to know where you stand. It was complicated work, some made it a career, and he had enough on his plate with his job, Lauren and maintaining an A average in order to keep his scholarship. He'd made a decision early on to remain an unknown quantity here in school, with the hope of being labelled enigmatic.

"Do you even have a personality?" Lauren had asked last month during their fight and her fit of confession, her face as helpfully earnest as a dog's. "Or have I been projecting mine onto you?" She didn't have a cynical bone in her body and these questions — for which he had no immediate answer and would later turn over and over in his mind searching for one — were asked with absolute sincerity.

"You never initiate," she said, leaving the sentence dangling. He finished it in his head: *You never initiate anything. You never initiate anything good.* "So I never know what it is *you* want."

"Sorry," he said, because he didn't know how to fix himself and he was ready to agree he needed fixing. He could initiate things when the outcome affected only him but when other people were involved, the possibilities multiplied infinitely, beyond sight. He was also sorry because he loved her, as much as he knew how. He loved the way she dragged her nails through

his hair when they kissed, loved the erotic hollows of her arm-
pits, her glaring excitement over random things — a new singer,
a YouTube prank, a book — and sure, he loved her initiative.
Stupid him thought she was fine deciding what movies to watch,
where to eat, how often they should spend the night together.
She'd seemed thrilled when he let her "outfit" him like her
favourite indie rocker: black jeans, boat shoes, pinstripe vest
over a T-shirt. He'd never had "a look" before and was grateful.

"I can't tell if you want to see me or even want to make
love to me," she said, and the punctuating tears made his gut
clench. "Just once," she continued with an emotional gulp of
air, "I would like to have to fend you off." She paused then,
her glistening eyes hopeful, as if to afford him one last chance.

But Quinn didn't have it in him to force himself on anybody, especially not on demand. That *was* what she was asking
for? Sex? Six months in, that mindless thrusting abandon still
required several booster shots of rum.

"Maybe I don't say it aloud, but I do love you," he said
instead, worried as soon as the words were out that they sounded
cliché. He was seriously planning to take her hand, then move
in for a "forceful" kiss. But in his moment of deliberation,
she'd turned and walked away.

"Yeah, come with us," says the girl named Mandy, who
looks as down-to-earth and easy as her name.

Vanessa hooks her arm in his. "It'll be fun."

Matching architectural style to personality — his private
game — Quinn had decided Mandy was a simple brick rancher
circa 1950 with large, friendly windows. Vanessa, the drop-dead
gorgeous girl in the program, who acted like a bimbo yet got
the highest grades (besides him), was a complex and innovative
subway system with deco mosaic detail. He'd fantasized about
Vanessa. She was in that category, fantasy, because he understood

that neither his personality nor his looks warranted someone this pretty. His brother Beau got the looks and he got the brains. He's come to accept it, but it does bother him that Beau is suddenly broader in the shoulders and soon to be taller.

"Don't tell us you don't drink," shouts Ritchie.

"Okay, I won't tell you."

"You don't drink?" Rebecca looks extra sad.

"Is it a religious thing?" asks a quirky Jewish guy whose name, Jehoy-something, Quinn can't pronounce. "You a Muzz?"

"I drink, all right? Like a fish."

"Fish don't actually drink," Vanessa says, dragging her reddish-blonde curls over one shoulder.

She sounds literal and serious, and it strikes him that in some fundamental way she might be as boring as he is.

"So you're coming then." Todd sounds impatient and this is not a question.

Suspension bridge is how he thinks of Todd, the one guy in the class he considers dangerous. Long limbed and long nosed, Todd has close-set eyes, white-blond hair and the cockiness of someone much better looking.

"Yes, okay. I'm coming."

Somebody behind him claps.

"Let the games begin." Todd starts towards the door and the group follows, jostling Quinn along. Ritchie, who has a car, takes orders and money. When Quinn orders a twenty-sixer of rum and a litre of coke, Todd smirks and says, "This should be good."

"Just being economical." Quinn pictures the near-empty rum bottle under his bathroom sink. He doesn't drink like a fish every day, just enough to free him from second-guessing and making knots out of everything – like how things could have

40

gone differently with Lauren if only he hadn't hesitated. At the very least, he could have stopped her from leaving, should have stopped her. Oh god, maybe even now she's waiting for him to initiate something more than text messages. To which she hasn't responded. He's on a sidewalk with these people. Maybe he shouldn't be. Maybe he should call, be walking in Lauren's direction. Maybe she would beam at the sight of him, helpless in joy. Maybe she'd sneer and close the door. Likely something in between. It had gotten complicated.

With its large rooms, low ceilings and shortage of windows, the girls' basement suite feels like a spacious cave. Somehow, maybe because of their mustard shade of yellow, the walls feel carpeted though they aren't. Around the circular coffee table sit a legless brown corduroy couch, a matching chair and two stained beanbag chairs. A tree branch has been rammed into a pot of rocks in the corner, random things hanging from its branches: key chain, candy cane, baby's soother, shoelace. A string of melancholy blue Christmas lights swoops across one wall.

The bottles — wine, beer, rum, cider, two litres of Coke — and assorted glasses are plunked on the table along with a bowl of red and green tortilla chips and salsa. Quinn takes a seat at the far end of the couch. When Vanessa sits at the other end and smiles at him, he responds with a finger-waggling wave.

Dork. He pours a shot, knocks it back when no one's looking and quickly mixes another with Coke.

Ritchie has produced a deck of cards from his backpack. "Ring of Fire," he calls out as he shuffles them, and people groan or laugh or both. "We need an extra glass," he yells to whoever's banging around in the kitchen. Todd appears with an extra glass and asks Quinn if he minds moving over.

"No, sure." As he slides over, the middle cushion dips

violently backwards and sideways, throwing him onto Vanessa.

"Sorry," mumbles Quinn, removing his hand from her thigh.

She laughs. "There are some missing springs there."

"Yeah." He adjusts forward to even ground, wonders if Todd, now nonchalantly examining the bottles on the table, knew perfectly well about the springs.

"Mind if I do?" Todd tips his chin at Quinn's rum.

"I'm happy sharing," says Quinn. Did he just sound like a kindergartner?

"It's nice you're here," says Vanessa, giving his knee a pat.

"Nice, too." What did he just say? He reaches for his drink. He could be home painting his newest miniature. He'd had to order four different figurines — maiden, farmer, dragon, scholar — to get the parts he needed: a staff to represent Lauren's love of Greek mythology; a dragon tail to make the mermaid tail and represent her love of the ocean; a book because she was an avid reader. It had taken him an entire weekend to solder the tiny parts, and he was proud of how it turned out. He'd planned to paint the hair brown with red highlights like Lauren's, the eyes her grassy shade of green, and paint on tiny fangs because of her guilty obsession with the Twilight series. Before she dumped him, the miniature was going to be one of her Christmas presents, and he's debating if it would be pathetic to give it to her anyway. He'd texted her last weekend. "Missing you, Laur. Wanting to hold you, and more." The word "want," he felt, was key. When he didn't hear back, he texted and said that his personality was "accommodating" — that was the descriptive he'd settled on because it contained the word dating — and that, if given the chance, he'd be more "demonstrative." He chose that word because it contained the word demon, a.k.a. vampire. His mother, the linguist, taught him that words had subliminal power beyond their intended meanings.

"You're from here, right?" Vanessa asks.

"Here?" He points to the table.

She smiles, waiting.

"Yeah."

"You live at home, then?"

"With my folks. I have my own entrance though." He just shouldn't speak.

She's still looking at him. Should he ask where she's from? In the gap, she looks away. Quinn takes a long drink.

Todd's voice next to his ear is a heated whisper: "Van loves to fuck."

His brain momentarily frozen, Quinn looks at Todd who shrugs, palms raised in innocence. Thrown off-centre in another way now, his brain races around the possible reasons Todd just confided or fabricated such a thing and glances at Vanessa to make sure she hasn't overheard.

"Quinn, know this game?" calls Ritchie.

"Excuse me?"

"Ring of Fire."

"Don't believe so."

"Everyone takes turns flipping over a card," Mandy says.

"Whoever loses the game indicated by the card," explains Rebecca, "has to take a drink and give one to the cup." She points to the empty cup in the middle of the table. "The game ends when someone turns over the fourth king, and then that person has to chug the mix of booze in the cup."

As Ritchie explains the rules for each card, Quinn only half follows. The cards are then spread face down in a ring around the cup.

"I'll go first," says Mandy and flips over a six. "Rhyme time. Okay, booze," she begins.

"Cruise."

"Lose."

"Fuse."

"Jews," says Todd and points to Jehoy-something who waves good-naturedly.

It's Quinn's turn. "News."

"MEWS and MUSE," spells Vanessa, then hikes up her legs to sit cross-legged on the couch. Her knee now pushes against Quinn's thigh. Accident or signal?

"Clues."

If he glances over at her or at her knee, he'll be making something of it when she might not be. Some girls are just naturally touchy. His sister, Pema, drapes herself over complete strangers.

"Glues."

If he doesn't glance over, she could construe it two ways: casual cool or indifferent.

"Use."

"Ooze."

Now the moment's past, so either he blew it or it didn't matter in the first place.

"Shmooze," says Todd.

Quinn can't think.

"Ten seconds," calls Ritchie and starts tapping a spoon against his glass.

"Screws," he blurts and people laugh out loud, Todd the loudest. Blushing, he forces himself to laugh along.

"BOOS," spells Vanessa.

"MOOS," spells the next person.

"Choose."

"Shoes."

"Dues."

"Poos," says Todd.

"Ruse," Quinn says, relieved.

"Hues."

"Fooz, as in fooz ball."

"That's not a word," says Mandy, but everyone ignores her.

"Vuse, as in pirating music."

"Coos."

"Blues."

It was back to him. "I'm out of rhymes," he says.

"Could have done crews or chews," says Vanessa, her head tipping right then left.

"Oh, yeah." He hits his head with an open palm, takes a drink and gives one to the cup. He also could have said accuse or stews. He wanted a drink.

Jehoy-something turns over a ten and makes index-fingers horns on his head. Quinn remembers, too late, that horns stand for Viking and therefore is the last person to pretend to row the imaginary Viking ship. He drinks and adds the rest of his glass to the cup.

"You'll get the hang of it," says Vanessa with another pat to his knee.

Quinn's the only person with a full glass when Todd turns over a five — a "make-up-a-rule" card. He takes one look at Quinn and proclaims, "Chug time," and everybody downs the remainder of their glass. Quinn knows Todd's watching him and knocks his drink back in one go.

His self-consciousness deliciously fades to white noise, so when Ritchie calls a time out to use the bathroom, Quinn has enough careless confidence to ask Vanessa about her holiday plans.

"Home to Calgary for the dysfunctional Christmas," she says with a meagre smile. "My parents are divorced and can't be in the same room together. One brother's a geological engineer who works for an oil company and one's a radical environmentalist, so they can't be in the same room either. My sister's a paranoid schizophrenic. Though she claims that's just my projection."

"God, I'm sorry. That sounds seriously tough," he says and means it.

She shrugs. "Gotta love family. Yours?"

"Parental unit still together, brother and sister like this." He holds up crossed fingers. "I do have a depressive aunt but we only see her when she's manically happy."

He mixes himself another rum and Coke. "Me, I'm the Lone Ranger in the family."

She laughs while giving him a quizzical look. Ranger contains anger, he thinks, pleased with himself.

Ritchie's back and it's Quinn's turn. He flips over a jack for jackass, which means whenever someone loses a round and has to take a drink, he has to drink too.

"Shit," says Quinn and people laugh. He says it three more times, having fun playing the new guy who doesn't understand the rules.

Ritchie's volume has gone up, Jehoy-something is flirting with Mandy and Todd's meanness is more direct.

"It's people like you," says Todd, stabbing a finger at Quinn's shoulder, "always on time, always prepared, wearing your fucking little vest, that make the rest of us look bad. Why do you want to make the rest of us look bad?"

Nothing sticks to Quinn now because he *is* the Lone Ranger, dodging bullets or coolly shooting back. "From now on, I'm a new man. Promise. I mean I'll even dress shitty like you. Little golf shirt. Like where do you shop? Sears fucking Walmart?"

Vanessa spits with laughter.

"Whoa," says Mandy.

Todd stares at him, expressionless, and a soft bull-like snort escapes his beak of a nose.

Jehoy-something has flipped over a card and is once again making finger horns on his head. Quinn makes horns a second before Todd. He raises hero eyebrows at Vanessa as Todd drinks and adds to the cup.

When someone stops the game to take a phone call, Quinn confesses to Vanessa he's recently been dumped. She's all coos and comfort, knowing, so she says, just how he feels.

"No way. You," he says, pointing, "are toooo smart to have ever been dumped." He's proud of himself for not saying hot.

Vanessa looks past Quinn at Todd, who's checking his cellphone.

"What," says Todd.

Quinn looks at one and then the other. "Oh my god, you two were an item?"

"Item?" says Todd. "You sound like my grandmother."

"Suspension bridge and subway system?" Quinn laughs. "I mean, guess it makes sense."

"Whaddaya you talking about now?" says Todd.

"Yeah." Vanessa leans in closer and he inhales the flowery scent of her shampoo.

Quinn explains his anthropomorphic game and the whole room is suddenly listening and asking his opinion on their "building type."

"Ritchie here's a sprawling monster home in a gated community. With monster fuckin' pool, hot tub, SUVs in the double garage. You," he says pointing to Jehoy-something. "Serious ultramodern movie theatre or library. Lotsa glaaaass. And Rebecca here, sorry, Rebecca, is your third-world modular housing unit." He has people laughing, exclaiming agreement, arguing for themselves.

Quinn hums inside. He feels profoundly connected to these people, his fellow architectural students. In fact, he fuckin' loves every person here and feels their love in return. He feels the love of the architects of this basement suite, of the people who made these clothes on his back, of the brewers of this rum and everyone behind the Coke feel-good empire. *Making things is love* he wants to tell this long-legged tragedy beside him. His parents made him. God, he loves them. He loves his macho brother, his frivolous sister. He loves his demented grandmother and his munchkin-sized aunt. He loves Lauren and knows she loves him back. She loves him.

"What about the Quinn man here," says Ritchie, "What's he?"

"Japanese hotels," says Jehoy-something. "The beehive kind with those little sleeping holes." He starts buzzing.

"I'd have said energy-efficient townhouses," says Vanessa. "But hell, after tonight, I realize I don't know you at all."

Quinn leans over and tucks a tendril of hair behind her ear, thinking it's very small for an ear. "If you'd like to get to know me, I'm all yours."

Her laugh is a trilling songbird. Whether that laughter is directed *at* him or *with* him, he suddenly understands, is completely up to him.

"You're so pretty," he says.

"You're pretty drunk."

"You're fucked-up drunk," comes Todd's voice behind him.

Quinn laughs. "My grandpa used to sneak me sips of his whiskey. Been drinking since I was five."

Someone lights up a joint. Quinn rarely smokes dope, and never socially, but after Vanessa takes a hit, so does he, holding it in like a pro.

His last memory of the party is of Todd pushing a card into

his hand, the fourth king?, of people cheering, squealing, him stepping up onto the coffee table and in a grand gesture hoisting over his head the Ring of Fire cup.

•••

After his breakfast of boiled egg, dry toast, two slices of orange and a dehydrating coffee — still no water — he's cuffed before being taken outside the cellblock to make his one phone call. Then, so he can actually use the phone, one hand is released and, as if he's some dangerous criminal, the other cuffed to a ring on the wall beside the phone.

His sister, Pema, answers, rap music in the background.

"Hi Pema, can you put Mom on, please?" His headache has settled into an even throb, his stomach a nervous swirl of caffeine.

"She's in bed."

"She's sleeping?" he asks, though can't imagine it. She's always up early.

"Don't think so. Where are you?"

"Just put Mom on, please."

"Only if you tell me where you are."

"Pema." He grinds his teeth, knows she won't back down.

"Tell me where you are or I'll hang up."

"I'm in jail for sexual assault."

Her laughter is so spontaneous, he laughs too. Yeah, it's so impossible it's funny. The music grows fainter as she walks the phone to another room and he scrambles to remember what the hell he did last night. He doesn't want to lie to his mother.

"Hello?" His mother's voice is at once a balm and a censure. He wants to stop there with her open expectation, her not knowing who and what is on the other end.

"Hi Mom. It's me, Quinn."

"Quinn," she says.

"Mom, sorry about this morning. I know I promised to help you move your office and I still will, but there's been some weird mix-up and I'm actually, if you can believe it" — he huffs a laugh — "calling from jail."

A silence at the end of the line and he imagines her frowning. "Are you all right?" she says, and the concern in her voice makes his eyes prick.

"I, I don't know." It's his first honest thought all day and he feels the relief of it.

"I called your cellphone."

"Yeah, I think I left it in my coat and I —"

"Lauren's roommate answered," she says quietly.

Lauren? Lauren. He starts to sit down though there is no seat, and the hand that's hooked to the wall tugs him back up.

He has the driver drop him at Lauren's. His girlfriend's place, he tells Todd.

Oh god.

"I told her that my son wasn't capable of attacking anyone." She chokes on a sob and Quinn, his stomach threatening to heave, hangs up the phone as the last piece of the puzzle floats up through the darkness.

Rum slicks back his hair, vampire style. She answers the door, bleary-eyed, in the pink fuzzy robe he gave her for her birthday. Its lapels are soft in his fists and he kisses her forcefully, taking initiative. She starts to fend him off. Just like she wanted.

Siblings

···········

In the kitchen, Beau shakes salt over the bowl of popcorn.

"What are you going to get me for Christmas?" Pema calls from the couch in the family room.

"That leather backpack you saw online."

"Really?"

"No. It was like two hundred dollars."

"You and Quinn could go in together."

"Yeah, right."

"What then?"

"I don't know. A gift certificate to the mall."

"That'd be good."

His sister, who doesn't do surprises, needs to be told what her gifts are ahead of time or she goes ballistic.

"Did you put yeast on it?" asks Pema.

"Yes."

"Turn off the lights."

He turns off the kitchen light then comes and knocks back beside her on the couch. The DVD is paused on a fishy close-up of an eye.

She runs a curious finger over a scab on the side of his knee, a gift from yesterday's club game.

"Metal cleat," he says.

"I want to pick it off."

"Leave it." He jerks his knee away.

"Get under," she orders and throws the comforter over him. "This part coming up freaks me out."

"Then why are we watching it?"

"I knew you'd like it. You like it, right?"

"It's pretty twisted." He loves it.

"DiCaprio's nuts. I don't mean really nuts, you have to see for yourself who's nuts. I'm saying too much. Forget everything I just said." She takes a handful of popcorn and restarts the movie where it left off. "Lotsa butter," she says happily.

He takes a drink of the milk he mixed with vanilla protein powder. His goal is to gain ten between now and spring season, and he needs a minimum number of grams of protein each day to build muscle mass.

Pema makes a face. "Milk doesn't go with popcorn."

"Shut up already."

She smacks his shoulder with the butt of her palm. He's long since learned that she needs the last word and lets it go.

In the dark, the flickering light of the TV paints them a frozen blue and their hands knock together in the popcorn bowl perched between them.

"Oh gawd, this part coming up." Pema falls sideways against Beau and tugs up the front of his rugby jersey to hide behind.

Her breast presses against his chest and some reptilian part of his brain stirs awake. He'd missed Pema so much when she was away last summer it hurt. But when she finally came home, he barely recognized her. Her face looked different. She was taller and she'd filled out in new places. Since then she'd filled out even more.

Pema peeks at the screen and in the underwater light he sees someone other than his sister and a primitive thrill takes him by surprise.

"Get off," he says in his confusion and gently pushes her away.

"Is it over?" she asks still clinging, still peeking, still pressing.

He wrenches his shirt free. "Move over."

"Did you see that?" says Pema, scooting over, eyes glued to the TV. "Freak me out."

"Yeah," Beau lies.

She stops the movie and jumps up on her knees. "Should we watch that part again?" She stares at him breathless and eager, and because he's just got a glimpse down the gaping v-neck of her nightshirt, he keeps his eyes stiffly on her face. His neck burns with shame. He throws off the cover and is about to get up when Pema jumps on him, straddles his lap and straight-arms him back against the couch.

"Where do you think you're going?"

"Bed. I'm tired."

"No. You can't go to bed," she says in that despairing way she uses to make him do something. "I can't watch this alone."

"Watch *Glee*." He feels an erection starting and shoves her off him more forcefully than he meant to.

"Beauuuu."

He's up and moving towards the stairs.

"I hate you," she whines.

"Good," he says and takes the stairs two at a time, horrified she might see. The phone rings and, praying it's not for him, he hurries into his room and locks the door.

Quinn is in his room, putting the final touches to the fig-urine he made for Lauren, and can't help answering the phone imagining it's her. "Hello?"

"Is that Quinn?"

"Hi Auntie Annie, how are you?"

"Oh god, you don't want to know, it's been a day, a week, totally wasted making a dress with a see-through waist out of six-pack rings, you know, the plastic circles? Was thinking sixties retro, bad idea, the edges curl and then pinch, but you don't need me to dump on you. Heard about last weekend. A drunk and disorderly, huh? You? Did someone slip you a roofie or something? When I was your age, Jesus help us, we drank, popped Quaaludes, Orange Sunshine, mescaline…"

His mom had talked Lauren and her parents into dropping the assault charge, convinced them that knocking her to the ground and dislocating her shoulder was a drunken stumble. An accident. He'd made a formal apology to Lauren's roommate and parents — Lauren wouldn't see him.

"…ecstasy, coke, Windowpane. That was back when you could trust what was in those things, more or less. Before the gangs got in on it. So how are you?"

"I'm fine."

His aunt's laugh is so loud it sounds more like an angry shout. He has no idea what's so funny.

"Heard you aced your exams."

"Yeah."

"Burning the candle at both ends. Excellent."

Auntie Annie never fails to make him feel better about himself.

"I'm looking for your dad. I tried his cell but no one answered. He's at the new job?"

"Yeah, he's at work."

"Can't pick up the phone with a new boss looking over his shoulder. I think he just needs to be his own boss. I don't blame him quitting that last place. I mean, at his age, having to take orders from a snotty thirty-year-old?"

"Hey, Mom's here. You want to talk to her?"

"Oh, is Jill there? I'd love to talk to her but she's probably busy and I'd hate to bother her… Is she there?"

"Hold on, I'll go get her." Unable to stomach the hurt on his mother's face whenever she lays eyes on him, Quinn calls out for her to pick up the phone.

"Thanks sweet boy," says his aunt. "A drunk and disorderly, eh?"

"Yeah. Bye Auntie Annie."

"Bye Quinner."

"Hello?" says Jill and Quinn hangs up.

"Jill, I'm so glad you're there." Annie hates interrupting Jill, knows how busy she is, but is busting to tell someone.

"Hi Annie. What's up?"

As if it was a command, Annie's up out of her swivel chair and then walking clockwise around the large cutting table in her loft, too excited to remain seated. "I was trying to reach Les but Quinn said he's at his new job. Always trying to move up in the pecking order, eh? It's a tough business, that chef business."

"He won't be home until after midnight."

"I've never seen a restaurant where you can order takeout online. That should keep the place in business. And I might have ordered from there tonight if my Internet wasn't still down with some virus. Smallpox, I think. Andy said he'd fix it but the shithead never did" — *don't curse, Jill doesn't like it*— "so I'm having to call all my clients, which is costing me, and my studio looks like a bomb's hit it because I couldn't find my fucking pins this morning then I couldn't find red bobbin thread —"

"What's wrong, Annie?"

"I have some great purple leather pockets for Pema, for her jeans? They're heart-shaped, will look great with her jacket."

"Slow down," Jill says in such a calm, measured voice that

Annie stops pacing. "Tell me exactly what's going on."

She sighs. "I'm an idiot, sorry."

"No, you're not. Is it Andy?"

"Andy? I gather that was obvious to everyone but me. Me and my Raggedy Annie and Andy crap."

"You can do so much better."

Criticism totally throws her and she's unable to think, much less respond.

"Annie, what I meant is, is that you deserve better."

Now she feels badly for thinking Jill was being critical.

"Come over," Jill says, clearly worried. "Have you eaten? We have lots of leftover lasagna. Pema would love to see those pockets."

Jill's sweetness and concern chokes her right up. How did she get so lucky to have such a family?

"Annie, don't hang up."

"I'm fine, Jill," she says, finding her voice again. "And it's not about Andy." She'd never told Jill or Les that the asshole turned out to be married with a kid on the way. "They found our mother, Jill," she says, the tears rising. "I need to tell Les."

"Annie, now wait. Are they absolutely sure?"

"In New York City. Her name's Faye. Isn't that the most beautiful name? And the coolest?"

"It's very pretty but —"

"I can hardly believe it myself and couldn't wait to tell someone." Her tears erupt in a gagging cough, and "They finally found her," comes out in a blubber.

"Annie," Jill says gently, "so you're absolutely sure this time?"

THREE MONTHS LATER

ANNIE

· · · · · · · · · · · ·

"This plane smells," Annie says to Les as she twists the air knob one way then the other for a lukewarm blast.

Her brother's eyes are closed, his head pressing the back of his still-upright seat, desperate for sleep, she knows, after six days in a cheap room in Times Square that vibrated when the traffic barrelled down Broadway. All night long, light from the Square's giant TV screen bled through the curtains, so Les reported, to bathe the room in "the colour of nightmares." Unlike Les, Annie had slept like a log. External chaos calmed her right down — what a former boyfriend called Ritalin logic.

To help Les get caught up on the plane she gave him a few Ativan, memory erasers as she thinks of them. Before yesterday's meeting with Faye, their so-called real mother, they both should have popped a handful.

"Don't you think it smells?" She knocks her knee against his.

"Like what?"

"Like the inside of a dry-cleaning bag." She reaches and twists on his blower too. "The air from these fans is more of the same."

"It'll change when we take off." His voice is groggy and he looks incapable of opening his eyes. Was three Ativan one too many? She just thought because he's so tall...

As the plane taxis out to the runway, instructional videos flare onto every seatback. She's in the middle seat, Les and his long legs on the aisle while a large man reading the *New York Times* fills the window seat. Wearing pressed chinos and collared polo, the man has a storm of dark grey curls on his square head, a defined goatee. She guesses fifty-five to her forty-five, a Spanish background, from Barcelona, no, Brazil, Buenos Aires. Good Air? Is that what that name means?

Under the armrest, his generous thigh, like that of a body builder gone to fat, presses warm along hers. She doesn't mind. There isn't nearly enough touching in this world. Faye, her own flesh and blood, didn't even bother to stand when she and Les arrived, but shook hands across the table. Shook fingers.

Annie pretends to read the airplane magazine as she checks out her neighbour. He's big, but big all over, well-proportioned. She's never had a really large lover. Markus was chubby but not what she'd call fat. Charlie had a beer gut and lovemaking required angles. Faye, who at sixty-five is a Pilates instructor, looked shrink-wrapped in her skin, her posture a goddamn pencil. She'd ordered sashimi, steamed vegetables and seaweed salad, announcing to no one in particular, "I don't do starch or red meat." That was after Annie ordered udon noodles with pork. "A large hot sake," she added to her order in terror, her morning lithium be damned. When the sake arrived and a third doll-sized cup was placed on the table, Faye held up her palm like a stop sign. "Not for me."

"So," Annie leans in behind her seatmate's paper. "Are you coming or going?"

His paper collapses in a heap on his generous lap. He looks amused and she likes how he takes his time answering. The skin on his face is smooth and lightly tanned. He doesn't have a fat face.

"If going means going from home then going."

"Oh?"

"Brother's wedding. Second marriage."

No foreign accent, an educated-sounding voice. "You're from New York, then."

"Jersey."

"So what does a man from Jersey do in Jersey?"

"Architect."

"Wow."

Bowing his head slightly, he raises a humble hand that has dimpled indentations where knuckles should be. "Industrial designs, not art galleries or skyscrapers."

"Still. Wow. My nephew is studying architecture. In British Columbia."

She'd done a handshake analysis workshop last year, a kind of prescreening for men. To make better choices. Glad to have chosen a flattering push-up bra this morning, she wants to shake his fat hand.

"So you're coming?" he asks.

"Coming home, yes. I'm in industrial design too, sort of. Clothes. I repurpose used fabric among other things."

"Repurpose?"

She pinches up her pants. "Canvas tarp dyed navy blue. These?" Maroon braids run down the pant leg's outer seam. "Vinyl upholstery from old diner booths."

"I'm impressed."

She lowers her voice. "Lined with wedding gown satin. Lovely against the skin. In the early days of women's pants, they were all satin lined. Keeps you warm in the winter and cool in the summer." Annie had driven Les crazy fretting over what to wear to meet Faye. In her more youthful fantasies, she wore white, billowy skirts and peasant blouses, bare orphan feet.

Yesterday she finally settled on skinny jeans and a white ruffled blouse. And, for a touch of high fashion, red spiked heels, red lips. She limited her jewelry to silver bracelets and one pair of earrings. All tattoos were discreetly covered. Not that Faye took any notice. In her sleek black sweatsuit and runners, Faye had just come from teaching what she called "a private." Her words were directed to Les, always Les, her grey businesslike eyes hooded to look professionally bored. Dyed blonde hair, bone straight like Les's, was pulled back into a whisk of a ponytail that tugged at the corners of her makeup-free eyes to make her look vaguely Asian. So this is what a murderer looks like, thought Annie. A murderess?

A flight attendant drifts by, eyeballing seatbelts and chair backs.

"So you were in New York on business?" asks her seatmate.

"Well, I did show my work at e-MERGE, a trade show for new designers, and actually got a couple of commissions out of it." She hooks her thumb at Les. "My brother's idea, so I could write off my expenses. I really thought my flapper tops made from plastic straws would be a hit but no, leather cummerbunds." She shrugs. "The main reason was so we could meet our birth mother. Well, so I could. Les didn't have the same compulsive need but kindly came with."

"You mean this was —"

"First time, yeah. Finally tracked her down after all these years. Planned to spend the week with her but she put us off until yesterday. Gave us a whole hour and a half."

"I'm sorry."

"At least I can let that fantasy go." The plane turns onto the runway and squares-off with the sky. "Ooh, I love takeoffs."

He lets go a long exhale. "Flying unnerves me. Especially takeoffs."

"No, no, I'll guide you through." The engines rev to a high whine and the plane shudders. "Listen, flying is so totally out of your control," she says over the noise.

"That's what I find —"

"So liberating." As the plane starts forward, she grips the back of his hand and lifts it, raising her arms in the sign of surrender. When he tries to tug free, she holds on and he laughs, a deep purr of a laugh, and lifts up his other hand. "Lean back and close your eyes," she tells him. The plane picks up speed. "Feel the power of this amazing machine...exhilarating... vroom... Feel it?"

"Yes."

"And now...oh yeah...listen for it...that hush as the wheels...release us from the earth." The plane lifts off the ground and noses skyward. "Ahh."

After another minute, she reluctantly lets him go. "Better?"

"The nicest takeoff I've ever had. Thank you."

"Annie." She holds out her hand.

"Jonathan." His hand swallows hers whole. His handshake, not too tight and not too loose, tells her he's sensitive, considerate, self-aware. And the subtle squeeze before they let go of each other's hand, that he's interested.

Les is reclined and asleep when the trolley rolls by with complimentary drinks and Annie orders him a Bloody Caesar so she can have two. Jonathan orders a minibottle of red wine.

"It's called the Reunion Registry. Reunion. Makes it sound all happy tears. As if you had something to reminisce about. Remember when you abandoned me as a baby?" She drinks and then raises her glass. "Tastes terrible. Yours?"

"Terrible." They tap plastic.

"My mom, the one who adopted me, that is — Gerry, short

for Geraldine — single after I came along, worked in a bridal shop. Taught me to sew. She was a rock, a practical throw-a-can-of-mushroom-soup-on-it kind of person and used to answer my questions about my birth mother with "no use digging up what's already buried," so of course I registered the day I turned eighteen. But you see, your birth parent has to put their name in. That's how it works. They're not like a private-eye business. We resorted to that later." Faucet mouth, a little voice warns, but she's helpless to stop. It always happens when she meets a man she likes. "So there I was, waiting with bated breath for the phone call. You dream about it a lot. I was depressed for a year after Joni Mitchell was reunited with her daughter. Not that I look anything like Joni but I loved Joni and, you know, there's such a shitload of possibilities you can't help but dream big. I was banking on Dad being Bill Clinton for a while." She takes a long drink.

"You'd have Hillary as a stepmom."

His wry smile makes her laugh.

"You know," she says, pausing, "I realize I just assumed my father was dead so didn't even think to ask yesterday." She huffs, mentally kicking herself. "So Hillary might *be* my stepmom for all I know."

He laughs though she wasn't being funny. "Anyway, not too long after I'd put my name in, I finally got the call."

"But I thought you said you had to hire a private —"

"It wasn't my mother they found. Annie Kellman, they said, did you know you have a brother? I had a brother! I danced around my room for an hour." She slips the second Bloody Caesar cup inside the empty first one and pats Les's sleeping leg. "Gerry died when I was twenty, dropped dead of an aneurism, boom, on her way home on the bus."

"I'm sorry."

"Yeah, I was devastated. And permanently stoned on something or other for the next two years. Les is my family now. Nicest man, I can't tell you. Gentle, kind, funny. Loved him the moment we met and the poor guy hasn't been able to shake me since. The truth is I probably wouldn't be here if it weren't for him."

"You're very fortunate then."

She loves the elegant way this man speaks. "We were never sure if we were full or half siblings, since we hardly look related. Me the size of a pygmy and, he six two. And the hair." She grabs a swath of her dark, wiry curls. "Though I always thought we had the same mouth. Not that it really matters whether we're full or not, but that was something we wanted to ask our mother."

"And did you?"

"Oh, I'm getting to that." The food trolley is making its way down the aisle. "I'd really like some cheese and crackers. Stuffs me up, cheese, so I shouldn't eat it, but I love it. Lost my appetite after yesterday but am getting it back talking to you."

"Glad to be of service," says Jonathan and empties the rest of his bottle into his glass.

"Because of Les, I've got this amazing family: Jill, his wife, who's stupid-smart, a university prof, linguistics, and beautiful and organized and sane. Very few sane women on my planet. Two nephews, Quinn's the one who's in an architecture program, and Beau's in high school, a rugby man; and one niece, Pema, who's a fashion hound like me. She's adopted too. Tibetan. Well I'm not Tibetan. I helped them find her through this meditation group I was involved with. Oh, god, those kids are the best things in my life."

"Those are interesting," he says with a graceful gesture towards her earring.

"Thank you. I make them from Scotch broom pods." She

gives them a little rattle. "Seeds."

"That's very clever," he says. "May I buy you some cheese and crackers?"

"Why yes, yes you can."

"Would anyone care for a snack?" The flight attendant leans in to snatch the empty wine bottle.

Annie raises her hand. "This nice man wants to buy me some cheese."

Twenty minutes later, she knows Jonathan has two grown daughters, the younger one a veterinary nurse, the elder a graphic designer recently married and unable to have children. He says nothing about his wife and is not wearing a ring. She buys him another wine and herself another Caesar and tells him the story behind believing Faye did something criminal to her father.

"I did this retreat led by a spirit guide, amazing woman, a psychic really. The work was done in groups and so when it was my turn, I stood in the middle of the circle and had to ask the group my question: Why is it that all my relationships with men end badly?"

"Fair enough."

"Oh god, yeah. Not to scare you off or anything."

"I'm flattered," he says in a humble, adorable way that makes her heart sway.

"The group was instructed to tune in to me, meditate on me while holding my question in mind, and then they were to spontaneously express whatever feelings or words or imagery came to them. One woman screamed, more angry scream than fearful. One guy crouched and covered his head. Another woman kept repeating I love you, I hate you, I love you, I hate you, while another said I had big black shoulders."

"Very odd."

"Very, but wait. So the leader's job — she called herself a spirit guide — was to interpret everyone's response then give me my answer. Oh yeah, one woman was hugging my thigh and another guy was running around the perimeter of the room at a pretty brisk pace. Anyway, do you know what the spirit guide said?"

"Couldn't begin to —"

The plane takes a hard bump, then another, and Jonathan sucks in his breath, his eyes darting out the window. The seatbelt sign pops on.

"Out of your control, remember?" Annie says, lifting up her hands. "And turbulence is nothing to worry about."

He sighs. "Tell that to my racing heart."

She places her mouth in front of his chest. "Turbulence is nothing to worry about."

She's made him smile his wry smile again. She likes making this man smile. "Do you like to cook?"

"Love to cook." He touches his stomach. "My downfall."

"Not at all." She hates to cook. "Food is life affirming." Faye was a human portrait of denial. At lunch, Les had offered Faye a piece of his untouched mahi mahi because she commented on never having tasted it. He cut off a small section, described it for her, "mild like sole but a meatier texture," extended the plate, and the look in his eyes, thought Annie, was as if he was offering a piece of himself.

Faye said one word, "No," and smirked as if he was being ridiculous.

The plane bumps again and Annie bounces in her seat just to tease him out of his fear.

"Oh, don't do that," he says with a shaky smile. "Keep distracting me. Now what did your spirit guide tell you?"

"She said and I quote: 'You — meaning me — are carrying around your birth mother's guilt.'" Annie raises her eyebrow and her index finger. "*Birth* mother, she said, though I hadn't told her I was adopted."

"Hmm."

"Said my mother transferred her guilt onto me and I was carrying it right here." She taps the back of her left shoulder. "And her guilt was from murdering my father."

"Your birth mother?"

"Murdered my father."

"That's a bit hard to believe."

"Well, yes, and I had let the whole strange idea slide until I saw a shaman three years later and asked the same question: Why do all my relationships with men end badly? He, I swear, pointed to my left shoulder and said I was carrying around my birth mother's guilt over murdering my father."

"Astounding."

"He and that spirit-guide woman both said that if I wanted an answer to my relationship question, I had to ask my birth mother about it."

"So, I'm sorry, was she in prison for the —"

"I don't think so."

"Or was this murder figurative?"

"Hmm. Like he died of a broken heart? I guess I don't exactly know."

"Continue please."

"So, we're at this restaurant and Faye is yabbering on about her husband, Nickel — What sort of name is Nickel? — and their apartment on Central Park West. On and on about the cost of slipcovers and new drapes. Les and I politely let her talk about herself for an hour straight." Annie turns to look squarely at Jonathan's warm, brown, tolerant eyes. "She didn't ask one question about our lives, our upbringing, what we did for a living, if we had any children. It was unbelievable."

"Perhaps it was her way of protecting herself from the pain of having abandoned her children?"

"Well, like Les said, she didn't do it once, she did it twice, so how painful could it have been?"

"But perhaps it wasn't…how to put it delicately, the same father?"

"Well, after enough warm sake shooters I finally cut right in and asked just that – did Les and I have the same father? She looked like I'd just punched her in the stomach. The hoods lifted on her eyes and I could see her making an enormous effort to continue to sit there, and I thought, with sudden hope, that she was going to crack and we were going to meet our real mom."

"It sounds heartbreaking."

At that, Annie can't help but give his big hand a stroke. "In a rather cold voice, Faye told us, 'Yes. You had the same father.' It was very satisfying to have that confirmed."

"How odd to give you both up then."

"No kidding. So then, despite Les nudging me under the table, I had to ask the next question: Why did you give us up?"

"She must have expected that."

"'If you want to blame someone,' she said, eyes wide open now as anger crept into her voice, and, I thought those were good signs, 'blame your father. He was the one who was married with his own -'"

Without warning the plane has tipped its nose into a dive. What happens next happens all at once. A forward thunk of luggage overhead, Annie's ears pop and fill with cottony silence. The flight attendant hits the deck and a hundred yellow fez-shaped masks attached to opaque plastic bags drop from overhead compartments with the click-shuffle of jack-in-the-boxes. In the near distance the plane screams obscenely at the ground and the little vodka bottles topple soundless over the edge of Annie's tray.

She flashes on the instructional-video parent placing a mask over her own face first but believes there is all the time in the world to fit Les's bendy rubber mask over his sleeping nose and mouth, slip the elastic behind his head onto the remarkably handy slots behind his ears. He blinks at her, groggy eyed, and she loves him completely. Her own mask smells like the inside of a Canadian Tire store, and when she breathes in, the oxygen bag collapses in on itself. She breathes out and still no movement of air. One more time and it's clear to her that it's not working. Slipping off the yellow cup, she places it on her head, the strap under her chin, and turns to Les. His face is sweetly confused as she hunches her shoulders and grunts like a monkey. She turns her monkey routine on Jonathan, who's pushed back against his seat, hyperventilating into his own deflated bag. And as she laughs at him, herself, at the whole insane situation, the plane levels off and its sharp whinny fades and settles back to its quiet roar. Less than a minute has passed.

A man's southern accent oozes from the walls. "This is Captain Kyle Hue speaking. Very sorry about that quick descent. We lost our cabin pressure and had to get, right quick, to a breathable altitude. But no worries, everything is under control."

There's a collective sigh like a balloon's slow hiss, followed by bright but subdued chatter. The flight attendant stands, feels her hair and makes a pleased expression as if she's just been pranked.

"That was some weird dream," Les says, taking off his mask,

his speech slurry. "My sister turned into an organ grinder's monkey."

"Mine wasn't inflating." She tugs off the yellow cap.

"It's not supposed to inflate," he says, which sets her off again, a giddy, manic laugh.

She turns to Jonathan who's slumped in his chair, his masked face dipped towards his shoulder. Eyes closed, he looks so perfectly relaxed that for a happy second she thinks he's sleeping. The next second she realizes otherwise and is ripping off the mask and slapping his face. "Jonathan! Les, press the button for help. Help!" She strokes a cheek then pinches a cheek and now pounds his chest over his heart. "Wake up! Jonathan!" She's crying, fighting off Les as he tries to pull her away and a man says, "I'm a doctor, I'm a doctor," like in some B movie. She grabs for Jonathan and a piece of him comes away, wedged between her fingers by small threads. A shirt button.

"With kids of his own," she calls out to him, desperate to go back in time, pick up where they left off. "My father, he already had his own kids."

She is being wrestled backwards towards the rear of the plane. Faye, she wants to tell him, wants him to know, wore perfume, White Shoulders. She left money on the table, to cover her lunch only, and Les made her take it back.

The same doctor who is supposed to be saving her new friend's life is now holding aloft a needle. Les has her in a bear hug to keep her arm steady. "It's all right, Annie," he whispers. "It's okay."

She looks at her brother's worried eyes, which are the same rainy grey rimmed in blue as their mother's, winces at the needle's sharp jab. And now she hears something else under Faye's admission, and stops her struggling. "She never told him about us," she mumbles to Les. "Our father never knew we existed."

"Maybe," says Les, as if it doesn't matter to him, but she knows it does by the way his grip loosens as if in surprise.

She murdered his existence she means to say, but her tongue has lost traction in her mouth. Which means he might still be out there.

The plane makes an emergency landing in Chicago and everyone is instructed to remain seated. In her haze, she sees two, or is it three, men stride down the aisle. They're dressed in white, are barefoot perhaps and take what seems like hours to unseat the nice cheese man she freed from gravity and heft him onto a narrow bed so he can sleep more comfortably.

Les strokes her hair, just like her father might have done if given half a chance.

Lovers
....

"The place is clean and safe," says Les as he lies in bed, Jill tucked up into his side. Her head is the perfect weight on his chest and her delicious bare leg crosses over his thigh. He's hoping to make love to her but knows she needs to talk first. "Nancy's eating three square meals, being looked after day and night. And, most importantly, she has plenty of companions and they aren't imaginary."

He's relieved to be back in his own bed in his clean-aired suburb, doesn't believe sleep is even possible in Manhattan without narcotics. It's clear Jill's secretly pleased there's not going to be another parent in the family to worry about. And he's a bit less eager to unite Pema with her birth mother. A damaged mother, it stands to reason, will pass on that damage to her children. But he blames his father, because what sort of selfish moron would be so careless as to knock up his mistress not once but twice. And not even be aware of it. He'd like to meet the man just to shock him out of his dream world.

"I'd feel less guilty if she was in a facility over here," says Jill.

"That's a second waiting game over which you have no control."

Jill had spent last summer living with and taking care of her mom, getting her assessed and on the wait-list for a care facility, meeting with estate lawyers and bankers and interviewing caregivers in search of someone to take over when September rolled around. Jill had settled on a kind and respectful Vietnamese woman named Lien who, after a month's time, Nancy decided she didn't know or like and flatly refused to let in the house. Which meant Jill had to take time off work, return to Vancouver and find someone new. The second caregiver was a ballsy Montrealer named Odile who made silver jewelry. She was a terrible cook, an even worse housekeeper, but she played cards and didn't put up with Nancy's moodiness. Then, just after the ordeal with Quinn, which put Jill in bed for three days, a room came up in what the social worker said was the best facility for dementia patients on the whole North Shore.

The holidays had been gruelling. He was working holiday hours, trying to stay on top of things at home while on the phone with his distraught wife every chance he got. The worst part for Jill was having to trick her own mother out of her beloved home into the car and then abandon her at the facility. Les had come up with the pretense that Nancy's doctor had ordered some tests that required sleeping over. After dropping Nancy off — "You'll pick me up tomorrow, right dear?" — the nurses sent Jill home with the order not to come back for five days, at which time she could bring more clothes and some household treasures to personalize Nancy's room. Jill had cried herself sick. This horror show was followed by having to clean out the house in order to put it on the market. The whole family helped out and it was a heartwarming couple of days, Jill putting on her best face in front of the kids. Now, months later, Les is still having to comfort her.

"There's a clique of women in the home," says Jill, who visited Nancy while Les was in New York, "all Mom's age, all middle class and proud of it, who sit together in the TV room. Each has a purse upright on her lap as if she's out visiting."

"Sounds all right to me."

"And anticipating going home. Anticipating someone who loves her coming to take her home."

"Stop torturing yourself."

"There's no love in those places," she says, lifting her head to search his eyes for answers he's not sure he has.

"You don't know that," he says and strokes her hair, gently forcing her head back down.

"I looked in her purse for cards to play a game of rummy — which she can still do with prompting — rather than sit in that sterile room and let her introduce me to the other patients again and again. Every three minutes. And not one of them remembers having been introduced and I'm greeted in the exact same way each time, same tone, smile. You start to think you're losing *your* mind. Anyway, there was nothing in it."

"Nothing in what?"

"Her purse. Well, there was a picture of some man in a nest of Kleenex."

"The man was lying in Kleenex?"

"The picture."

"Oh. So whose man was he?" says Les, trying to keep up.

"Haven't a clue. When I moved her in, I had to take away all her cash, credit cards, IDs... Odd symbolism to have stripped her of all identification."

Jill's voice is shaky and Les pulls her closer.

"But I'd left her wallet in there with the kids' school photos, pictures of me and Kenneth, Dad."

"No picture of me?" he tries for levity.

"And her little book of verse, car keys, reading glasses and a deck of cards."

"Car keys." Jill's mother hasn't driven for years.

"She loves that oyster shell key chain. The one she says Dad found that pearl in."

"So where did it all end up?"

"I asked a nurse, who said 'patients forget whose things are whose. It's like sharing toys to them.' Then I realized it wasn't even Mom's purse!"

Les snorts. "Who's on first?"

"This tiny lady named Bea had it."

"You switch them?"

"I told Bea she had the wrong purse and she smiled a great big smile and held on tighter. Got one of the male nurses to do it. The women of that generation listen to men."

"Was everything in there?"

"Her wallet was, and the cards, but no glasses, book or key chain."

"Do you think the nurses steal stuff?"

"Les, don't make me paranoid."

"I wasn't serious," he's quick to say, admonishing himself for planting that seed. "You know you did the right thing," he repeats. "It's the best facility in the area."

"Apparently Nancy has begun to undress herself in the public areas. Unbuttons her blouse, leaves it open, especially when one of the male nurses is around."

"That's interesting."

"No, that's weird. Awful. That's so not her."

"I know it's not her but, Sweetheart, dementia is progressive. Personalities change."

"They keep it awfully warm in there. I think she's too warm and is too polite to say, can you open a window? Turn down the thermostat?"

"Oh," he says, having forgotten to mention it and thinking this an opportune time. "I read this article in *Time*. On coffee. That studies are showing something in coffee slows memory loss in Alzheimer's patients."

"Mom loves coffee," says Jill, sounding hopeful. "I'll ask them to serve her more coffee."

On this positive note, he rolls over to face her, hoping his erection isn't too soon.

"What you do think about Beau going away for grades eleven and twelve?" she asks, and he knows the change in subject is a good sign. "That sure surprised me. Leave all his friends. Pema. Grade ten and he's already star of the senior rugby team."

"If he's serious about pursuing rugby, I guess that school's the place to be," says Les and kisses around her ear. "He'll have to get accepted first."

"He'll have to get financial aid, you mean. Are you aware of the cost?"

He starts down the side of her neck and she leans away, making room for him. Under his lips, he feels her faint shiver.

"With room and board it's forty thousand a year. We'd have to remortgage."

"I want you," he exhales in her ear.

"He kept asking so I went ahead and set up an interview."

"Door locked?"

She nods. "The entrance exams could be a problem."

He cups her face, a gesture she once told him never fails to make her feel beautiful.

"Pema's not happy about it," she says, then allows her eyes to close as his lips find her mouth and she kisses him back.

With his finger, he outlines her breast — how he loves her breasts — and as she exhales with a soft moan, he can almost see the thundering train of her thoughts derail, feel her sink into the forgotten home of her body. He marvels at her respon-siveness, the apparent magic in his hands. She pushes back against him and as her hand disappears under the sheet, his own thoughts crash and burn.

"Ow," he says in surprise.

"Ow?"

"A pain in the old rucksack."

"You have to get that checked out."

"Standing on my feet too long at work."

"I'll make an appointment."

"Shh…" He doesn't want to get off track here.

"You sure you're okay?"

"Am I okay?" he asks and takes her hand. "Come on."

He knows she's tired and was probably hoping to remain horizontal this time but he gently encourages her up off the bed.

NINE MONTHS LATER

· ·

BEAU

············

"Think of each boney angle, each indentation, as being shaped by personality," Ms. Jameson says into the quiet. "Trust the pictures that come to mind. Remember them."

Beau wishes the art teacher would shut up already. The girl's hands, soft as if covered in flour, are tracing the spiral cartilage of his ears. Here in grade eleven art, they have started portraiture and today are "going in blind." He could hardly believe it when he was paired with an Asian girl. No, focus on this girl's hands, here, right now probing the weird dips and bumps of his skull. It's like getting shampooed in slow mo and his eyes drift closed. Being touched is heaven.

Each of her fingers deserves a first and last name, he thinks, as five of them convene behind an ear to examine a trough of scar. His diving score too close to someone's cleat comes back to him in high def. Some scars are totally worth it, he wants to tell her and steals a look.

Her short, chubby lips are parted, as if in awe, and the black blindfold swallows her bean of a nose. She's kind of boxy, flat-chested, has a boyish haircut. He's been at St. Paul's two agonizing months now, in this girl's same art class, yet swears he's never seen her before. Asians, both here and at his public high school — which he misses so much he could puke — tend to hang together, speak their unintelligible codes outside of class, and Beau can never tell which side, exactly, is doing the ostracizing.

As her hands linger over his ears, she makes small snufflings through her nose and he remembers how his right ear sits higher than his left. She skims her fingertips from his hairline down to his eyebrows and back up again. Down and up, again, again, so ticklish he bites down and wills her to dig in her nails.

"Don't move," she whispers, more to herself.

"No problem," he whispers back, to no reaction.

He hopes he doesn't smell. Having failed room check this morning after putting his washed-out chip bag in the wrong recycling bin, he'd had to run three kilometres. His roommate, Alexei, had to run too because, according to the school's motto — One for All and All for One — no one ever acted alone. Alexei is a musician, spends most of his time sedentary and couldn't begin to run that far, so Beau, feeling guilty, piggybacked him whenever they were out of sight of the monitor.

The way her fingers poke and stab around his eyes, she's disturbed by his eye sockets. She smoothes his eyebrows, roughs them up then smoothes them again. She runs a fingertip along his lashes, the sensation like the butterfly kisses Pema once pestered him with.

Judging by the time she spends on his cheekbones she visualized them instantly, but then she fondles his nose as if it's some archaeological curio. As her thumb and forefinger measure the bridge of his nose, it dawns on him that smelling is a nose's secondary job. First it leads the way into battle, offers itself up to protect the more vulnerable eyes and brain. A nose is dispensable. The rugby coach, Mr. Dugan, broke his three times. When Beau saw the picture, which hangs in the hall down to the gym, of a young Dugan when he played for the national team, he barely recognized him. She pinches Beau's nostrils closed, forcing him to exhale out his mouth with a huff.

Her hands remain cupping his jaw for a weirdly long time until it feels like he's grown a meaty beard. He has a sudden image of her chubby lips kissing him and opens his eyes just as she moves on to his chin. Something about his chin dimple makes her laugh. Hey, what? he wants to say but doesn't. Pema calls it a butt chin. Is that what she's thinking? She mashes the skin around his mouth as if to assess the size and spacing of his teeth. This *doesn't* feel good but he lets her do it. Her fingers make him aware how the long roots of his teeth are embedded in his jawbone. And that teeth can probably only get knocked out from the root end. He wonders what the difference is, if any, between teeth and ivory.

As if she totally owns him, the girl pushes a confident finger between his lips to ease his mouth open and something in him lets go. Relaxing to a degree he didn't think possible in this place, he's hit by a new wave of homesickness because only Pema has ever touched him as freely.

Her finger slides along his lips and he involuntarily shudders. She lifts it away.

"Sorry," he breathes and she puts it back.

Now she toys with the dip beneath his nose and he knows she knows that he couldn't grow a moustache if he tried. Last year, after Quinn starting growing a moustache, Beau shaved his face with Dad's electric because Pema insisted that shaving makes hair grow in faster and darker because that's what happened when she first shaved her legs.

"Finish up now," warns the teacher and Beau's anger flares. "And no matter how strong the urge, when you remove your blindfold, no looking at your subject. Just turn directly to your easel."

He reluctantly opens his eyes to see the girl wheel back to

her easel and her hands become her own again as they remove her blindfold, take up her stick of charcoal and attack the paper with alarming confidence. Makes him think of Dad and the way he chooses a certain knife for the job, then chops with speed and abandon. God he misses his dad's cooking.

He turns to face the blank paper taped to his easel. He's supposed to transfer the image in the mirror clipped onto the side of his easel — a self-portrait — onto the paper. He does some careful measurements so that, at the very least, he'll get his features in the right places. He looks at the Asian girl's drawing. The hair she's drawing actually looks like hair, and he tries to mimic the abrupt, wispy motions of her hand.

"It's all in the shading," chimes the teacher as she passes behind him. "If you forget the rules for shading, look in your book." Beau opens his book.

He's trying to get his lips to look less wormlike when the girl appears beside him. She's only a foot taller than him seated.

"Turn to me, please." She doesn't know his name either.

He turns and she takes his chin in hand to study his eyes. Her irises are so dark they bleed into her pupils. Seal eyes, he thinks, and pictures Pema's, which are a more velvety brown.

"Smile," she whispers and smiles herself as if to show him how. She has a sly but sweet smile, dimples. When he mugs a grin, she tickles his ribs, hard, and he laughs — more because it hurt — smiling for real as she objectively studies his face.

"I'm a lot bigger than you," he threatens.

"No looking at your subject," calls the teacher.

Poker-faced, the girl returns to her portrait of him, which he sees is finished except for the empty eye sockets. She's caught the greasy shine to his nose which he hates, and she exaggerated, he's sure, the cleft in his chin, but still it looks like him, which is more than he can say for the monkey face on his easel.

After the bell rings and he's gone through the receiving line to thank the teacher formally for the class — a ritual inconceivable at his public school — he goes over to where the girl's packing up her things. "I'm Beau," he says and holds out his hand.

She looks at his hand then at him. "Tu es beautiful?"

"Yeah," he snickers. "I, I didn't name myself."

"You've got classic good looks," she says, glancing at her portrait of him. "It fits."

"You made me look good." He's blushing now.

"I was going for realism."

"Well, yeah, it's good. I, I, I won't come anywhere near capturing your face." He apologizes ahead of time because next class they're switching roles. "And your name is?"

"Satomi. Means fat fish in Japanese."

He smiles, unsure if she's joking or not. "Well, that doesn't fit."

She puts on her backpack. "I'd like to draw your hands."

He looks down at his hands. "Sure."

"Bye Beautiful."

"Bye Fat Fish."

She smirks. "Satomi, Beautiful."

He watches her leave, her pleated skirt swinging over strong shapely legs, and tries to recall what he knows about Japan: samurais, sumo wrestlers, kamikaze, sushi, atom bombs. *Mulan* had been Pema's favourite movie when they were little, and she'd make him watch it with her then proceed to block the TV screen as she performed each of the songs. He never did see the whole movie. She can't sing worth shit, he thinks smiling. Or was Mulan Chinese?

Beau thought he might have the dorm room to himself for a few minutes, but Alexei is there, leering into his computer. The constant companionship of boarding school is overwhelming and he doesn't know how kids stand it. It's Pema times ten, times seven hundred. Morning chapel, meals in the dining hall, classes, afternoon practices, mandatory group study in the evening, house meetings. At night, the shared bunk makes him aware of Alexei's every move, and self-conscious of his own. The bathroom's the only place he has any privacy. Pema made him promise to Skype her every night at bedtime, and he kept his promise for the first couple weeks before managing to get it down to Saturdays. School rules, he lied. Last Saturday he kept the video off so he couldn't see her. That made it easier.

He sometimes wonders why he misses his mom but not his dad and why he feels that missing in his throat when they talk on the phone. Realizes how Pema's famously purple bedroom, which is so chock full of photos, stuffies and souvenirs from every day of her life that you can't see the colour of any wall or surface, is the place he feels the safest. He was desperate to come home for Thanksgiving but there was a rugby clinic that weekend, a renowned coach in town from Argentina. The cafeteria made a traditional turkey dinner and he was tempted to get his dad to call the cafeteria and tell the cook to put curry and a single whole clove in the gravy.

"Hey, Alexei."

"What's up Bobo?"

He hates being called Bobo. "Game day."

"Oh, yeah. Rah, rah for the good guys."

"You know a girl named S...S...Satomi?" Beau can't believe he's starting to stutter again.

"Artist?"

"Yeah."

"Came the year before my incarceration. Tragic background

if I remember." He spins in his chair to face him. Alexei's lip hitches up on one side making him look like a Russian gangster. "Why, you want to toss her the dog water?"

The expression makes Beau both feel guilty and want to shower.

It's hard to believe he and Alexei grew up in the same country, much less the same province. Alexei plays piano, is into music composition, a hybrid of baroque and folk rock. Beau had to look up the word baroque. Alexei's father is rich, his mother Persian, and the guy speaks five languages. While Beau spent his summer working at a pizza joint and racking up kills on *Call of Duty 4*, Alexei was dancing in taboo nightclubs in Tehran and having his V-card punched in Paris. And, despite his sophistication, or maybe because of it — Beau has no idea — Alexei is crude around the subject of girls.

"Just think she's funny," says Beau and grabs his pumice stone.

"Good. Gay as a parasol is my guess. But the Japanese, hey, they'll let anybody on their swing. Satomi reminds me of Hello Kitty, if Hello Kitty wasn't a kitty, or a doll."

Beau drops the subject, sits and pulls off his socks.

"Checked out Jenna?" Jenna was one of the girls on Alexei's list of hot girls.

"She's all right." He files the ridge of callous that's forming on his left heel.

"I hear she's drooling to get her hands on you, Bobo. And Melissa too. You know her. She's the blazing redhead in your English class."

Beau, perversely, is never attracted to girls attracted to him.

"Talks too much," says Beau, blowing away the dead skin.

"Tell them that whoever gives the best blow job can go out with you. Have a blow-off." He laughs, a tight high trilling.

"Best of three," he adds laughing harder, the sound like his head's coming unscrewed.

Beau forces a snicker, keeps pumicing.

"Speaking of gay." Alexei scoffs at Beau's foot then spins back to his computer.

"Keeps the blisters away," he says checking his other foot. Alexei wouldn't understand the truth. That soft-skinned feet means he can feel the ground, meld with it, like an exchange of fluids. And though he thinks this contact makes him infinitesimally slower, it also makes him infinitesimally harder to knock over.

He opens his side of the closet and takes out the brand new uniform. He likes "suiting up" as he thinks of it. Likes the way his black underarmour hugs his thighs and butt, defines the muscles of his chest and arms. Loves this black and gold jersey with his number, 18, and the warm-up jacket with his name sewn in perfect cursive on the sleeve. Beau Wright. Great rugby name, people always say. He pulls on the used shorts he bought from a guy in the house who claimed they were worn by Stephen Jones, captain of Wales and a friend of a cousin back in Ireland. Alexei said Beau'd been had, but whatever, they were top quality, only a small tear that he easily stitched.

Dressed, he admires his body in the closet door mirror, flexes his neck and practices his "cannibal" look. "The other guy should be convinced you're about to take a bite out of his face," coach Dugan said at last week's practice.

He fusses his hair into place then shuts the door, grabs two protein bars. He'll eat one at halftime, one directly postgame.

Alexei swings around in his chair. "You could strangle someone with those thighs, you know."

Beau snorts to hide a smile and grabs his bag. "Have a good

jam," he says. Alexei's afternoons are spent with a quartet of student musicians.

"Make someone ugly, Bobo."

•••

"Beau-man!"

"Killer." Beau stops to let his teammate catch up and is glad to see Killer's black eye has healed so fast and so well. Dropped a dumbbell on it was his story.

"How's it going?" Killer is beaming. "Game day!" He's always happy as far as Beau can tell. The kind of happy, though, that looks like a decision, and effort.

"Yeah," agrees Beau. Today it's only an exhibition game, but he's more nervous than pumped. He's here on a scholarship after all, and it isn't for his good looks. Or, as Quinn likes to point out, for his grades.

"I saw a picture of you," Killer says.

"Huh?"

"Art class. Ms. Jameson was using it as an example. Was totally you."

"A girl named S…S…Satomi did it."

"Satomi's gifted, man. Going to be famous some day. Like you."

"Yeah, sure." Killer's always gushing high-flying compliments.

"She lost her parents and sisters, you know, in some freak train accident in Japan. She was like, eleven."

"Satomi?"

"Yeah. Lives here year around."

"That sucks." Beau hates stories like that. Makes him want to hit something.

...

It's halftime and an enraged Coach Dugan has called a huddle. Sweaty and mud splattered, the players stand with their arms wrapped around each others shoulders and encircle the coach. "Not fucking good enough." He whips off his ball cap and drills it into the ground. "Who's your check, Moore?"

"Twenty," mutters the guy on Beau's left.

"Fucking look at me when I'm talking to you."

Lyle Moore lifts his head, his arm tightening around Beau's shoulder. Beau's arm tightens back.

The coach's face is flushed, his cauliflower ears inverted conch shells, his nose something deflated. Dugan is a god among coaches. Under his five-year reign, St. Paul's has won more rugby games than any school in North America.

"Then why do I see number twenty *pussy-skipping down the field*?" Dugan's saliva warms the side of Beau's face. "Everybody pulls his own weight and stays on his check." His eyes lands on Beau's. "That one tackle was yours, Wright."

Beau was distracted by a woman on the sidelines wearing a purple jacket like Pema's. "Y...y...y...yes, sir."

"Y...y...y," says the coach, then moves on to a grade twelve named Mick. Beau seethes, hating himself.

"A little late, Mick," says the coach.

"If it wasn't for fucking Phan," says Mick. Andy Phan, one of their own, was the touch judge who called Mick's try incomplete.

"Were you fucking Phan?"

Nervous laughter loosens the circle.

"Remember, you're only as good as your team." Dugan doesn't seem to realize that he's stepping on his ball cap, pushing it into the mud. "You're one machine out there. One."

"One," echoes the captain, and the team follows a beat later. "It's a question of?"

"Honour!" they bark in response, their deep voices deeper on purpose.

Dugan gives them a sad, even loving, smile, as if any second he might tear up. "Show me what I know you can do."

Beau's never had a coach who cared about the game as much as this man, and by extension cared about him as a player, and can't help but want to please him.

From the start of the second half, Beau is absorbed to the point where anything beyond muscling towards one united goal is background noise. He makes every one of his tackles, two huge kicks downfield and a crucial fake-then-pass to Mick, who scores. When he plays well, he's free from thinking about things he has no business thinking about. This is why he loves the game, why he needs the game. And what always amazes him is how he can never tell which comes first, his playing well or his team playing well. Chicken or egg, Coach Dugan is clearly the wise rooster.

Though they lose four tries to three, Dugan's ecstatic in the dressing room. "That's what I like to see," he booms, "one pumping heart out there. One heart." Smiling so broadly Beau can see a molar missing on one side, the coach thuds his chest with the butt of his fist. It isn't the first time Beau makes note of the size of his fist.

"We're going to need that same aggressive teamwork Thursday when we play the Irish lads. Play it forward in your brain. Just like you played now...play it forward."

Eyes open behind the blindfold, Beau reaches towards Satomi's face but doesn't find it. A second later, she takes a firm hold of his hands and draws them down on top of her head.

He smiles his thanks.

Her head shape feels like a rounded-off square and he can't stop picturing Hello Kitty. She scratches her scalp, pushing aside his hand. He waits until she's finished. Her hair is almost as short as his except for a silky curtain of bangs that hangs just past her eyebrows. Pema has the same bangs except that the rest of her hair hangs to her waist. His thoughts return to Satomi as her head pivots left. Though she was crazy focused when doing the touching, now she won't stop fidgeting. She turns her head right. She shivers. Then sucks her teeth — at least that's what it sounds like — making it impossible to concentrate. Sure, he's no artist like her, but he can't afford to blow the assignment either and she knows that. Any mark below a C+ puts him on the bench. She scratches her cheek, knocking his hand. He feels dismissed, even disliked, and that whatever connection they made two days ago was in his mind only.

Satomi sighs as if waiting for him to get on with it which makes him even more pissed off. Doesn't *his* touch feel good to *her*? She starts to turn her head and he stops her, forces it forward and holds it still. Her face sandwiched between his hands, he waits for her reaction. She doesn't resist, doesn't say anything, but then, slowly and with deliberation, she starts to turn her head again, forcing it against his hands. He forces it straight again.

"I'm stronger than you, remember?" he whispers and feels her smile before all her resistance seems to disappear. "Okay," he says with a nod.

Except for a small rough patch on either cheek, her skin is ridiculously soft.

When he touches her ears she makes them wiggle ever so slightly.

"Talent," he whispers.

She wrinkles her nose and somehow stresses it the tiniest bit to cause it to vibrate.

He knows she'll bite him when he comes to her lips, and she does. It hurts but he doesn't let on, just leaves his finger there until her teeth give up and release him.

Nearly finished, he cups her chin with both hands just like she did to him. When he hears the teacher speaking to someone on the far side of the room he leans over and, teasingly soft and brief, kisses her lips. And she, who would have seen it coming, doesn't stop him. As soon as he pulls away, she slips from his hands with a screech of chair wheels along the floor.

He yanks down his blindfold to see Satomi slumped in her chair, arms crossed, eyes down, knees bouncing against each other under her tartan skirt. He can't tell if she's furious or about to cry. He runs a hand through his hair, thinking how to explain himself. Why *did* he do it?

When he starts to apologize, she wrinkles her nose to its vibrating point and flashes a tiny smile. He laughs to himself, you win, and drops back in his chair.

His portrait of her looks like a cross between an alien and a panda bear. Hello Kitty, in other words, if Hello Kitty wasn't a kitty. When Satomi turns in her chair and sees it, she bursts out laughing, which prompts an invitation up to Ms. Jameson's desk. While Satomi gets in trouble, he checks out her self-portrait; an arty, exaggerated likeness with oversized features as if she's making fun of herself. The inflated lips have a light shining on their centre. He scoots over in his chair and takes a closer look. The light's in the shape of puckered lips. His kiss?

Satomi is now walking towards him and he wheels back to his easel. She comes and stands beside his chair.

"I want to apologize for laughing at your picture of me," she says, unapologetic, then whispers, "You are free to whip me."

"Hmm... Start with a walk after dinner?"

She covers her mouth to keep from laughing aloud again. "But Beautiful," she whispers, "fish don't walk."

"We could go to the pond?"

"So what *does* Sa...Satomi really mean?"

They're walking the chip path around the school's perimeter. Well, he's walking and she's sashaying or clomping or sliding on her feet while making mini-breaststroke and diving motions.

"Wise beauty," she says. "Not to be confused with your kind of beauty."

"Dumb beauty?"

"No. Easy. Easy beauty."

"It's not my fault I...I look a certain —"

"I know. It's just good face-fortune."

"Hey, I might not have lost my family, but that doesn't mean my life's easy."

"Oh, you've heard my sad story," she says and walks hunched forward, arms crossed over her head. "Poor fat fish."

"Wise beauty," he says.

She straightens and begins walking sideways, crossing one foot over the next. "Everyone has a sad story. But you see I now speak perfect English with no accent and will be able to get any number of jobs in Japan. And, before coming here, I knew nothing about art. So, happy ending. But I have vowed that after I graduate from this school I will never eat another potato, never go to any form of chapel and never recycle anything ever again."

Beau laughs and tells her how he failed room check on Monday.

"I failed room check so many times my first year, my room-mate hated my guts, sad story, but I was in the best shape of my life, happy ending." She runs on the spot, makes an ugly determined face, then walks backwards, facing him. "So tell me your sad story."

"I'm here for the rugby, don't really have a sa...sa...sa..." Embarrassed, he looks at her and is grateful when she looks away. "God, I haven't stuttered since I was a little kid."

"This place takes getting used to."

"Yeah."

"How did you get over it? Stuttering. I mean before."

"Well, it was Pema really."

"Pema?"

"Ma...ma...my sister. She's adopted. Mom couldn't have any more kids after me. My aunt was raising money for Tibetan orphans. So —"

"Pema."

"Yeah."

"She older or younger?"

"Almost a year older but in my s...same grade. Mom kept her back." He takes a breath. "First you should know that my mother's a linguist who considered my stutter her personal failure, so tried all these exercises on me and when those failed put me in speech therapy. All of which made it worse because I became super self-conscious about it."

"I know that one."

"Anyway, new country, new family and all, Pema cried a lot in the beginning. I mean, like all the time. Couldn't under-stand a word of English."

"How old was she?"

"Three almost four. So, the story is whenever Pema cried, Mom dragged me over to talk because it would make Pema laugh instead of cry. She has this great laugh," he says, smiling, "like sheep bleating. Anyway, my stutter became the best joke ever and I was like some big hero so, naturally, I started to try and force the stuttering. Was instantly cured."

She stops walking.

"Sorry, long story," he says.

"You didn't stutter once right then," she says, taking his hand and examining the back of it.

"Oh?"

"You miss your sister." She makes it a statement.

"We've always been pretty close."

"Pretty?"

"Too pretty," he says before realizing that's not what she meant. He pulls his hand away and strides ahead. He just sounded like a sick perv.

"Don't worry, Beautiful," she says, catching up. "Whatever your sad story, this place will beat it out of you. You know, I'd really like to draw your hand."

Owen Daily arrives at practice still in his school uniform.

"Why aren't you dressed?" Coach Dugan says as if confounded by what he's seeing.

"I can't see very well." Swollen shut, Owen's left eye is a fat clam, the skin muddied shades of yellow and purple. A cleat to the face was his story.

"You can walk?" asks the coach.

"Yes, sir."

"Then you can run. And I'm planning to start you in Thursday's game against JKS."

Owen's good eye perks up. He's also a grade eleven on the senior team but, unlike Beau, Owen has yet to start.

"Tomorrow go see the nurse to hurry that eye along. Now

run and get dressed."

Owen begins to leave.

"I said run," says the coach, and Owen breaks into a sprint and bangs his elbow on the door frame, stifling a squeal.

When it's *his* face that's messed up, thinks Beau, maybe the coach will let him play centre. And what will his story be? Diving try against the goalpost?

They have a warm-up run, stretch, and then, because the fields are dry for a change, the coach calls a game of touch. After the game, they head to the gym to weigh in before hitting the machines. Beau's sorry to see he's lost three pounds. He sets himself up on the rowing machine beside Killer.

"What's your weight, Johnny boy?" the coach asks a grade twelve, his tone too friendly.

"Same."

"You did write down the same weight as last month," he says loud enough for everyone to hear, "but you don't look the same to me."

Johnny continues adjusting the height of the pec press.

"Come on over and let's have a look-see together." Dugan grabs a fistful of Johnny's hair and leads the over-weight defenseman, hunched and helpless, to the scales. Beau can't watch.

"Two-hundred-sixty-one pounds," announces Dugan. "Whoa. Now that's what I call fat."

A couple of guys snicker.

"What are you laughing at?" snaps Dugan. "What's funny about one of your own being overweight? It means *you're* overweight."

He lets go of Johnny's hair and smoothes it back in place as he speaks. "At meals, vegetables and protein first. Have second helpings of these only, then go for the fruit. Hopefully you're pretty full, but if you must, have a little pasta or bread for dessert. It'll work. Trust me." He pats his own flat gut. "If I or anyone on your team sees you eating chips or cookies, you're on the bench next game. Right?" he calls to the room at large.

"Right," they echo.

Beau catches Dugan's eye and quickly looks away, rowing as if this stupid machine could actually take him somewhere. Namely back home. Imagines Pema's room, sunk into her beanbag chair, surrounded by the pictures of their childhood she's plastered over her —

"Wright, with a W."

"C...C...Coach?"

"Outside."

"Outside?"

"Outside."

Dugan disappears through the door that leads behind the gym. Beau gets up, his muscled legs hollow and weak.

"It's when you look up," whispers Killer, his eyes straight ahead as he slides forward and back on his rowing machine. "That's when."

Beau nods and forces his feet towards the back door. None of the other guys dare look at him, dare acknowledge this initiation they've each gone through or will go through. But they're with him every step of the way, Beau tells himself. They're his team. He's one of them. He presses down the bar on the door and steps out into the grey light of the afternoon.

"Shut the door, Wright."

Beau does as he's told. The gym backs onto a dense grove of evergreens, out of sight of other students, teachers, staff. Dead pine needles litter the narrow strip of dirt and gravel that runs the length of the building.

"Come over here."

Fixing his gaze on the man's immense running shoes, Beau goes and stands in front of the coach.

"To go to this school and play with these guys is a privilege and an honour."

"Yes, sir."

"And do you know that the methods I use, as your coach, are to help you become a better team player?"

"Yes, sir, I do." What would Mom say if she knew?

"Good. So I need to know if you, as one of our most talented guys, if I do say so, want to be on this team."

"Yes. Thank you, sir." His fear momentarily billows with pride.

"So you will keep what happens today between us."

"I will, sir." As he makes himself a promise that rugby will be the most important thing in his life, the strength returns to his legs. What's a little pain anyway? He raises his gaze to where Dugan's knees hide beneath his sweatpants. "I just want you to know, sir, that I...I...I...I...," Beau says, then hitches up his lip like Alexei's, "I want to toss the dog water to muh... muh...muh." He looks up.

The punch to his cheek is harder than he expected and he reels backwards, lights flashing in his head, but doesn't fall. Before he can feel the pain, he stumbles back up to the coach, looks him in his eye and says, "sister," before a second punch, in the nose this time, extinguishes light and consciousness.

He doesn't remember hitting the ground, but when he opens his eyes, a rusty taste tickles his throat and he's looking at the saddest-coloured sky he's ever seen. But what he notices more, lying here in the dirt, is the incredible relief he feels. As if he finally landed, planted his feet on the ground, after a long, anxious time hovering just above. The next thing he notices is that he isn't thinking of Pema but of Satomi and how different her next portrait of him is going to be and that he might have to change his fucking name. As he gently touches his off-centred nose, which is already twice its normal size, his laugh comes out as an ugly gurgle.

Brothers

∙∙∙∙∙∙∙∙∙∙∙∙∙

Quinn is at his desk listening to Fats Waller and staring at a picture of a Renaissance stone bridge brilliantly arcing the Tiber. He has a project due: Create a structure or structures that connect a city with its landscape. He scrolls down, reading about the social history of this Roman river, slips a mickey of rum from the bottom drawer of his desk and takes a long swig. Pictures a metal arch from riverbank to riverbank with something practical yet magical…huge dome-shaped building suspended from its centre and dangling mere feet above the rushing river. It would need walkways, but how…

The phone shatters his concentration. Irritated, he lets it ring before he remembers Pema's at school, Mom's at work and Dad's napping. With a grumble, he turns down the National's *Boxer*.

"Hello?"

"Quinn?"

"What do you want, Beau."

Early arena, gladiator style, perfectly symmetrical, made from cement and limestone blocks, is how Quinn thinks of Beau. It rubs him wrong that his jock brother is at a private boarding school with a stellar academic reputation. Quinn did his research.

"Nobody's around," says Quinn. "Well, Dad is but he's

sleeping, down with the flu or something. Call back later."

"When's later?"

"I heard you dove face first into a goalpost and that you're pretty ugly now?"

Beau laughs his menacing laugh. "Make up your mind."

Good one, thinks Quinn. "That you've defaced your face," he says, guessing Beau won't know what deface means.

"I still make your face look sorry."

"Pfft. How's school?"

"Imagine jail. Oh, you don't have to imagine. Beat up any more girls lately?"

Quinn shakes his head. Can hear Beau now, in the locker room, telling the story of his drunk brother, wearing it like one of his scars. "I was inebriated, that means drunk. I tripped and fell on her. End of narrative, that means story." A familiar emptiness hollows his chest, as though all integrity has been drained out of him. He hasn't dated since Lauren. Hasn't even gone out except to a movie or two with his friend Graham.

"She was kind of a bossy bitch anyway," says Beau.

"You're getting meaner *and* stupider?"

"No, but I'm getting stronger. I could crush you with one hand."

"I'm sure you can." Quinn hangs up, tired of sort-of joking. He can easily picture his younger brother beating the shit out of him, can sense he would find it really satisfying for reasons even he doesn't know. He cranks the volume on his music. Picks up a pencil, taps the eraser against his nose then takes another hit of rum. He opens his sketchbook and copies the picture of the Tiber, placing the stone bridge in the background. In the foreground he draws a metal arch the same height as the bridge, and from its center, a giant birdcage-like structure hovering over the river. Ballroom sized...diaphanous walls. The prof is all about natural light. And energy efficiency, he recalls, drawing solar panels all along the top of the arch. The circular floor is made of…plexiglass! The rushing water below taking your breath away. Giving people vertigo, fainting spells. Antique fainting couches around the perimeter of the room. Weddings. The symphony.

The diaphanous walls a pale blue to enhance the water effect. He pencils in walkways to connect the structure to either shore.

The apex of the dome will be one giant skylight. Sky above, water below, like standing in a vertical tunnel. Quinn smiles, rewards his brilliance with another drink.

The walkways also see-through, every step – he thinks with a mean satisfaction – will feel like falling, will be death defying. "Walking on Water" he could call it. Maybe the Vatican will fund it.

Below the window of Jill's shared office, students hustle to classes, faces tucked into collars against the blowing rain. Except for taking an unpaid year off for the birth of each of the boys, she's been at university since she was eighteen. She dials the number of her mother's care facility and it takes four rings before someone picks up.

"Cedargrove."

"The Alzheimer's wing, please."

Jill pictures the phone as it rings in her mother's wing, on the desk inside a glass-walled office.

"Cedargrove."

A rock station plays in the background and she knows it's the same music that's pumped throughout the wing, competing with the TV in the living room. Jill suggested they could play music from an era the patients might well remember and enjoy, but nothing came of it.

"I'd like to speak with a resident. Nancy Thomas." She considered installing a phone in Nancy's room but Nancy is rarely in her room except to sleep, and patients wander in and out of each other's rooms. She could end up talking to anybody.

"Nancy. And who is this calling?" The woman sounds impatient.

"I'm hoping to speak to my mother."

"Is it an emergency?"

Every minute's an emergency, thinks Jill. "I do need to speak to my mother. Nancy Thomas." Unable to come over this weekend, Jill just needs to hear Nancy's voice. Know she's all right.

"Hold on."

There's yelling in the background and Jill winces, pictures the heavy metal entrance and exit door. Every visit, there's one old woman with a walker watching that door as if for her parents, or God, waiting for someone, anyone to punch in the sequence of four numbers that adds up to liberation. On Jill's last visit, the old woman who blocked Jill's way out, edged closer and closer whispering "take me with you" before a nurse scolded her in a heavy Spanish accent and forcibly turned her around and steered her into the TV room. The defeated woman was visibly scared. Jill sat in the car and cried for twenty minutes before she was able to drive home.

Jill makes the trip over once a month and spends the day with Nancy, takes her for a walk or drive, out to lunch and sometimes dinner. Occasionally Les comes too.

"Some people just drop them off and leave them," a staff member, Filipino, who Jill has come to know, told her during one visit. "They think the person doesn't know who they are, so what difference can it make?"

"But you think it makes a difference?" Jill asked.

"Oh, yes. On the days that family visits, patients sleep better. Eat better."

"I work full time," Jill needed to tell her, "and live in Victoria but have her on two wait-lists for facilities over there."

"Hmm... Moving can be terribly disorienting. She's not unhappy here."

Not unhappy.

In her absence Jill pays Odile to go visit twice a week to play cards, go for walks or ice cream and do any shopping Nancy may need, like hunting down shirts without buttons. Unbuttoning her blouse in front of the male nurses has become a habit.

"Do I answer this phone?" she hears Nancy ask.

"It's for you. It's your daughter."

Jill sees her mother standing in the office, on the wrong side of the glass, uncomfortable, no one offering her a chair.

"Mom? You there?"

"Hello?"

"Mom, it's me, Jill. Jillian. How are you?"

"Jill. I'm busy in the office."

"Have you and Odile been out for a drive today?"

"I went for a drive. All around the town."

"Good. Did you have an ice cream?"

"It's very busy here."

There's so much she wishes she could tell her mom. Her paper's been accepted for publication and, though she didn't make the short list for the tenure position, she should get a salary increase. And about Beau's broken nose and fractured cheekbone, how he's wearing a protective mask and hasn't missed a game. Quinn's straight As. Pema having her first boyfriend, going on dates and all. Les undergoing a series of tests for what they first thought was a hernia and now aren't sure about.

"I won't keep you. Just to say I can't make it this weekend but will come next weekend."

There's a scuffle and bang as if the phone's been dropped. Then it goes dead.

Jill waits for a minute, then there's a dial tone and she hangs up. The chronic guilt she used to feel is now closer to grief. And anger at her self-involved brother, Kenneth, for making her take this on alone. She's about to call back to say a proper goodbye when her two o'clock appointment knocks on her door.

FIVE MONTHS LATER

LES

· · · · · · ·

Eyes hunting in the dark, Les makes his way down the driveway, trips on a pile of pruned branches and rights himself with a clumsy skip.

Filmy pools of light illuminate their cul-de-sac and, like some invisible night janitor, a lumbering wind has swept dirt and pine needles neatly up against the curb. A cool moistness in the night air feels like pure oxygen, and Les breathes it in along with positive images of healthy cells.

What first sold him on this neighbourhood were the trees, so many you can barely see the houses. Garry oaks, juniper, red cedars, all of which appear curiously alive in the dark and make him wonder if trees could be somehow nocturnal. Or maybe they're just insomniacs like him.

Last night, at three in the morning, he made a batch of phyllo pastry, the night before, french loaves. Tonight he had to get outside and walk. The oncologist warned that the hormone therapy could cause insomnia but failed to mention this nervy, phantom feeling in his lower legs that makes him have to move them. Either that or ram a paring knife into his calves. When Les described the sensation to Jill, she said she'd had the very same when pregnant, her smile strained. "I don't *think* I'm pregnant," he joked to cover their mutual pain.

A chip bag cartwheels past and he grabs it, crumples it into his jacket pocket.

They bought the house the same year they brought Pema and a recipe for momos home from Nepal. Bought it outright with the money from his parents' estate. He's not a great provider but he did provide a roof over their heads. He's proud of that anyway. God, that was a stressful year, moving house, Pema having night terrors, Beau acting out, Jill getting more teaching work all the while fretting she wasn't there for her daughter. He ended up the stay-at-home parent — cooked, kept the house somewhat in order, played one game after another with the kids. Something he wouldn't trade for all the truffle oil in the world. God, you blink and they're all grown up.

He'd woken tonight to Jill's breath warming his shoulder. When he removed a tail of hair from her eyes, she'd made a sleepy sound of annoyance and turned to her other side. She's frustrated, angry even. Not about the lack of sex, he hopes, but with the fact he's only forty-eight. Hell, he'd be angry too if the estrogen pills weren't turning his blood a passive pink. Instead, he's on the verge of weeping half the time. Like at Sunday's game when Beau made that unbelievable tumbling kick down the sidelines then dove on the ball in the try zone. His pug-faced, teeth-gnashing coach had leapt on the field and hugged Beau as though he were his own son while Les had to duck behind the stands to hide the tears raining down his face. Beau would have been embarrassed beyond belief.

It's after three and the neighbourhood is quiet except for a feeling like static electricity in the air, a vibration that dogs might hear. Is he imagining it or is it the pull of the moon, or maybe the invisible cross-hatch of wireless networks? He's read that where networks cross over, the recognized safe level of waves in the air is no longer safe, especially for kids. When he logs on to his computer, three other wireless networks pop up. Maybe they should change back to plug-ins.

He passes Jim and Liza's house. They have two kids, eleven-year-old Hailey who's musically precocious, if not a genius, and her younger brother Darwin, who has Down's syndrome. He loves that they named the kid Darwin, and how every time he says hi to the kid, Darwin gives him this look of superior disdain. Darwin loves Pema, who has babysat him since he was two. "Pretty Pema," he calls her and loves to touch her hair.

Les picks up his pace, counts his blessings for having had healthy children. He'd take being sick any day over one of his kids being sick. Hell, fifty was considered a long life a hundred years ago. Still is, in some parts of the world. You get old, you get sick, you die. Everybody does it. Every second of the day. Doesn't mean you're special.

Annie had found out that their father, a man named Frank Chapman, owner of Chapman Realty, had died a mere two years before they found Faye. Frank and Faye. Chapman sounds English, or is it Scottish? Would have liked to have seen a picture. There's an animal satisfaction to knowing what you're made of. Who you're made of. He suddenly wants to know what Frank died of, how old he was. Maybe he'll send Faye a note and ask. He's left that sort of thing up to Annie, but Faye would have his home address then, in case she wanted it.

There are no stars out tonight, only a bruise-coloured sky with a patchy highway of cloud crossing its middle. As he turns down Parkside, a couple of street lights are burned out and it's hard to tell what creature is crossing the road ahead of him. His eyes adjust in time to make out a raccoon's hump-backed lope. He once read how the invention of street lamps changed people's biorhythms so they stopped going to sleep with the sun and, as a result of the increased "daylight" hours, crime increased a hundred percent. The article declared progress an illusion, that a step forward in one direction was inevitably a step back in the other. Like when Les asked his oncologist, why him?

"Petrochemicals and their by-products are a root cause of carcinogenic cell mutation. Of course, reproductive organs are the first to go." The man used that gloating factual tone scientists are good at, then patted the vinyl-covered examining table. "Ubiquitous now. We're stuck with finding a cure."

It was a survival-of-the-fittest answer Les couldn't argue with. But later it made him angry to think that no one was doing anything about these man-made cancers and that his sons might also be vulnerable, with their lives compromised some day.

A pushy wind at his back makes him pick up his pace before a tweak in his groin reduces him to one anxious thought: it's back. A minute later the pain's gone. God, he's fretting like an old woman. Man up. Where's the guy who prefers his sex standing up? He laughs weakly. And he thought having his wife be the breadwinner was emasculating. These little pills take the prize.

Around the next corner someone is crouching in the street and Les slows his step, considers turning around. It *is* the middle of the night. Why the hell is he crouching?

"Hey," says Les, twenty feet away.

"Hi there." The man unfolds to standing. To Les's relief, he's short and pudgy. "Letting my cats out for a whizz."

Les sees the cats then, Siamese, one large, one small, curl out from the man and come toward him. "Same litter?" he asks.

"Brothers. Rescued them from the reserve," the guy says proudly. Les can't tell in the half-light if the guy's Native or not.

It's Les's turn to squat, let the cats sniff his hand, but they veer back to their saviour.

"Bubbles and Monkey," says the man, and he makes a kissing sound. "Bubbles is the runt."

"Bubbles and Monkey." Good name for a dessert, thinks Les as he stands. Something with pink meringue and chocolate and some kind of fruit or nuts. "See ya."

"'Night," says the man, and Les likes that he wasn't asked what *he* was doing out this late.

At the end of the block he turns into Orchard Meadows, the new subdivision, named after the dozens of apple trees the developers toppled. The wind sounds lost as it races down this street with nothing to rustle, no blossoms to scatter like confetti. One balmy summer night years back, returning from the grand opening of a restaurant where he once worked — the manager couldn't taste the difference between real butter and margarine, shallots and yellow onion — and having indulged in the free champagne, he and Jill snuck into this former orchard under cover of darkness and had the best sex he can remember. Dr. Linguist was a drunken harlot. Normally quiet when love-making, she let loose these sounds, growly and breathy and round, like a lioness letting her hunger be known. Makes him horny just thinking about it. They found petals, later, pasted on their backsides.

He walks up the street, past the sprawling but close-set homes, their postage-stamp back yards. When did mowing and gardening a patch of earth become undesirable? The street ends in a cul-de-sac and as he circles back he hears a screech owl. Peers up at rooftops hoping to see one when a second-storey light comes on in a house ahead to his left. Not an owl but a child with a nightmare? He's back to that year with Pema and her night terrors. Emitting heart-shattering screams despite being sound asleep, she woke the whole house and made him worry they'd made a terrible mistake. That no amount of riches, education, nutrition and love could fill the emotional chasm left by one's missing mother. He used to sit by her bed, hold her stricken little hand and talk to her over the screams. Tell her about all the things she had to look forward to in her new life. Tell her that he also had two mothers, and that because raising a child is the best job ever, they have to share it or it wouldn't be fair.

They'd received a second letter from Pema's birth mother after he convinced Jill to send pictures — ones not just of Pema but of the whole family — and to be straight about wanting to wait until Pema was older before letting her come to visit. The woman was very understanding in her response, though Les has been thinking it's time now. Two years have passed and Pema is sixteen, not the most mature sixteen, but still.

He passes the house with the light on when another screeching cry is followed by banging, like someone pounding on a door. Then a man's voice yelling. The lit window rasps open and a woman appears, leans forward and peers down at the ground as if judging how far it would be to jump.

"Are you okay?" Les calls.

She looks out in surprise, quickly steps back and closes the window. More yelling, pounding. Adrenalin strides Les up the woman's driveway. He takes the three steps to her door in one, and knocks with a firm fist before punching the doorbell.

The yelling stops. Les knocks again, a little less firmly, and scrambles for what to say and how to react if the man is hostile, or armed. Scans for a weapon of this own. Flower pot? A hall light comes on and he's drenched in porch light, exposed and feeling way less certain. The door opens and it's the woman in the window, a pale blonde, slight, wearing a dazzling lemon silk kimono and holding a sleepy baby who blinks at the brightness. Les strains his neck to make sure no one's behind them.

There's no sign anybody's been hurt. He can't help wondering, as he often does with strangers, if she's eaten in one of the restaurants he's cooked for. If he's cooked for her and maybe, by proxy, the baby.

"May I help you?" Her expression is unreadable, its frank lack of curiosity whisking him back to his mother Faye and that horrible restaurant meeting in New York.

"Hey, my name's Les. I live over on Thurston and was out walking. Everything all right?" He can't help smiling at how the baby smushes his cheek against his mother's shoulder, grips her kimono in a fat fist. He wants nothing more than to protect these two strangers. "I was just wondering —"

"No thank you," she says, as if he were selling magazine subscriptions. She drops her gaze and for a still second seems to hold her breath as though about to confide in him but then slowly shuts the door. The porch light vanishes and he stands there, more in the dark than ever, feeling helpless and then blindly furious. He kicks the banister, possibly fracturing a toe, gets control of himself and leaves.

Was the baby a red herring? He looks back at the house, the light still on upstairs. He'll make a point of walking this way if he's up in the night again. "I've got my eye on you, buddy."

At the end of the street he stops and rakes a hand through his hair wondering which way to go? May not be able to sustain an erection, he thinks, but at least he's kept his hair. "Girly thought," he mutters and turns right along the main road.

He cuts down a path between houses that leads back into his subdivision. Penned in by chain-link fence, he passes indecently close to windows on either side, treads through the sound of snoring. Halfway down the path he gets a distinct whiff of skunk. He's never seen or heard of skunks around here and guesses someone's got a few pot plants filling out their garden.

Cannabis, he read somewhere, releases a perfume at certain times of day that allows police literally to sniff out crops. He walks backwards to recatch the scent, but the wind whips up and it's lost. His oncologist told him that if he wanted a prescription to buy medicinal marijuana for "insomnia, anxiety, discomfort" he only need ask. He thought the man eyed him sideways for a reaction.

He hasn't gotten stoned for at least two decades but used to make delicious mint hash brownies. He'd told the doctor, "No thanks," thinking Annie could probably hook him up if he went that route. He really needs to teach her how to keep her own books, fill out a tax form. Wishes he could know for sure that Jill will be there for her. He emerges from the path into a cul-de-sac and there's an insane yapping coming from the house ahead. He sees the shadow of a bearded face trying to eat a hole through the picture window.

"Hush before you wake someone." He jogs out of view and the small exertion ignites a chaos of sensations. More volcanic surge than hot flash, some hidden arson begins radiating outward and upward and, as he pictures his hair bursting into flame, his head erupts in sweat. Ducking under the large oak on the corner – the climbing tree as his kids used to call it – he removes his jacket to wait it out. Sweat streams down his face to sting his eyes and soak yet another shirt. These pills better be working, cause he doesn't know if he can take -

"I've dialed 91, just need another 1."

"Jesus!" Stumbling to look up into the dark branches, he swoons slightly before locating the pale gleam of a rubber sole. Wipes the sweat from his eyes. "What are you doing up there?"

"I'm going to do it." It's a female voice, a scared one.

"Stop that. I live down the street. I'm just out for a walk."

A hesitant pause.

"I'm not dangerous. I'm on this damn medication and can't sleep." He pulls his shirt away from his skin. "Makes me sweat. Excuse me."

He hears her breath let go.

"Where do you live?" she demands.

"Fifteen-eighty Thurston."

"Beau's house?"

"You know Beau?"

"You're his dad?"

"Yeah. How do you know Beau?"

"We were in school together, before he went private." She talks fast, each word tailgating the next. "He doesn't know me from garbage but I've always known him."

Okay. "Now it's your turn to tell me who you are and why —"

"I think maybe I used to be in love with your son."

Les strains to see a face but can only make out one pantleg and high-top runner. "He's not as perfect as you might think."

"I don't. I think he's kind of mean and egotistical but that's just to cover up the hate-on he has for himself."

Les laughs under his breath. "I've often thought he was hard on himself. Worried I didn't spend enough one-on-one time with him."

She huffs. "It's *always* about the parents."

"Fair enough." He gazes through the dark, homeward, thinking he could sleep now. Wants to lie down anyway. Stangely, it doesn't seem all that special that he's talking intimately about his family with someone up a tree in the middle of the night. "You haven't told me why —"

"What are you sick with?"

"I'm battling cancer." He likes that word *battling*, the noble implication of a good side. "Why are you up a tree?"

"I had something I needed to tell it."

He can't think of a response.

"You think that sounds stupid."

"No, no, not at all." He's glad she can't see his face.

"I have a book by this Ecuadorian shaman. Indigenous peoples, you know, have a connection with the natural world that we've lost."

"You and my sister Annie would get along famously."

"There are three steps."

"Steps?" Clearly she needs someone to talk to besides a tree.

"You can talk to a rock, the wind, a flower, a bug, whatever. The first step, and you have to be sincere," she says, pausing to send home the point, "is introducing yourself and then letting, say, the tree, introduce itself."

He looks at the tree trunk, tries not to imagine a cartoon mouth and eyes.

"Then you give the tree something you no longer need like depression, fear, anger, unrequited love."

"Wait a second," he says. "Don't you think that's a bit selfish? To dump your problems on some poor unsuspecting tree."

She groans with impatience. "That's the problem. We humans think we're the big cheese sandwich and the tree some poor unsuspecting retard."

If his politically correct wife heard her use that word. "Okay."

"Nature can take it. Taxo says Nature likes it, because when we give up our crap, we get closer to our true nature, which is Nature with a capital N. And then neither the tree nor we are as alone."

"No shortage of leafy friends around here," he tries.

"You should do it sometime," she says.

"I will," he promises, starting to enjoy this disembodied conversation.

"So what's cancer like?" she asks in the same tone one would use to ask the time.

The thought comes right out of his mouth. "It's like having someone sit on your shoulder and whisper 'you're sick, you're sick, you're sick' in your ear while you're trying to think about something else. You're only half there, half present to your life and can't commit to anything because you don't know what you're up against tomorrow." He hadn't verbalized it before, but it's true.

"It's called obsssesssive." She draws out the s in a kind of sexy drawl. "Just say STOP." She's mocking someone. Her therapist?

"You're absolutely right. I shouldn't indulge those thoughts."

"The scariest part's getting back to my house."

"Oh." He's having trouble keeping up. "Youuu want me to watch you?"

"Yes."

"Okay."

"Move so I can get down."

Les moves and a girl drops out of the tree. Dressed in dark clothes, a thief's hooded jacket, fear or maybe embarrassment propels her across the lawn. She's all knees and elbows, a fleeing insect. Reaching her house, she slips inside the front door. This is followed by a clunk of a deadbolt. He didn't see her face. Pema might know her. He starts to put his jacket back on, his hot flash having passed without him noticing. He looks again at the tree, whose dark surfaces shimmer like a charcoal drawing. Takes a couple of steps forward.

"Hi," he says, suddenly shy. "I give you...my fear...of

dying." His arms, he sees, are flung out wide, his stomach going sideways at what he holds and is truly trying to give. He waits, for what, he doesn't know, then laughs. The girl never told him the third step.

Walking home, he thinks what a bizarrely eventful night it's been. Annie would blame it on the moon conjunct with Saturn squared with Venus or some such thing. In any case, he'll have a story to tell Jill tomorrow. Passing another large oak, he glances upward. Are there other owly teenage girls perched inside other trees? For all he knows Pema's up a tree right now, relaying *her* troubles to the poor stiff.

Random encounters with strangers. Is family any different? He'd have to say that Pema, oddly enough, feels more knowable to him, more familiar, than either of his sons whatever that's about. He turns down his street. Thinks of Faye and feels glad, despite what happened or didn't happen, that he got to meet her. Really, the woman did the best she knew how with a bad situation. It's really all any of us can do.

He eases into bed so as not to wake Jill. As soon as his head meets the pillow, his thoughts race to next month's checkup, the monstrous industry of cancer cells, dividing and multiplying, starved of oxygen and — Stop.

I'll come back, he tells himself. Or I'll die. It's really not up to me.

He rolls over and wraps his arm around Jill. When she moans and starts to pull away, he doesn't let her.

Sons

·······

It's one in the morning on a Friday night and Les thinks he's alone when he steps quietly into the kitchen only to startle himself and his son. "Whoa. You still up?"

"Studying for an exam." Quinn is in the middle of topping up his glass with orange juice.

"Juice, the healthy choice. We drank coffee in my cram-exam days."

Quinn smiles briefly, glances at the floor and sips his juice. Les wants to throw his arms around this cerebral son of his, tell him he should be out partying, finding himself a new girl. Here are the keys to the car, money for a six-pack, no hard stuff. Don't tell Mom.

"You're up late," says Quinn.

"A little discomfort from the operation. Keeping me awake." A simple hernia operation was what they'd told the kids. The kids had worries of their own and didn't need his. Besides, his prostate cancer may already be a moot point.

Quinn nods then takes a sip. "That's a drag."

"Just a muscle ache."

"Okay good. Well, I should get back to it."

Les appreciates his son's concern and has to ask, "So how're you doing?"

"I'm fine." Quinn's cheeks light up as if embarrassed by

the question.

Les wants to say something fatherly, something helpful. Since meeting Faye, he's determined to be there for his children. From the utensil jug, he slips out the spatula designed to look like an Imperial Stormtrooper's helmet that Quinn gave him for Father's Day a couple of years back. It came with a matching Darth Vader that Beau somehow managed to break. "I love this spatch," he says, tapping it on the counter. "Lot of fish in the sea, ya know."

"Don't worry about me." Quinn downs his juice and sticks the glass in the dishwasher.

"Personally and pathetically, I found it hard to get over one fish until the next fish came along. And you know, the next fish is usually bigger and better because you've learned shit about fish from the first one."

This gets not only a smile but a chuckle. Now he can let his sad diligent son escape back to his books.

Brainiac kid'll be rolling in dough one day, thinks Les as he watches him go, women swimming all over him.

The liquor cupboard door is partly open and Les goes to close it. Peeks inside and sees the top is missing from the vodka bottle. He checks around but doesn't see it anywhere. A twinge in his groin makes him flinch.

Les knocks first then opens the door. Doesn't say anything, just raises the bottle.

Quinn's eyes widen for a telltale second, then return to his book. "What's up?"

"Can't find the top for this."

"Oh yeah?" He squints at his book as if to delete Les from his peripheral vision.

Les leans against the door jamb, tips the open bottle to

his mouth and drinks. A darting glance from Quinn. For no good reason, an old incident comes to mind. "I haven't told anyone this story ever, but when I was thirteen, I burned down the small woods in back of my middle school." Quinn's eyes are up. "It was a really dry summer. Didn't take much. Roaring flames fifty feet high. Pockets of sap exploding. Boom. Boom. It was very very cool." He can picture it perfectly. "I never felt so alive. Firemen came with axes, hoses. No one was hurt and no one got blamed." Les laughs. "Now that I'm all grown-up I'm reduced to setting fire to desserts."

Quinn points to his own eyebrows, long since grown back after the cheese flambé incident.

"Yeah," says Les and starts to close Quinn's door.

"Dad?" Quinn doesn't look up and barely pauses in his typing. "I'll look for that top."

Les pauses in the doorway until he sees nothing more is forthcoming. "Thanks," he says, and closes the door softly as breathing, lest a sound ruin the perfection of the moment.

TWO MONTHS LATER

PEMA

· · · · · · · · · ·

Pema follows Les and the meander of people into the next
room of the Tibet exhibit where, penned in by braided rope
and a whispering mill of people, four maroon-robed monks
kneel over a low table. She recognizes a guy from Beau's old
rugby team leaning against the wall to her left. Matt? Cute, in
a jock sort of way; she rates him a seven point five. She steps
closer to the rope to see what everyone's ogling. At snail speed,
the monks shake primary-coloured sand out of ornate silver
straws creating some sort of design.

"Is this, like, Tibetan busking?" she asks Les.

"Kind of, I guess," he says with a laugh. "It's called a sand
mandala."

Though it was a sincere question, any time she makes her
dad laugh a small explosion of light – part happiness, part vic-
tory – goes off in her stomach.

Behind the hard-at-work monks, picture windows reveal a
Japanese garden with Tibetan prayer flags flapping overhead,
strung zigzag, the way Dad does the Christmas lights over the
back patio.

"Be a shame if there's an earthquake?" whispers Les, nodding at the monks.

Pema smiles up at him. "Or one of them sneezes."

Already two feet in diameter, the sand mandala is divided

into coloured quadrants, not a single particle of one colour mixing with another. The monks, she guesses, are in their early twenties, with the exception of one who's maybe forty. Their shaved heads and flat faces remind her of gingerbread men. She takes a picture of them with her phone and then one of herself. Sends them to Katie with the text: *truth. do I look like a gingerbread man?*

Non-Asians are always mistaking her for Chinese and she doesn't correct them. Sometime she says she's Chinese because it's simpler. Her boyfriend, Cody, thought at first that she was from the Philippines.

"Who're you talking to?" asks Les.

She leans all her weight back against Les and holds up her phone to read Katie's message *i would happily kill you if that meant i could look like you.*

Pema smiles and texts back: *liar. mall later — check out shoes for prom.* Cody is in grade twelve which means she — a grade eleven — gets to go to his prom.

"Don't think modern technology is allowed in here," whispers Les.

Blue, medium heel, she finishes and sends. Wonders if she should change her purple highlights to blue for the prom. Or a silver blue.

Pema agreed to go to the exhibit only because her parents had promised brunch after at the gallery's Café Cezanne, which was rumoured to have excellent French toast. Jill had planned to come along but ended up having a department meeting. She was going to catch up with them at the café. "We have something to discuss with you," she'd said on her way out the door, her tone an eight and a half — meaning hovering between serious and grim. Gauging her mother's tone helps Pema know what to expect and prepare for. Could be her grades, which have taken a dive since she's missed so many morning classes. Which is Beau's fault for not being there to wake her up.

Her phone trembles. Katie texts: *my mom has blue heels you could borrow.*

Patent leather?

Just leather.

Maybe. Bored, need French toast, she sends, just before Les slips the exhibit's brochure between her phone and face and reads: "'The mandala's four colours symbolize the four emotional patterns of envy, hate, pride and greed.'" Her dad's breath smells of his morning mocha espresso. "'Each of us has a dominant emotional pattern that is our entrance or gate to the spiritual path or mandala.'" He lowers the brochure. "See, each quadrant has a gate?"

Ornate little gates open on each side like the start of a maze. One monk pauses in his painting to scratch at his bum, not so discreetly. Worms, thinks Pema. She'd had two types of worms when she arrived from Nepal and can still remember how the nervy itch made her head swim. Her phone goes off and she ducks out from under Les's arm.

Olivia says you gotta order The Masterpiece.

What's —

"Come on, Pema. Let's be here while we're here," says Les.

The slight irritation in his voice shames her and she quickly types *that?*, snaps her phone closed and hooks her arm around his. "Read," she says determined to only half listen. Anything Tibetan makes her think about her birth mother who she understands is poor and probably sick — she's seen enough homeless people here in Victoria to know those things go together — if, that is, she's even still alive.

"North is envy and represented by green. That makes sense. East is hate, represented in blue."

Last year, Jill took her to a talk by a Tibetan lama who picked his nose. Over Christmas, Les rented not one but two sleep-inducing Tibetan movies with subtitles.

"South is pride, represented by yellow. West is greed, represented by —"

"Greed." Pema raises her hand picturing her bedroom.

"Red."

Too sentimental to throw anything out, she has a lot of stuff. Every sports participation ribbon, photo, stuffed animal, poster, the smallest memento from the smallest occasion, she not only keeps but displays. Every surface and wall is pretty much splattered with memories. The exact opposite of Beau's room, even when he lived at home.

Last night, Beau had called her "needy." Rhymes with greedy. Actually it was "stupidly needy." Freaked out by a horror flick she'd gone to with her friends, she'd forced him to stay up on Skype until she fell asleep.

The older monk points to a part of the sand painting and says something in Tibetan and one of the others responds.

"Did you understand any of that?" asks Les.

"No," she sneers, though somehow she believes the younger monk said "Yes, I will."

"Bet you'd get it back though. If you were around it."

"Bet if these guys had a choice of being here or at the mall, they'd choose the mall," she says and Les snorts — not quite a laugh — plops his palms on her shoulders and steers her through the crowd towards the next room. "You come from a fascinating culture, you know." His hands squeeze her shoulders a little too hard.

"Ow," she says, but he doesn't let go.

"It's something to be proud of."

"My culture," she repeats and shrugs his hands loose.

They've been watching bald guys in dresses paint with sand, and before that they saw trumpets made from human thigh bones and baby-sized skulls turned into bowls.

Through the far doorway she glimpses the clothing section and wonders if Aunt Annie has some cotton lace she could tack to the cuffs of her purple jacket. And around the lapels. Dye it grey to match her jeans.

"Dad?"

"Question?"

"Have you heard of a dish at this café called The Masterpiece?"

During Pema's first couple of years in Canada, whenever a babysitter was needed, Jill hired a Tibetan woman named Tsogyal in order for Pema to have a chance to use her native tongue.

In her soft-spoken Tibetan, Tsogyal told Pema things she already knew. "You are a lucky girl to have been able to come here." "Your name means Lotus and represents something beautiful growing out of mud and muck." "You have such pretty black hair."

Pema wasn't interested in Tsogyal or in speaking Tibetan. She was too intent on decoding the strange but wonderful food, the cars and who sat in what seat, the TV set and all its important confusion, and the secret sounds erupting from the exciting boy who was the same size as her.

"Do you have a favourite colour?" Tsogyal asked as she and Beau drew pictures at the kitchen table.

"Monster," Beau would yell as if Pema were deaf, thrusting his picture under her nose.

She'd plug her ears and shake her head at him, point to his drawing and repeat, "Mon-ster."

He'd growl and shove the paper against her face, but not

too hard. When he laughed, she laughed too and then it was as if they were speaking the same language.

Tired of drawing, Beau would dump a bucket of tiny coloured bricks at her feet.

"Would you like to build something?" said Tsogyal in Tibetan. "A house?"

"Lego," Beau roared.

When he gave her one word at a time, she could repeat it. But when he strung them together in long necklaces, her shrug would draw disappointment on his face. She didn't care about disappointing Tsogyal, but this boy's disappointment felt like her own.

"I don't know," she learned to say and "What what?" so Beau would try again and she might catch the important words, hoard them like treasure. And when she became certain of the meaning and sound, she'd give him the words back and watch him smile as if he'd done it, not her. When Beau's face was happy, it reminded her of the cutest of puppies. When big brother Quinn's face was happy, it still looked worried.

Two giant metal cylinders covered in what looks like Tibetan Braille stand in the entrance to the Thangka Room. A staff woman, short with cloudy grey hair, is encouraging everyone to "Have a go."

"Spinning the prayer wheel accumulates merit and virtuous karma," she broadcasts, "ensuring a favored birth in your next life."

"What about this life?" Pema whispers.

Les puts a finger to his lips.

Pema steps up and gives the dirty-grey cylinder a hard whirl. Expecting the metal to be cold to the touch, she's grossed out to find it warm.

"Clockwise," corrects the woman.

"What?"

"You're supposed to spin it clockwise."

"Or what happens?" she asks.

The woman's eyes cross before she looks away and encourages the next person in line.

"I have to use the washroom," Pema tells Les. "'Cause how many jabillion hands have touched that wheel thing over the centuries?"

Les gently pushes the back of her head in the direction of the washrooms. "Hurry up."

Her parents blame her germ phobia on the unsanitary conditions of the refugee camp where she was raised, where washing hands was a religion. Or so she was told. She has zero memories of her birth mother or of Nepal, as if it truly was another lifetime. Jill had made a photo album of her adoption trip and every photo of the refugee camp is slightly hazy as though the camera lens was covered in grime. In contrast, all the pictures on the plane and of Pema's "home-coming" are bright and clear, the world suddenly come into focus. There was only one photo of her birth mother because apparently she'd refused to have her picture taken, something about it stealing her soul. Though Pema doesn't remember doing it, apparently she tore that picture up and flushed it down the toilet.

She angles her hand underneath the soap dispenser to make it auto-pump soft pink foam, and again for a double helping. Inhales its watermelon scent. The pictures taken on the airplane show her on Les's lap, wailing, and asleep in her seat with her mouth slung open. Most of the pictures are of her arrival.

Her first memory – not just a picture memory – is of seeing her new home, towering green trees hiding a white two-storey palace with yellow window boxes spilling the most beautiful red flowers. There are pictures of Auntie Annie wearing a tie-dyed turban, of Quinn, seven, smiling dutifully for the camera, and Beau, three, scowling. Another shows Grammy Nan, making a sad face as she sits in a chair and holds crying Pema's hands in both of hers. In one picture a beautiful cake covered in snow-white icing and edible orange and yellow flowers is in front of her, her face scrunched and crying. Her favourite picture is of Beau pushing cake into her wailing mouth to get her to shut up already. Beau was the only one who wasn't cautious around her, who didn't pretend to love her. She trusted him instantly.

Pema finds Les in front of a painting of a naked white woman with three eyes, straddling the lap of a naked blue man, also three eyed, who's holding a sword in one hand and what looks like flaming molded Jell-O in the other. She leans her head against his shoulder, wraps her arms around his elbow.

"The union of male and female deities represents the indivisibility of form and space," he reads.

"Like whatever that means."

"Well, it's interesting when you think about it," he says.

"Mind if I go see the clothes?"

He sighs and shakes his head, making her feel dumb. She slips her arms from his. Jill sometimes makes her feel dumb, and Quinn, but never Dad. It's a new feeling and she doesn't like it.

"I'm interested in fashion like Auntie Annie," she says, defensive. "I want to see the clothes."

"That's fine, Sweetheart," he says, his tone softening. "I'll meet you there."

Two headless mannequins wear sleeveless wraparound dresses the colour of dirt over a yellow shirt with flared sleeves. A plaque reads: *These everyday chubas are made of cotton and wool.* The word chuba she does remember. Her phone vibrates against her thigh and she reaches for it when Les comes up behind her.

"You had a chuba just like that one," he says.

"I did?" She doesn't remember that chuba and loves hearing stories from when she was small and new and an object of so much careful attention. When she was the luckiest girl in the world.

"Brown with white stitching. But you left that behind because your birth mother had a fancy silk one made for your departure, though she couldn't afford it." He pauses as if to let this information sink in. "It was a very pretty sky blue and you wore that thing every day for months. You knew how you wanted it tied and if Jill —"

"If Jill or you tried to help, I smacked your hands away," she says.

"Didn't want your chuba messed with," he finishes. "When we finally got you into shorts and a T-shirt, you never touched it again. Though didn't Auntie Annie re-make it into a regular dress?"

Her sixth birthday, all eyes on her as she opened Auntie Annie's box. "It's an old dress made into a new dress," her aunt had explained before passing it over. When Pema saw the watery flash of blue silk, she shut the box again and Beau said, "She's gonna blow." And she did, unable to explain why it embarrassed her to see her old chuba again after believing it had gone safely away to the Salvation Army.

"I'm really hungry," she says. "Is it time to eat?"

Jill is already downstairs at the café, sitting in a booth, wearing a stiff, troubled smile. Haven't cleaned my room like forever, thinks Pema. Is that it?

"Hi sweethearts one and two," she says, too brightly.

"Hey, Mom."

Les bends to kiss Jill's head then slides in beside her. Having the long seat on the other side of the booth all to herself makes Pema wish Beau was here. He'd stick up for her, whatever it is she's done. A distracted smile occupies Jill's lips as she glances at Les, the table, then out the window.

They can't know about the joint she smoked with Olivia, which was painful to inhale and just made her sleepy. Or the twenty-dollar bill she found on the floor in the front hall, which *could* have been hers. She hides behind the menu, reluctantly skips the French toast section and locates The Masterpiece. Gives it a quick read.

"Can I get the Masterpiece?" she blurts, hoping to delay whatever's coming. She points to the description. "It's the chef's special, which today is a..." she sounds out the word, "frit-ta-ta."

"You like eggs. It's like an open-faced omelet," says Jill.

"It's what I'd call an egg pancake," says Les. "Usually thickened with milk powder."

"Oh." She's doesn't like unfamiliar foods and would rather have the French toast but cares more about having a story to tell her friends. "The thing is the waitress —"

"Server," Jill corrects.

"Server, flips a coin at the end of the meal and if you win you get your meal for free."

"And if you lose?" asks Les.

"You pay double. But it's only ten dollars and I can pay the other ten if I lose."

"Curious business ploy," says Les. "One assumes they'd break even in the long run,"

"You don't have to pay," says Jill.

"So I can order it?" asks Pema.

"Yes," says Jill, her clipped tone pushing nine.

The server is a waiter with a long narrow face and thick lips that pucker when he talks. He reminds Pema of Nemo in *Finding Nemo*. She orders hot chocolate, Jill and Les coffee. Is he wearing guyliner? In a solemn voice, Jill orders the smoked salmon benny.

Pema leans over the table towards Les. "Please get the French toast," she says, putting on her own worried face, "in case I don't like my frittata?"

"Sure."

"With blueberries?"

"What if I don't like blueberries."

"Don't you?"

"With blueberries," he tells the waiter.

"And I'll have the Masterpiece," she announces.

"Alright!" The waiter flings a hand in the air as if for a high-five then points a finger at her. "Hope you're hungry."

"I'm hungry." She points back. He is definitely wearing guyliner.

"You think he's gay?" she says after he's gone.

"Who?" asks Les.

"The waiter."

"Server and it's his business," says Jill.

"I know," she says, hating how easily her mother can shut down a conversation before it's even started.

Jill asks about the exhibit.

"Auntie Annie would have approved," Pema says, thinking that she can potentially redeem whatever it is she's screwed up. "They repurpose, like, everything."

"They repurpose everything," says Jill.

"They repurpose everything," she repeats. "Like, there

were... I mean there were these crazy hats made out of horsehair. Hand drums made out of skulls and horsehide. Religious objects made from the metal from space." She looks to Les.

"Meteoric iron."

"Something falls from the sky and they're on it," she says, hoping for a laugh and having to settle for distracted smiles. "Some of the jewelry was pretty cool, lots of turquoise and amber."

"Any Tibetans there?"

"Besides the monks?" says Pema, thinking it a stupid question. As far as she knows there are maybe five Tibetans in Victoria, and she's one of them.

"No," says Les.

Their drinks arrive. Pema takes a spoon to her whipped cream and watches Jill absently stir her coffee and stare out the window at nothing. Les, who never looks uncomfortable, looks uncomfortable. How bad can it be? Quinn lost his car privileges last weekend after he puked and passed out on the front lawn. Whatever she's done can't touch that. She grabs the plastic card on the table to read about *Dessert Impressions*. She can ignore them too. Jill's phone rings. She takes it out, checks who's calling and turns it off.

Another long minute goes by and Pema's about to take out her own phone to text Katie when Jill says in an earnest voice, "We need to talk, Pema." Jill's face is so serious Pema almost laughs. But then Les lets go a big fat uncharacteristic sigh.

"What is it?" It's big. A two-parent problem is rare, and not knowing is making her anxious. She knows her dad has been sick. Her stomach falls.

"We've waited to show you these," Jill says, digging in her

bag, "until we felt you could handle..." Her voice cracks and she covers her eyes.

Pema can't remember ever seeing her mother cry. Jill never loses it, is the most together mother of all her friends' mothers. Les slips his arm around Jill and presses his head against hers, causing Pema to feel startlingly alone on her side of the booth.

"What aren't you telling me?" She feels her own tears coming.

Jill takes a big breath and wipes her eyes with her napkin. "I'm sorry, Pema. It's actually a happy thing."

She sees the letters in her mom's hand. "You don't look happy."

"It *is* a happy thing," says Les, practically snatching the letters from Jill. "It's from" — he reads from the top envelope — "Jampaling, I think that's how you say it, in Nepal. Pema, these are letters from your birth mother, Datso Tsering."

The waiter sweeps over with their meals. "Your benny, ma'am. And for the young ma'am, one bacon, swiss cheese and sun-dried tomato frittata, drizzled in a tarragon cream sauce and served with our fab hash browns, sourdough toast and homemade fruit salad."

Pema smiles up at him, willing his gay fish mouth to keep talking.

"I'll be right back with your French toast, sir."

Les places the letters on the table and slides them towards her until they touch her napkin. Pema lifts her napkin and puts it in her lap because she likes small formalities.

"You don't have to read them now, but you should know that she's doing well," he says.

There's a date stamped on the first envelope. 2006? She pulls her eyes away, pokes at her frittata to make sure the waiter's description is true. There are small green bits among the bacon and tomato. The waiter didn't say anything about green bits.

"She's living in a refugee village in rural Nepal. It's a community of a thousand Tibetans?" Les turns to Jill for confirmation.

"Right," Jill says in a small voice.

The waiter arrives with Les's plate and Pema asks about these green bits.

"Those are scallion." His tone is tantalizing. She likes his spiked belt.

"Thank you."

"Not a problem."

Her potatoes look exactly the way she hoped, a crispy brown the way Les makes them.

"She's remarried," says Les, "and she and her husband both have jobs."

Using her knife, she makes a space between her potatoes and the cream sauce. Ketchup goes with potatoes. Where's the ketchup? She signals the waiter, who hurries over, breathless. She asks for ketchup and laughs when he says, "Righteolly."

She wishes Les would be quiet and eat his French toast now, but he seems keyed up and unable to stop.

"They have two children," he continues, though Jill has grabbed his arm as if to stop him or tell him something. "Two girls."

Pema squeezes the ketchup bottle, which farts noisily, unable to believe the amount of food on her plate.

"So you have two half-sisters," he says as if she didn't get it the first time. "Eleven and four."

Pema waves for the waiter again then realizes there's nothing she needs.

"Let her eat," urges Jill, her hand fisted beside her plate.

The whiteness of her mother's skin reminds Pema of the time she smeared Coppertone Instatan over Beau's face and arms to try and get his skin colour to match hers.

"It's a happy thing," says Les, sounding almost angry now. "She wants to meet you, wants to know you."

With her fork Pema turns over her potatoes in the ketchup to coat them. Wonders if her sisters have ever seen so much food on one plate.

Clearing his throat, Les manoeuvres out of his side of the booth, mumbles something about the washroom and walks away, leaving them in silence.

"Is everything all right with the food?" the waiter asks.

"Fine," says Jill. "But maybe we'll take it to go?"

Pema nods, eyes on the table, not the least bit hungry any more.

"Nada problemo," he says and begins collecting plates.

As soon as he leaves, she can't help herself and lays down on the booth's cool vinyl surface, tucks her knees into her stomach and stares at the silver pole holding up the table.

"Pema, sweetheart," says Jill, her tone a gentle number one.

Her breath comes hard and fast to keep from crying or yelling or throwing up, she's not sure which.

"Please, let's not do this here," says Jill, up to number two and a half.

Did they purposefully tell her this in public so she wouldn't make a scene?

"Sit up, please." Number four.

She wipes at her eyes and closes her mouth to quiet her breath, thinks how she's always felt scrutinized by her adoptive mother and slightly afraid of her.

"Pema," says Jill, her tone pushing six.

She slowly sits back up, hiding behind a curtain of hair.

"Thank you," says Jill.

Pema can't think about it, any of it, and slips her phone out of her pocket to send Katie a text to see if she still wants to go shopping. For shoes for prom. And maybe a new necklace. Auntie Annie and she are designing the dress. They've already bought the material.

The waiter reappears with their boxed-up meals then holds up a quarter and beams at Pema. "We have to do the Masterpiece flip."

She scans the room for Les, wants him to be here for this, but doesn't see him. Seems he's been gone a long time.

As the waiter takes a dramatic stance and balances the quarter on top of his thumb, Jill reaches for the letters as if to put them back in her purse and, without thinking, Pema slaps a hand on them and their eyes meet. Jill's smile wavers as her eyes and hand retreat.

"Feeling lucky?" he says, one eyebrow cocked. People at nearby tables have stopped eating to turn their heads and watch.

She smirks at his puckered smile. She's the luckiest girl in the world.

"Heads or tails?"

"Heads," she says, and he flips the coin high into the air where it disappears in a glare of light.

Sisters

· · · · · · · · · ·

"What colour do you call the satin part?" asks Pema.

Annie bunches her lips. "How about dewdrop green. Or forest sunlight . Or underwater dwelling."

"And the velvet? Is that turquoise?"

"Turquoise green, not blue."

"Cody and his friends are renting a party bus for after the grad ball."

"Sounds like fun, fun, fun. Is he coming here to pick you up?"

After Pema found out that Jill and Les had kept her birth mother's letters secret for more than two years, she stopped speaking to them and moved in with Annie. It was only going to be for the weekend but then she decided to stay. Annie couldn't be more thrilled to have her.

"Yes. His dad's driving us. I wish Katie was going too, or Olivia. I think I'm the only grade eleven except for some guy who I don't really know."

"Next year you and your buds will all be together. Think of this as a practice run."

Pema doesn't respond.

"Cuddly Cody. He's got the best hair that kid." Annie scrunches her nose. "You just want to roll in it."

"He is cute, isn't he?"

"Yeah, cute, but you're a stunner and are going to be the bomb in this dress," says Annie, which wins a brief smile.

"So Cody's wondering what colour tie he should wear."

"Black suit?"

"Yeah."

"White shirt?" asks Annie.

"We were thinking a black shirt might be —"

"No. White shirt. And I'll make him a velvet tie out of your dress material."

"Cool."

"But it's going to be a bow tie."

"Bow tie?"

"Bow ties are so in, trust me. And one of my leather cummerbunds. And tell him to forget the vest and we'll make him some suspenders."

"Love suspenders."

"Braided ones. We'll braid some leather strips" — Annie points across the studio where used belts dangle from hooks along the wall — "maybe weave in some strands of your velvet."

"Cool. What about corsages?"

"Pale yellow, but don't get chrysanthemums. Cheap funeral flowers. Lilies would be good. Or roses. Yeah, get roses. They'll bring out the texture of the velvet. Maybe," says Annie, thinking aloud, "the criss-crossing part across your boobs should be leather. No, no, stupid idea. Too Harley D. We're already getting a bit matchy matchy."

They work quietly for a while, Pema cutting the skirt material, Annie pinning the bodice.

"Katie always dreamed of going to prom with Beau. Confessed she's always had a crush on him."

"I'd have a crush on him too if he wasn't my nephew and I was a child molester. No reason the sexy beast can't go next year to both his own and yours. We'll send for him. Say his favourite aunt had a heart attack, might not make it, is asking for him."

"You know what he said when I told him about the letters?"

Annie holds a pin between her lips and can't talk.

"'So?' That's what he said. I'm crying my eyes out and he's says, 'So?'"

"Guys turn and run to the nearest hockey bar, rugby bar, when women get emotional."

"We used to be, like, so close."

"That closeness is getting stretched, sure, but like a rubber band it'll snap back once he's home."

"Last time he was home, Katie had a party and he didn't even come. If he wasn't sleeping, he was hanging out at David's. Barely said two words to me."

"Just a phase, Pema Pea. Both your brothers love you and always will."

"Auntie Annie?"

"What? Pass me the scissors, Sweet Girl. No, the shears."

Pema passes the shears. "Do you think I should go to Nepal?"

"Gawd, I certainly would. Be knocking on my dad's door as we speak if he was alive, hoping he was the next best drug. The key" – she raises her hand holding the shears – "is not to expect anything and it'll be great."

"My birth mom doesn't speak English."

"You'll pick up Tibetan again. It'll be like déjà vu."

"I don't think so."

"Think so."

"I'm so mad at Mom and Dad."

Annie bites her tongue. It's the first time Pema's brought up the subject of why she's sleeping in Annie's bed.

"They think I was too stupid to have a say about it. Two

years. And what if, like your dad, my birth mother died in those two years." Pema's voice is building to a crescendo. "Or dies next week."

"They were just scared of losing you, Sweet Pea. That's all. Don't be too hard on them."

"After prom, I'm fucking going and never coming back."

"Whoa, whoa. Come here girl."

Pema drops her scissors and walks around the table where Annie grabs her by the shirt and yanks her in for a hug. "You swore on your mother's grave you wouldn't get taller than me."

"Which mother?" Pema buries her face in Annie's shoulder, her body stiffening like it does before she cries. "The one who got rid of me, or the one who lied to me."

Annie holds her tighter. "I'm also adopted, remember, and if I have learned one thing in life it's not to try to figure out who you are. If you just think of yourself as everybody's daughter, a daughter of the world, it's much easier. And more inclusive."

An explosive gulp of air lets loose the demon and Pema is blubbering that she's so confused and wishes she was never born.

"Nobody said life was a bed of roses," says Annie. "Well, maybe somebody did, some fool, but anyway, it's going to be all right." She strokes her niece's hair. "I'm almost sure of it."

THREE YEARS LATER
SPRING 2011
••••••••••••••••

CHASING THE CIRCLE CLOSED

Les rearranges his pillows so he's semi-upright, the only position he can sleep in and still breathe comfortably what with the fluid making a swamp of his lungs. R2D2, his nickname for the oxygen machine he's tethered to, drones in the corner of the room, the fat silver canister a constant reminder of his dependence, and noticing it seems to make him feel weaker still. He removes the tubes from his nose to scratch an angry itch then reaches for the cream beside his bed. The oxygen dries the hell out of his nasal passages and he doesn't want another nosebleed.

The mattress tilts as Jill steps up onto it and wedges the Windex between her knees.

"Why didn't you get Sylvia in?" he asks and instantly regrets it.

"I can do a better job," she says, though he knows the real answer is monetary.

"As if the kids are going to notice the dead moths in our bedroom fixture."

"I wonder how old the kids have to be before we stop thinking of them as baby goats," she says, the first of the screws scraping against metal on the overhead light.

His laugh comes out as a congested snort, a piglet's snuffle.

"It's true, though," she says, "I still view them as the kids.

There must come a time."

"When they hit forty-five." That was the age when he came to the abrupt realization that his youth was forever behind him. It was as if he'd reached the top of a beautiful mountain only to see where he was headed: downhill, on the rocky side that didn't get much sun.

Jill pockets the screws, dumps flaky grey carcasses onto her rag and sprays the inside of the glass.

"I'll remind Annie to pick up Pema at the airport," he says, glad to have thought of it.

"Katie's getting her, remember?"

How did he forget?

"I wonder why Beau insists on taking the bus from the ferry," says Jill. "I should just go get him."

"He may be a baby goat but he's not helpless." Finished with the cream, he refits the tubes into his nose. "What's Quinn's girlfriend's name again?"

She doesn't answer.

"Jill?"

"What?"

"Quinn's girl's name?"

"Woman friend. Holly."

"Girlfriend," he says and clears his throat. "Where'd they meet?"

"Didn't ask. Just hope it wasn't rehab."

"Not good enough for our addict?"

"He needs strong people around him."

"You're judging her before you've even laid eyes on her?" Trying to talk over R2D2 makes his lungs wheeze like a feeble accordion. "You can control the moth count in your fixtures" — he breathes deeply through his nose — "but you have to let the kids bed their own choices."

"Just wasn't expecting him to bring her."

"My fault." He reaches for his water. Quinn had asked if it was all right and he'd said please do. He doesn't want to put things off any longer. He picks up Le Carré from the pile of espionage books Annie brings every week from the downtown library. Fast-paced thrillers are the only thing that knocks down these four walls for a while and distracts him from the headache in his bones, as he's come to think of this dull, insistent pain that keeps reminding him he has a body, a failing one. He sips his water through a plastic straw with faint red candy stripes and bendable neck, the very kind, he's almost sure, that he used to drink chocolate milk when he was a child.

"I was thinking maybe, for Quinn's sake, we shouldn't have wine or beer around," says Jill.

"I don't want a heavy-handed occasion. And maybe pandering to his weakness isn't helpful."

Jill fits the fixture back in place and Les opens to his bookmarked page and the Hallmark card he received from Faye. Annie had insisted on calling Faye to let her know his condition. "She's your mother," Annie said in that tone one doesn't bother arguing with. "She'll want to know." He rereads the words:

> Healing takes time, so please,
> take it easy.
> Wishes for a speedy recovery.
> Faye and Nickel

He holds the card to his nose then remembers he can't smell with these tubes in, tucks it back inside the book which he lays face down on his stomach. "We're doing this thing in the family room?"

"We'll do the ceremony, yes, in the family room."

"Ceremony? Less scary than Living Wake, but do we have to call it something?"

"Celebration. Life Celebration is what I've been calling it."

"Just keep it informal, please, or I'll wish I was dead already." He picks up his book and Jill frowns at him from her lofty angle.

"Come on, you said you liked the idea. I've worked hard on this."

Les looks at her. Amazing, really, that they have grown so used to his dying that they can bicker. That his tender, sympathetic, frightened-to-death Jill has grown used to it. Can you get used to anything? Even being dead?

"And we've talked about the importance of ritual," Jill adds. "For the kids."

"Stage fright," is all he tells her, out of breath, and waves an apologetic hand. What bothers him most about this Life Celebration is going public with the understanding that this is it. This thing tomorrow will put the formal stamp on it. No more treatment options. No *speedy recovery*. There's something to be said for self-deception and having the people around you playing along. Not so unlike a good escapist novel.

He eyes the bottle of Percoset beside his water, wonders if he should damn the constipation and take a half of one tonight to ensure a decent night's sleep, maybe feel a little stronger for tomorrow.

A screw slips from Jill's hand and lands in the valley between his feet. She picks it up and gives his foot a squeeze through the covers. "It's your party, Sweetheart. You can just sit back and take it all in."

Like a decadent, feeble king, he thinks.

"We'll do the Life Celebration in the family room with drinks and appetizers, and eat dinner, more formally, sorry, in the dining room. Then we'll retire to the family room again for dessert and coffee."

"All planned out."

"You know me." The fixture now screwed back in place, she climbs down off the bed. "It'll be strange seeing Kenneth after all these years."

"Looking forward to it." And he was. The Kenneth he remembers, with his macho disregard for convention, was bullishly entertaining. It had always been hard to see him as Jill's brother.

"I'm trying to," says Jill. "He could have made more effort to see Mom. We've never even met his wife."

"We could have gone to them." And Japan would have been a treat.

"We had kids to raise."

When we went to Nepal, he doesn't say, only watches her go into the walk-in closet, take off her shirt. Then, like some modest ingenue, she turns her back to him before unhooking her bra, sliding the straps down her shoulders. It's been her habit for the last ten years and he's never figured out if she turns her back because she's embarrassed her breasts aren't what they used to be or if she's afraid he'll get turned on when she isn't up for it. Whatever it is, it saddens him. He loves her breasts and misses seeing them. Funny, or not funny, how after twenty-seven years of marriage, he's shy to ask her to turn around.

"I imagine living in Japan would make a person hypertidy," he says.

"That should be a word, hypertidy." She takes off her jeans, folds them onto the closet shelf. "Such crisp happy beats. Onomatopoetic really."

He thinks of Ned Flanders for some reason, and the word

hypertiddly. As she reaches for her nightshirt, he catches the lovely outside curve of her breast.

"I asked my etymology class," she says without looking at him, "to come up with new viable words and their meanings and one kid came up with overstand. Instead of understand? Means one truly understands, beyond what is required or useful. Or it can be used when someone is belabouring the —"

"I overstand already. What's Kenneth's wife's name?" Names are so elusive these days.

"Kimmie. Kimmie. Infantilizing sounds, like a diminutive on a diminutive. A name for a three-year-old."

"And this infant is how old?"

"Thirty-two to his forty-nine. Typical Kenneth." She shakes her head.

"You're so tough on him. Hey, they've lasted ten years."

"I'll give him that. And she's educated, has a masters in history, I think it is."

"I thought he wanted kids." He should stop talking, but the thought of seeing his own kids tomorrow has him keyed up.

"Said he wanted a baseball team. Maybe they couldn't have any." Done buttoning her nightshirt, she finally faces him. "Probably best not to have kids in Japan right now. They say the next generation is where the fallout, so to speak, will start showing up. So awful. I'm just glad they live where they do."

Les has avoided the Fukushima stories in the news. It's too much. Though he did make Jill go out and buy kelp tablets to send to each of the kids. "I'm happy he's bringing Nancy," he says, changing the topic.

"I'm happy you're happy," she says on the downslope of a sigh, disappears into the bathroom and returns sawing a piece of floss between her teeth. "Kenneth insists Mom wants to come. As if she knows what she wants. I'm concerned she'll get upset without her routines."

"Routines? Breakfast, TV, lunch, TV, dinner, TV." Les has visited the facility where Nancy lives and seen how utterly useless those people are made to feel, and most of them in decent physical health.

"That's not fair."

"Give her potatoes to peel while she's here, some mending. She'd probably weed the garden if we pointed her in the right direction."

"I've told Kenneth that Mom's *his* job," says Jill. "I'll be overwhelmed as it is."

He clears his throat. "Cause you like being overwhelmed."

Jill smiles blandly. It's hard to get a rise out of her any more.

"I'm putting Mom in with Pema," she says. "Tempted to tie a string around their wrists."

"In case she wanders?"

"Or turns on the gas stove."

"Has fun with knives and furniture."

"Oh God," laughs Jill.

"Put her in with me," he says with a cough. "I'm up all hours. We can share afterlife notions."

"Don't be too morbid, please. It makes people nervous." She returns to the bathroom.

He didn't think he was being morbid. He thought he was being funny. Staring up at the ceiling, his eye comes to rest on the spray of faded brown stains, the explosive result of a shaken beer when this was Quinn's room. Back when the house was filled with the complications of living. Last summer they'd moved out of the master bedroom upstairs and onto the main floor because he could no longer handle stairs. Les has never pointed the stains out to Jill because he's afraid she'll scrub them away or paint them over. He picks up his book.

"Is the lamb marinating?" he thinks to ask.

"In your recipe, followed to the letter. Potatoes too."

"The skewers —"

"Soaking." She sticks her head around the corner, a toothbrush full of paste. "I'm the worrier around here. Quit trying to take my job."

"Have enough triplesec to make a scene with the dessert?"

"Stop it," she says and he hears the faucet turn on.

"I want serious flame action," he calls, too loudly, setting off a coughing spasm. The word "action" hurt his throat.

As soon as her head hits the pillow, Jill moans, "I wanted to do the bathroom fixture."

"Tomorrow." His breathing has strained shallow, his voice a hoarse whisper.

"Tomorrow all our children, and Annie, Mom, and my baby brother will be sitting around the dining-room table," she says in a awed voice. He can hear in it that she wants nothing but to stop his suffering, and is tired not knowing how.

"Don't forget Quinn's witch of a girlfriend," he whispers. What the hell's her name?

"I always imagined our boys would be closer," she says.

Les finds Jill's hand and hooks his fingers through hers. Her warm moist hand makes him aware of the dry cold of his.

"I'm going to make flower arrangements with the lilacs and tulips." She gives his hand a squeeze. "God, I'm nervous about seeing Pema. She sounds so grown up in her letters."

"Yeah."

"Oh well, it's good she's had the chance to see how the other half lives."

Pema. His eyes involuntarily fill and he turns his head towards the aquarium housing the two angelfish Jill brought home one day to "watch over him" while she was at work, before Annie began coming over.

Under the dramatically bright warming light the winged fish hang suspended, facing one another, eyes wide open as ever, and he wonders if they're asleep. The floor of the tank is littered with neon pink, yellow and green stones and, to one side, a gloomy castle grows dark with algae. He read about a memorial reef off the coast of Miami, where people have their ashes mixed inside concrete sculptures and dropped onto the ocean floor. The accompanying photos for the article showed an underwater graveyard, fish swimming in and around what looked like giant chess pieces and a series of archways, black with algae and crawling with invertebrates. An eerie notion but no worse than the obliterating horror of being underground. Jill knows his wishes; cremation and ashes scattered in the place of her choice, a place that'll best house her memories of him. He joked about her mixing some of his ashes in with the peppercorns in the pepper grinder. "A little bone meal for you," he'd said, secretly liking the idea.

He wipes his eyes. If he was doing the cooking tomorrow, they'd start with Pema's favourite soup – french onion – followed by halibut in a lime and Pinot Gris reduction, the risotto cakes Quinn likes so much, and fennel beet salad. He tries to think if there's something Beau especially likes, but food is simply fuel to that kid. He's an eating machine, Les decides, smiling.

The last time he tried making an Alaska bombe for dessert, on their wedding anniversary – tenth? twentieth? – something didn't work. What was it? The meringue. It didn't lift.

...

Beau steps off the ferry bus in front of the Pharmasave at Royal Oaks Mall, his backpack hanging from his one good shoulder, his other having been dislocated so many times it now requires a twenty-minute tape job before games. He checked his suitcase at the Marseille airport, but it never made it further than London, or so he was told when he arrived in Vancouver last night. The baggage claim people said they'd deliver it Monday, at the earliest, which means the only clothes he has are these ones he slept in. His jeans are frayed at one knee and after twenty-four hours of travel he can smell the stink of his T-shirt under his hoodie. He wonders when the next bus is due and taps his pocket for his phone but remembers, for the tenth time, that he packed it.

In that suitcase, painstakingly rolled to avoid wrinkling, is the outfit he'd planned to wear tonight: black Italian-cut jeans that cost him nearly two hundred euros, a white silk shirt that had made the saleslady's eyes widen. He imagines his leather loafers and favourite belt being tried on by British custom guards. Mom had wanted him to dress up for this party but his only thought was impressing Pema. A bullshit idea, and his lost luggage serves him right.

A woman and her preteen daughter come towards him, the daughter cooing endearments as she coaxes along a puppy gnashing on its leash. Damn, his little speech is in that bag. He'll have to wing it. Mom had suggested a gift too, "something meaningful to you both," as if he would've given Dad one of his jerseys or some old, rancid cleats. She'd made this celebration thing sound all happy so he ended up buying an expensive bottle of real champagne, although for all he knows Dad can't drink, a can of duck pâté and hand-dipped chocolates.

He breathes in the heavy but clean west-coast air, catches the cat piss perfume of that bush that blooms every spring along the path connecting their street to Cedar Hill. The smell brings an instant memory of biking up that path with Pema, him in the lead. And of capturing her in the pirate game at school, trying to outperform her on the trampoline. Everything in his old life was a competition, either with her or with Quinn, but mainly with himself. He thinks of himself now as more of a team player. That, for good reason, his individuality has been beaten out of him, literally.

A blue-smocked woman steps out of the Pharmasave, plants her back against the glass and lights up a cigarette. She draws in the smoke like nourishment and his stomach sputters a long growl. He's hungry but also nervous. Nervous about seeing Dad — Mom implied he looks a lot different than a year ago — and nervous about seeing Pema. He used to check out her Facebook page obsessively and follow her posts. Couldn't get enough of her face, so he stopped.

"You just missed the bus," says the smoker. "Next one comes in an hour."

He's surprised for a second that she didn't speak to him in French.

"I appreciate that, thanks."

Was nice not having to scramble to form a coherent response. After two years in France, the language still takes a lot of brain power.

Beau is ten, fifteen minutes from home by car. An hour by foot. He's only got the backpack, which is light — laptop, toiletries, an extra pair of socks and boxers — why not walk, maybe even jog away some of this nervous energy? But first he'll buy a few protein bars.

The cashier's Harry Potter glasses and thin tie scream

college boy. He drones off the total, then gives Beau a superior glance reminiscent of Quinn. Beau hands over the cash. Quinn and rehab. Weird. Things might have turned out differently if Mom had forced him to play a sport, anything to get him out of his head. Golf, even.

Maybe he'll offer to take Quinn along to the gym tomorrow. Teach him a basic routine or two. If, that is, he doesn't mock the idea.

...

Placing his pencil back in its holder, Quinn blows on the graph paper. He's almost caught up on his work. Next time, though, his boss may not be so generous, so understanding. He catches his negative thinking and amends it aloud: "There will not be a next time."

He swivels his desk chair to face the bed where Holly sleeps on her back, slack-jawed, arms and legs a far-flung tumult under the covers.

He met Holly in Jasper House. The first time they slept together was instant sexual ignition and so good he was afraid they'd already peaked. The second time was even better, coming at the same instant as if it was a single shared orgasm. They'd both spontaneously cried after, the heaving sort, and then — he was so thankful — she didn't feel any need to talk about it. They'd fallen asleep holding each other and woken to the morning chimes in the same knotted position only to skip breakfast for another equally unified go. Sex took alcohol's place, which made withdrawal a lot easier. "Do you want a drink?" became their private euphemism for making love. Relations between patients that went beyond friendship were frowned upon so they did a lot of sneaking around which only made things more exciting.

Holly approached sex as if it was a wholesome meal and no more complicated. She kept her eyes open and made slow disjointed conversation. For Quinn to do anything else but the same felt oddly embarrassing. With his eyes open he fell in love with the walleyed angle of her breasts, her boxy shoulders and surprisingly muscular arms, her small mound of a belly with its ghostly language of stretch marks – Holly had a four-year-old son, Owen. There was a weight and bovine deliberation to her movements that put him at ease, a lack of boundary in her gravel-coloured eyes that made him trust her and want to protect her. He thinks of her architectural equivalent as an old-style cement water tower on a smooth expanse of prairie. Instead of a white stencil-painted town's name, it's HOLLY, bold and wholesome.

He has yet to tell his parents that he's moved out of the sunny bachelor apartment Jill found for him in Nanaimo and into Holly's basement suite in Duncan. Is planning on revealing information about her in increments. The fact of his having a girlfriend was increment number one, her name increment two and today's introduction increment three. Luckily Owen is with his grandmother this weekend, he thinks, slipping his work into his briefcase. Between the cigarettes and crow's feet, Holly will be more than enough for Mom to digest. He catches himself. It's not his mother's business to love Holly, it's his.

The clock says 3:10. Holly worked the night shift last night at the seniors' home and wanted to be woken at three. Though he'd prefer to waltz in as dinner is being served, after people have had a few and are distracted by their appetites, he knows it would upset Mom. He's been out now for two months and twenty-six days, and today will be the first time he's been around booze. Holly says she'll be fine and not to worry about her. Though of course he does, because if she goes AWOL, he doesn't stand a chance. He'll be focused on Dad, he tells himself, the incredible shrinking man as he's come to think of him. He hopes Dad will meet Owen some day.

Owen's the first kid Quinn has ever paid attention to, or maybe it's the other way around; Owen's the first kid who's ever paid Quinn any mind. Four-year-olds are from another planet, a planet where everything springs fresh out of the sky for the first time. Each morning, he wakes to Owen leaping on his chest demanding a wrestle and answers to his questions: What keeps the ceiling from falling down? Can we eat acorns? Why don't dogs and cats get married? When he's on Owen's planet, there's no time to dwell on himself and his problems. Therefore no problems. If there was a pill to keep children four years old, he'd be tempted to give it to Owen.

When Holly's on night shift, Quinn makes the boy breakfast and walks him to junior kindergarten where Owen, as openly affectionate as his mother, bear-hugs him goodbye. It's only recently that he's stopped being surprised by this.

He lets Owen play with his old Lego ships, watching with a shaky kind of euphoria as Owen crashes them into the couch and sends pieces flying. Then he helps rebuild them according to Owen's eccentric specifications.

Quinn goes to the closet and rechecks the pocket of his vest to make sure what he wrote for Dad is still there. Hopes he's not expected to read it aloud. Mom wants him to wear a suit and tie. He'll give her the tie but chooses one of his aunt's creations: narrow blue suede with brown leather piping. Mom will think Holly's not good enough for him, not educated enough, but Holly's a social genius compared to him. And compared to her, if she wants the truth. And if universities gave degrees for being real, Holly'd have a fucking doctorate.

The thought of spending the weekend with his family

propels him to kneel at the end the bed, where he carefully tugs up the sheet. As he plants a slow row of kisses along the flat arch of Holly's foot, she half sighs, half moans and he moves to the inside of her ankle.

"Is that a sea anemone on my leg?" she says with a rumbling laugh.

Yesterday at the beach with Owen, they were gently sticking their fingers in the creatures' centers for their contractive rubbery kisses.

"Yes," he says, adding suction to his kisses and continuing upward.

Arriving a little late should be okay.

...

The weather has been clear and blue right across the country but now, just past the Rockies, the windows darken and the plane jerks and dips, overhead bins rattling.

"You call British Columbia home?" pipes up the woman beside Pema as she lowers her book to her lap. Except for exchanging smiles at the start of the trip four hours ago in Toronto, they haven't spoken. Clearly the woman is anxious.

"Yes," says Pema, to keep it simple. "You?"

The woman speed-talks about having visited her son in Guelph, his course of study at university, then moves on to her home in Brentwood Bay and some invasive weed "with sticky-fingered hands" overtaking her garden. Westerners, thinks Pema, are quiet on the outside and noisy on the inside, while the Tibetans and Nepalese are noisy on the outside and quiet on the inside.

The woman describes her basement flooding last spring and Pema wonders what home really means beyond walls and a roof. Pictures the two-room house in Jampaling, the grass-stuffed mattress on top of two wool carpets that was her bed, a bed she shared with her two half-sisters. Datso and her husband slept on the other side of a thin cotton curtain in the same small room. When she first arrived and saw the set-up, Pema wanted to stay elsewhere, even pitch a tent outside. For as long as she had memory, she'd slept alone in her own bed in her own room. Her fourteen-year-old sister, Kitsi, blatantly resentful of Pema, had been all for the tent idea, but Datso wouldn't hear of it. That first week was painfully awkward, Kitsi's random kicks in her sleep always finding their mark, Datso's snoring, some invisible night bug leaving welts on her face and arms, her gut reacting badly to the food and therefore her having to use the outhouse in the middle of the night, terrified of snakes, which Kitsi assured her were deadly. But it wasn't a month later that her stomach problems and bug bites were gone and it became only natural to fall asleep surrounded by warm bodies and synchronizing her breath with another's. And as if Datso knew it would, sharing the peace of sleep eased Kitsi's jealous anger – though it could also have been the shared care package from Jill. And if Datso and her husband did make love behind the cotton curtain, it was after Pema and her sisters were long asleep.

Last night she slept in an airport motel in Frankfurt. For two months she's been pumped about the idea of a real bed, a shower with hot water, being able to spread out and watch that most modern of contraptions, TV. The shower was heaven and she can't remember ever feeling that clean before. In Jampaling she has 'washcloth' showers from the kitchen sink, cold water only, her own precious sliver of soap. Once a year, on the eve of the lunar calendar new year, Datso boils water for a hot bath in a large steel tub. But since everyone takes turns, oldest to youngest, the water never feels quite clean.

All the TV programs at the motel, with the exception of the BBC news channel, were in German or French, and the advertisements with their rapid-fire images, felt like a physical assault on the brain. Once night came, she missed the village's evening whir of prayer wheels, the chanting songs to unseen protectors, and had trouble getting to sleep. And without the physical presence of family blurring her boundaries, she became weirdly self-conscious and decided that to sleep alone was unnatural, even dangerous.

On Pema's last night in Jampaling, Datso had broken down, wailed for her not to leave, certain she'd never come back. "I'll come back," she told her, crying too, her tears mixed with a profound happiness that her birth mother was so distraught. "Or maybe you can come to Canada."

The plane takes a couple of hard bumps in a row and the woman's fast talk halts in anticipation of a third. When it doesn't come, her words tumble along again. Pema had expected Datso to be a sad person, unwell, and in the beginning was secretly angry that that wasn't the case. Laid-back and quick with a smile, Datso appeared to be both happy and healthy.

The opposite of Jill in ways that made Pema feel better about herself, Datso disliked hard work, didn't do math and was a passionate gossip. Known in the village for her match-making skills, she tried to fix Pema up with the gap-toothed mailman from Pakhara.

"Mail delivery," Datso would remind her, "is a Nepalese government job. Benefits," she'd say, rubbing her fingers together.

The night before mail day, Datso would make momos, put three aside to steam the next morning, invite him inside. With his receding chin and saucer eyes, the mailman reminded Pema of an ugly lemur. Datso would make Pema stand beside her and together they loomed over the young man as he juggled eating and smiling and answering Datso's inquiries about his family and job, job and family. Occasionally he'd flash shy, excited eyes at Pema's exposed legs beneath her shorts. The noisy way he breathed through his nose never failed to remind her of the time five-year-old Beau put a dried bean up his nose and couldn't get it out. Pema even tried the vacuum hose. By evening it had started to swell painfully and Jill took him to Emergency.

"And you're coming from?" asks the woman.

"Nepal."

"Nepal?" The woman leans slightly away as if it might be catching. "You've come a long way."

Pema smiles at the truth of this statement. Her biggest concern in life used to be matching the colour of her highlights to her shoes.

"Are you a student?"

"No, but I'm hoping to go to school next fall."

"In what field?"

"Well, eventually I think I'd like go into immigration law."

"Really," says the woman, a challenge to her voice. Whatever a lawyer looks like, thinks Pema, I'm not it.

The woman starts in about her sister, a paralegal, who lives in Ottawa and works for the Crown.

Pema's glad Katie's picking her up. It'll give her a chance to ease into this homecoming.

"Your parents are Nepalese?"

"Tibetan."

"Oh." The woman nods as if with new understanding. "Does Tibet technically still exist?"

Pema wonders what she means by technically. "Not if you listen to the Chinese government."

"A powerful force, China," says the woman, glancing back at the novel open on her lap. The seatbelt signs have switched off, the turbulence gone along with the woman's interest in the conversation.

Pema suddenly wants to tell her the story of her birth parents walking for fourteen days out of their Tibetan village to the Burmese border and being forced to turn back when they found the mountain pass covered in snow. And about their second attempt, when, after a fifteen-day walk, this time to the border of Nepal, they were caught by Chinese police and, fortunately, sent home and not to Chinese jail to die like many others. On their third escape, Pema was with them, "a precious jewel" hidden inside her mother's belly. After walking for a mere seven days they were picked up by a truck which, three days later, drove across the Nepalese border without being stopped. Because of this, Datso still referred to Pema as her "good luck child." The following year, only months before the Chinese shut the Tibetan border for good, Pema's father travelled back over the Himalayas to try and bring back his sister's family, along with Datso's mother and younger brothers. Neither he nor any of her family members were heard from again. These are stories Pema learned as she relearned Tibetan which, after months of stupefied resistance and struggle, came rushing back like the lyrics of an old, beloved song.

She catches glimpses of green through the clouds, a hint of metallic-blue ocean. The air here is probably one reason Jill, despite being twelve years older than Datso, looks the same age.

Datso was the one who kept in contact with Jill and Les. She made Pema translate their letters aloud so that, despite herself, she vicariously kept in touch. Jill sent regular care packages — a big occasion in Jampaling — of notebooks and pens, tooth-brushes and soap, and some of Pema favourites: dark chocolate,

Triscuits, sardines. Everything was shared with neighbours, friends and the old folks' home, and Pema barely saw any of it except for the sardines. Not accustomed to eating fish, no one could stand the smell, and sent her outside to eat what the villagers considered "dog food." In the box was always a bundle of clothes from Annie. For reasons Pema never understood, the clothes were not shared outside the immediate family. And though Pema's family was not the best dressed in Jampaling, they were the most interestingly dressed. Her youngest sister, Maitreya, wore her flapper shirt made from recycled straws every day for two months until a large patch of it melted when she left it on a chair too close to the stove. And Datso and her husband were both very proud of Datso's peekaboo nightgown made from a rainbow riot of scarves.

Datso was the one who was most upset when they received news of the aggressive return of Les's cancer, which had wormed its way into his bones and liver. And though Datso never pushed, never said a word, Pema began writing her own letters to Jill and Les, it feeling strange but also a relief to be using the English words she'd been teaching the surrounding village kids all day, for pennies. She's hasn't told Jill and Les how teachers are revered here, how discipline is not a problem in kids who are grateful and who all have crushes on their English teachers. She has not told Jill and Les that she has never felt so wealthy in all her life.

The pilot announces the time and weather in Victoria. She's sorry to have stayed away so long. Though it may have appeared selfish or childish on her part, it has taken her this long truly to believe she wasn't the reason Datso gave her away.

She pushes her tray upright, twists the plastic latch. She's been craving Les's homemade pizza, his lemon ricotta crêpes, his french onion soup. Anything with cheese. A shiver of excitement straightens her back. She's psyched to see everyone. Except Beau, that is, who never answered any of her letters. Such a shithead. She promises herself that she will not say hi to him until he says hi first. Won't even look at him. She pictures him all Paris vogue, sneering at the dirt-hippie she's become with her long shapeless hair, baggy pants, flip-flops. A taste for rancid butter and dried yak. She scratches the back of her head. She'll pick up some lice shampoo, take a shower at Katie's and change into the only dressy thing she owns, the navy-blue brocade chuba Datso made her for the Dalai Lama's visit. She'll look déjà-vu, like she just got off the boat.

...

Standing in her studio Annie kicks off her pants which are impossibly tight around the waist. In underwear and bra she steps up to the full-length mirror, squints to see better and pinches the tire of flesh crowning her hips. Jesus. The new meds didn't just make her a dullard but a fat dullard. A mallard. She'll have to start designing goddamn caftans.

Her downstairs neighbour, Eloise, says the weight gain is menopause — "At fifty, the waist thinks outside the box, period" — but Annie's convinced it's the antidepressants she's been on, and so yesterday she stopped taking them. She went online to read up on potential sudden-withdrawal symptoms, which include nausea, delusions, mood swings and hallucinations and sound far more interesting than how she's been feeling lately. And the nausea will be a blessing because she won't feel like eating and might be able to fit into some fucking pants.

She's determined to wear this plum satin suit because the cigarette pants show off her one still-slim feature, her ankles.

She grabs a strip of elastic and sits down at the sewing machine. Not that anybody notices what she looks like any more. At the deli counter the other day, she thought a distinguished doctor type was mesmerized by her chest until he pointed right through her and ordered a pound of smoked turkey. Then two giggly college girls with their pop-up asses tripped past and, as if he could smell them, his head did a one-eighty.

She sits sewing, crucially aware of the glasses perched on the end of her beak, the picture of a librarian spinster. Since the last of her eggs have hatched, she's not only become invisible to men, but salespeople call her "dear" and even with glasses it takes her fifteen minutes to thread a needle. She thinks of Les and stops herself, incredulous. "Annie Kellman, who the fuck are you to feel sorry for yourself?" Hit by a flash flood of tears, the force bends her over her sewing as grief rolls through like seismic thunder. Losing Les is unbearable. Get it all out now she tells herself, having promised Jill she won't lose it today and will keep it on an up-note. Jill doesn't like *scenes*.

She grabs a scrap of fabric and wipes her eyes. At least her offering for tonight is cheery. Having done her research, she recorded the music hits that were number one during the important junctures of Les's life — birth, high school grad, dropping out of college and taking a pastry-chef course in France — which was the same year she and Les met — his marriage, Quinn's and Beau's births, Pema's arrival. Emailed the songs to Quinn who was going to synchronize the music to a slide show.

She bought Les the new Elmore Leonard and made him a pair of pyjamas from recycled silk ties, lined with satin to protect from bedsores. But really, her gifts feel paltry. They're just stuff. If she could give him half her liver she would.

Sniffing, she sews a buttonhole onto the strip of elastic

and pins the elastic to the waist of her pants. Remembers what a skinny whip of a thing she was when she flew from Cleveland to Seattle to meet Les that first time. He'd driven down from Vancouver, told her, "I'll be the guy wearing a Canuck poncho." She had to go to the library and look up *Canuck*. And there he was at baggage claim, a piece of paper pinned to the front of his goofy-looking poncho saying "Annie's brother." Though they were virtual strangers — they'd only had two previous phone conversations — she walked right into his open arms and scratchy poncho.

"I assumed you'd be taller," he said in his unassuming way. "Blond like me."

"I assumed you'd be disappointing," she said.

He laughed his silent, open-mouthed laugh.

She was going to stay in Canada for a week but ended up getting a job, a work permit and, two years later, landed immigrant status. Never used her return ticket, which she's kept in her Keeping Drawer along with her adoptive mom's sewing scissors and the small white button she got from a beautiful man she met on a plane. Also in her Keeping Drawer are locks of baby hair from Quinn and Beau, a strip of brocade from the chuba Pema was wearing when she arrived, birthday cards, letters and her collection of nineteen house keys stolen from lovers.

Finished securing the elastic onto the waist of her pants, she tries them on again and manages to do them up without pain. She steps back up to the mirror.

"Look at those cheeks." She grabs the fleshy pouches. Les's cheeks are caves under shelves of bone. She takes a handful of her curly hair, which has recently exploded with fine silver lines as if she stuck her tongue in a light socket. He's lost his hair, his eyebrows, even his lashes. She squints at her reflection. "While

I look like a poodle." It's not fair. She lifts the hair up over her ears and lets it drop. "Like a fucking poodle."

She goes to her sewing table and picks up her pinking shears, puts them down and heads to the bathroom. This job requires a razor.

...

Kenneth, Jill's brother, flew in from Japan two days earlier, arriving at three in the morning Pacific time. He spent a day recuperating at the motel, in no man's land as he thought of it, watching pay-per-view and ordering Chinese takeout because Vancouver's Chinese food was even better than the food in China. The relief of having an ocean between him and his screw-up back home was strangely euphoric.

The next day he and a rental car found their way to his mother's place of incarceration. She looked just like herself, had had her hair done — something Jill arranged — and was dressed respectably in brown slacks, a lavender blouse and her pearl necklace. She seemed so like herself that for a moment he imagined she was as coherent as when he last saw her more than a decade ago. She knew his name right off the bat, was thrilled to see him and they had a good hug before she introduced him to some of the inmates. Each elderly person shook his hand, smiling pleasantly. "A tall drink of water," said a petite woman with a beatific smile. "Do you live around here?" asked a man wearing a dapper silk cravat. To the expected oohs and ahs he explained where he lived. Finished talking, he then entered the twilight zone. Nancy introduced him again and he was received with the same smiling handshakes, the same "Tall drink of water" and "Do you live around here?" The cycle began again and he quickly asked Nancy if she'd show him around the place.

As they toured the facility, Nancy acted as if it were her private home, muttering about the guests she couldn't seem to get to leave then giving him a nasty look as if wishing him gone too. And that was when sorrow gutted his chest. Why hadn't he made more of an effort to see her while she was still the person he knew and loved?

He took her for a walk in the adjacent park then stayed for an institutional dinner of ham steak, boxed potatoes and canned peas. When he mentioned going to see Jill and family, Nancy perked up and asked with a kind of pleading clarity if she could come along. Her sincerity was so heartfelt, however temporary, and his guilt so replete, there was no way he could leave her. And when he called Jill and she said in that self-righteous way of hers, "No, it's a bad idea," he became all the more determined.

Now, as he and Nancy wait in a line of vehicles to exit the ferry, and he's lost his name and identity to someone named Harold, he's worried that Jill may have been right after all.

Kenneth punches his sister's address onto the rental car's computer screen.

"Fifteen eighty Thurston Court," the mechanized yet sultry female voice reads back to him.

Beside him, Nancy turns to look in the back seat.

"It's the car's computer talking," Kenneth explains and Nancy gives him a look like he's the one who's lost his mind.

He drives off the ferry into the narrow stream of traffic and sudden blinding sunlight.

"Like a herd of angry turtles," singsongs Nancy in what Kenneth thinks of as her former-schoolteacher voice.

"Yep, we're off and running to see your daughter, Jill, and your grandchildren, Quinn, Beau and Pema. Jill's husband, Les, is very sick." He drones out this information at regular intervals because Jill told him to.

"My husband's very sick," says Nancy.

"And very dead," he mumbles.

"Excuse me, Harold?" she says, her voice rising in alarm.

"Nothing, sorry." And he is, then reminds himself that in another few seconds all will be forgotten.

"What time is the ferry?" asks Nancy.

"Two o'clock." He looks at the car clock. It's three-forty.

"I haven't been on a ferry for a while."

Only three minutes ago.

Nancy goes quiet, hands plucking at the top of her purse with a kind of restlessness that prompts him to activate the child lock on the doors and windows. She taps out the syllables of her next sentence on the window. "I re-mem-ber."

"That we're going to your daughter Jill's house?"

"It's good to go back. Pin it down." She mimes putting a pin in the lapel of her rain jacket. "Otherwise, it's like salt over your shoulder," she says with a toss.

He doesn't ask. Has given up trying to make her make sense.

"Nice that we left the rain behind," he says. It had been raining in Vancouver.

"What time's the ferry?"

"Two o'clock."

"I haven't been on a ferry for a while."

Nancy was frightened by the ferry crowds and they'd stayed in the car until the car deck emptied out. Then he took her and her cane up in the elevator to the quiet buffet room where she had six desserts, a bucket of coffee and, also at Jill's suggestion, they played rummy, a continuous game of recklessly changing rules. His fingers ache from shuffling. When the "return to your vehicles" announcement came, Nancy was in the washroom. After ten minutes and some urging by the buffet personnel to head down to the car deck, he went and found her locked in a stall. Had to crawl under the door, not an easy manoeuvre with his height. Her sweater and purse were hung on a hook, her shirt unbuttoned to the waist. She mumbled something about "tickets to get out of here." It all would have been funny if it wasn't so sad.

"Minto?" Keeping his eyes on the road, he offers her the open roll. When she doesn't take it, he looks over and sees her staring at it as if he's offered her a rotten fish. "If you don't like Mintos just say so." He slips the roll back into his pocket.

"I have a son," says Nancy.

He sighs. "Yes, you do."

"He teaches baseball in China."

"English in Japan, though he does coach Little League." He presses his head against the headrest and sighs. "I've been away a long time and I'm truly sorry about not coming more often. But I'm here now, Mom. It's me, Kenneth." He glances over, hopeful.

"I'm tired of eating chicken." She's looking out her window. "It's chicken this and chicken that, as if the sky's falling."

Changing into the passing lane, he's eager to get to Jill. Things are a little too real for him these days and he needs a strong drink and his sister's advice. She has always told him what to do and hopefully will tell him what to do now. Back home he's fucked up big time, literally.

"Turn left in ten kilometres," drones the computer.

Nancy turns to search the back.

"It's the computer talking," he repeats for what it's worth.

She huffs and opens her purse and Kenneth glimpses what looks like the motherlode of paper clips. She shuts it again and clucks her tongue. "I've always liked the smell of a decent place."

...

Jill had risen early to ensure everything was done in time. She cleaned the final light fixture in the bathroom, did another dusting in the upstairs bedrooms and marked four test papers before Les woke and rang his bell for help to and from the bathroom.

After tossing the marinating potato wedges, she made Les his morning oatmeal then put together the Greek salad — keeping the tomatoes separate. She skewered the chunks of lamb, toasted pine nuts and diced mango and scallion for the rice, then froze her fingers struggling to embalm the mascarpone ice cream in thick slices of pound cake. "Form the cake into the shape of a hill or volcano," Les had told her, "with enough surface on top to place the demitasse." Her cake hill ended up lopsided, but the ice cream was beginning to melt so she wrapped it in wax paper and made room in the freezer. Figured that when the time came to make the meringue icing she could spread it on in a way that straightened up the hill.

She sliced celery, carrots and cucumber for the veggie plate, realized she was missing red pepper — Pema's favourite — and made a trip to the store. The moment she arrived back, Les was ringing his bell for lunch, last night's soup and a tuna sandwich. Having forgotten to eat breakfast, she grabbed a banana and poured herself a cup of tea, which ended up turning cold on the kitchen counter while she made her mother's pastry recipe for the miniquiches.

Now, as she fills the pastry cups, she reviews the order of the ceremony. "Welcome everyone home and give a short speech to set the tone. Invite each family member to light a candle on the mantelpiece, say their prepared words and finish by offering their gift to Les. Les opens gift. Invite next person.

Dinner. After dinner, ask Quinn to run slide show to Annie's music. Serve coffee, end with the flaming cake which Les will ceremoniously light."

She can't help wondering if Pema will even feel like hers any more. Oh, why the possessiveness? A child is not something you own. Les's bell rings. She's coming home, thinks Jill, heading to the bedroom, just be happy about that.

"I'd like my shaving things and toothbrush, please," he tells her.

Because walking takes so much out of him, these are things he now does sitting up on the side of his bed, over a bowl of warm water on the card table Jill carts to and from his bedside as needed.

She leaves him to it, finishes filling the quiches — swiss and cream cheese, parboiled broccoli — which she puts aside to cook just before serving so that they'll be warm the way her mother likes them.

"The egg whites for the meringue have to sit at room temperature," she intones, repeating Les's directive. She puts the required number of eggs in a bowl on the counter, then, to have at the ready, hunts down the old dented container of cream of tartar.

Her favourite chore, setting the table, she's saved for last. Cathy Benfey, the professional celebrant Jill hired, had encouraged her to incorporate familiar traditions. Therefore, like she's done every Christmas and Thanksgiving since starting a family, she uses her grandmother's damask tablecloth and napkins — dry cleaned for the occasion — the china and silver inherited from Les's parents, the crystal glasses that were a wedding gift from her parents and the brass candlesticks that Kenneth sent for their tenth anniversary but which arrived over a year late.

Cathy Benfey designed all occasions from baby welcomes to ash scatterings, menstrual beginnings to pet memorials. Living Wakes, though, were her specialty. Despite the grating sounds of the term 'celebrant," Jill had paid Cathy for an hour's advice. "Knowing that he or she has made a mark upon this earth," said Cathy, eyes drooping with sincerity, "makes the thought of an imminent departure more acceptable."

The woman tried to talk Jill into handing over the evening's reins — "So you can focus on your loved one and attend to your own grief" — but the last thing Les would want, and Jill too, was a stranger in their midst pretending to know what they were feeling. She did adopt Cathy's suggestion of semi-formal attire — Jill plans to wear her green satin cocktail dress because it's the one dress the kids never fail to compliment — and her suggestion to display things the kids had made for Les over the years. When sorting through the storage room, Jill dug up a dozen necktie-sporting Father's Day cards — an ongoing joke since Les didn't own a necktie — and the place cards with acrostic poems Pema had painstakingly made for somebody's birthday. She also found two well-preserved school projects that Les would have helped with and she thought the kids might get a kick out of seeing.

With Pema's place cards, she marks the immediate family in their customary seats with Les at one end and herself at the other. Nancy, she places to her right and next to Kenneth. Holly between Quinn and Les.

Curious all over again what Pema had written about her, Jill picks up her place card.

J uggles home and work

I nsists everyone speaks right

L oves words

L ong legs

She smiles and reads Les's.

L aughs a lot
E njoys cooking
S uperific dad

She rereads hers. Fair enough. She'd have been more fun if she hadn't had to work so much. If Les had stuck with a job and been more ambitious...some people find more reasons to laugh. Is anyone — Is anyone to blame for the way she is?

She displays the Father's Day cards around the table's centre, including the unredeemed remains of a coupon book Beau and Pema made for one of Les's birthdays. *Good for one Foot Massage. Good for getting you one Beer. Good for one Toe Paint.*

How many times did she arrive home from work to find this table strewn with Monopoly or a card game and Les in front of the cooking channel, his hair festooned with clips and ribbons, his eyelids a horror show of blue. Jill never once got her toenails painted with scented markers, each nail a different colour, sometimes polka-dotted or striped, smelling of watermelon, licorice and lime. She never got a coupon book either. But then she never asked for one. She asked for notebooks, transplants for the garden, oven mitts. Once she asked that no one say "like" all day, to try really hard, and no one found this funny or endearing.

She adjusts Quinn's first-place science project — a home-made seismograph — on the dining-room sideboard. Hardly fair for Quinn to be the only one not drinking. She can abstain too, provide moral support. She looks at her watch. Time to shower and get dressed. Also on the sideboard, though battered in places, is the elaborate diorama Beau and Pema made of Hogwarts. Jill had helped edit the book report while Les had helped with the diorama — quidditch balls and secret chambers — the fun part. Something's ringing somewhere. It's Les's bell.

As she heads to the bedroom, she remembers something her father, the armchair philosopher and drunk, once said when she was angry at her then boyfriend for blowing off a date. "'Tis good to be reminded that every relationship has its wows," he said in that bloated professorial way of his she'd vowed never to have. "It's a law of our solar system demonstrated by its elliptical, not circular, orbit." He'd swung his finger round and round in an elongated circle. "Its wow."

Occasionally what came out of her father had the ring of intelligence, and she was feeling dejected enough then to accept a little fatherly wisdom until he added in a bullying tone: "There are no perfect circles."

It was then that something inside her sixteen-year-old brain bit down and she became resolute to prove him wrong. To this day she's ever propelled by the notion that perfection is out there, around the next corner just out of sight but not out of reach, and if only she tries a little harder…

His dress pants are even baggier than he'd feared and they have to use one of Jill's belts to keep them up. The folds of his white shirt are hidden under a black V-neck sweater that Jill shrank in the dryer. On purpose, he thinks, despite her apologetic claim otherwise. The doorbell rings just as Jill is tying his shoes.

"Beau?" he says.

"I'm still not changed."

"Did you lock the door?"

"I guess I did."

"You have to answer it."

"I will, I will." She finishes tying his shoes and stands up.

"I wanted to be sitting in my chair," he says, more to himself.

"Well, here's the walker." She wheels it over.

He doesn't want his son to have to witness his old-man procession from bedroom to family room. Jill grips his elbow to help him stand but he hesitates. "I'd like not to be wearing the oxygen tubes."

"Let's get you to the chair then I'll take them off."

"Tell him you're coming," he says, and she hurries into the hall and yells, "Just a minute."

It's the first step that requires the most courage. An image has formed in his head of his cancer-riddled bones as porous coral that might fracture on impact and send the twin towers of his legs crumbling beneath him. He closes his eyes and steps forward. Still standing and the pain's bearable. The most efficient way of exerting himself is to take six even steps and stop for a deep breath, six even steps, stop, deep breath.

"Coming," Jill calls again.

When his easy chair comes into view, he has to hold himself back from hurrying. Finally seated, Les takes a couple of full breaths of concentrated oxygen, unhooks his tubes and hands them to Jill, picks up the ball cap he keeps handy. She hurries to return them to the bedroom when he stops her.

"What?" she says, exasperated. "He's waiting."

"How's my hair?"

That sober face of his wife's softens into a smile. Nice. He covers his baldness with a ball cap and she hurries down the hall to the door. He listens intently to the door opening, Jill's squeak of a cry.

"Hey Mom." Beau's jocular tone.

"Come here," she demands.

"I need a shower, badly."

Les pictures Jill giving him a hard squeeze and Beau sighing like he's doing her a favour.

"Tell him we gave at the office," calls Les.

Beau's chuckle gives Les a throat-swelling thrill.

"So am I the first one here?" Beau sounds tentative.

"Yes, thank goodness," says Jill. "I'm not even dressed yet."

Hurry in here, thinks Les. I can't stand it.

The smell of lilacs competes with something sour, thinks Beau, his nose wrinkling as he drops his pack. Glancing up the staircase, he flashes on racing Quinn and Pema down these stairs, round the banister, past the guest bathroom, slipping on his socks down this hall then hopping over the back of the couch in the family room, the first one in prime position for Saturday cartoons.

His mom's a fluttering bird behind him, winging him towards his dad's voice saying weakly, "Let's see you." The kitchen and family room are really one large room and between them, on the far wall, French doors open onto the back patio and yard. He knows the trampoline's been sold but is glad to see the ping pong table set up on the grass.

Dad sits in front of the picture window that frames a rhododendron gaudy with hot pink blossoms. He looks pinned to his chair as he leans back to see from under the brim of one of Pema's old softball caps. His narrow face is a chalky yellow, his lips a chapped stinging red. Beau hardly recognizes him.

"I'd hug you if I didn't think you'd snap me in half," says Les, holding up a hand.

Beau can't help but smirk. He squeezes his dad's hand, hears a small crack and quickly lets go.

"God, I think you broke it." Les grabs his hand and hunches over it as if in pain.

"Whaaat?" Beau is horrified and looks to his mom. "I didn't —"

"Gotcha." Les's laugh is strangulated.

"Jesus."

"Les," scolds Jill.

Beau forces a laugh. Remembers back in grade ten challenging his dad in kitchen doorway rucks to see who could push the other over the threshold. Les would hold back, give Beau the edge until the last minute when he'd put real muscle into it and easily win.

"You are even bigger than the last time we saw you," says Jill.

"You're a monster," says Les. "I bet you eat like one too."

"I'm actually one of the smaller guys on the team." Two-thirteen. But fifth best bench press. Second best fifty-metre sprint time. So-so tackler. Lousy kicks.

His parents are shaking their heads, smiles stuck on their faces.

"You can take a shower. Or are you hungry? Where's your luggage?" His mother is clearly in multi-tasking mode.

Beau tells the story of his luggage and Jill reminds him that he still has some old clothes in his room. "Though I doubt they'd fit you any more."

"You'd crush those clothes," says Les and breaks into an ugly fit of coughing that sounds like it must hurt.

Beau looks to Jill, who asks him in a strange upbeat voice if he'd fetch his dad a glass of water, no ice, then disappears down the hall. Though the kitchen's just on the other end of the room, he's relieved not to have to stand there and watch his father struggle. The phone rings and Jill calls out for Beau to answer it.

"Hello?"

"I know that voice, I do. That you, Beau?"

"C'est moi, ma tante Annie," he answers and her laugh

is maniacal. He grabs a glass for water. Dad now sounds like he's choking.

"I can't wait to see you, pinch your cheeky cheeks. So great you're home. So great. Just calling to ask if your mom needs me to bring anything other than all the shit I'm already bringing."

"I'll ask." He takes the glass of water to his dad who, still coughing, points to the table beside his chair.

"Who's coughing?" Annie asks. "Is that Les? Oh God, is he all right?"

"I'm just bringing him water. Here comes Mom."

Jill appears with a long transparent hose that his father fits into his nose. His ball cap has fallen onto the floor beside his chair and the sun shining through the window illuminates a large blue vein like an underground river arcing across his whiter than white bald head. An alien's head, thinks Beau.

"Thanks, Beau." Jill slips a bendy straw into the cup and Les's lips reach for it in sad fishlike motions. Beau looks away.

"Auntie Annie wants to know if you need anything else."

"Got it covered, tell her."

"She's got it covered."

"Of course she's got it covered," says Annie. "Okay, so how is he today?"

"Pretty good, I think."

"He's so amazing." A minute ago his aunt sounded insanely happy and now sounds close to tears. "You are one lucky kid to have such a dad. Sorry, this is a celebration. A happy day. I'm going to hang up so I can hurry over and see your handsome face."

"Bye, Auntie."

"And you can see what you think of my new look," she says. "God help us." And with a fresh rocket of laughter, she hangs up.

As Les's cough subsides, Beau, feeling like he's in the way more than anything, thinks he might escape upstairs. "So I slept in this shirt and should probably shower," he says.

Les just smirks and takes in Beau's bulked-up body, not with any hint of jealously, thinks Beau, but with something like pride of ownership, and Beau has a fleeting sense of himself as an extension of his dad or of what his dad once was.

"Okay, say it," croaks Les as he catches his breath.

"What?" says Beau and hopes he knows what his dad is asking. "That you look like shite?"

Les's head falls back against his chair. "Don't I know it. So how about a beer?" Another noisy breath. "Or you a wine snob now?"

"Beer sounds great."

"Beer. Coming right up," says Jill from the kitchen.

Annie parks in her brother's driveway, flips down the visor mirror and repowders a rogue freckle in front of her left ear, then a string of satellite freckles along her hairline. Les didn't have any spots under *his* hair. She turns to reassess the melted chocolate chip on the side of her head.

"Bull's eye," she mutters, "mole's eye," and doesn't bother to try and cover that one.

Convinced her head looks freakishly small without her mass of curls, she wore her most daunting earrings — four-inch bronze discs. And, to feminize her suit, sky-high heels and a ruffled blouse. Wouldn't want the kids to start calling her Uncle.

She had a difficult drive over because small animals, squirrels or cats, maybe rabbits she couldn't tell which, kept darting out in front of her car. After the sixth or seventh time it happened, she figured out that her missing drugs were playing games with her brain stem, which had branches that tickled the insides of her eyes.

A black sedan pulls in behind hers and she flips up the visor. Quinn? She can't wait to meet this new girl of his, and can sure use help carrying things. She grabs the two bottles of wine and gets out of the car as a tall, thick-shouldered man unfolds from the black one. Not Quinn. This man has a grey-streaked ponytail, a goatee ringing his full lips and is wearing a wrinkled sports coat. He bends down and announces, loudly, to whoever's in the passenger seat, "We're here." Sun reflects off the windshield and Annie can't see who's inside.

He turns to face the house and therefore Annie, rests his elbow on the car roof and his chin in his hand.

Annie gives a wave but he doesn't move. Can he not see her? Is her head that small?

"Do you happen to speak Alzheimer?" he asks.

Annie barks out a laugh. "You," she says and closes her door, "must be the infamous Kenneth?" He has a slightly bulbous nose and friendly, dog-eared brown eyes. She was picturing a Japanese aesthete not a St. Bernard. "I'm Annie, Les's sister."

"Give me one of those lovelies." He takes a bottle so they can shake hands.

His handshake is rugged and sloppy and she suspects the Japanese view him as a Canadian cartoon, a little barrel full of beer around his neck.

"That must be Nancy," she says, looking in the window.

"More or less." He slips the other bottle from Annie's grip.

"Thank you, kind sir," she says and starts round to the passenger door. "I haven't seen Nancy in ages."

"She's refusing to get out of the car." He shuts his door, presses his key chain and the doors click and lock. "Locking it so she can't escape. Got a window cracked."

"But..." Annie taps a finger on Nancy's window. "Nancy, hi. Remember me?" Dumb thing to ask. "Would you like to open your door?"

Deliberately ignoring her, Nancy stares straight ahead, her nose tilted an inch upward, her eyebrows arched.

"Infamous," Kenneth repeats and trudges up the driveway with her wine.

"Wait," says Annie but he doesn't. "Be right back," she says to Nancy.

She gets a bag of clothes from the trunk of her car, things she can no longer fit into that she trusts Pema or Pema's Tibetan family can use. She's received the nicest, most illiterate notes from that crew and is starting to think she'd do well to set up shop in Nepal.

Walking towards the front door where Jill's appeared, Annie sees something tan and fuzzy slip past her sister-in-law and into the house. Don't say anything, Annie tells herself, not wanting to add to Jill's burden in any way, shape or form. "Jill. How are you holding up?" she says. "I don't know how you do it." Jill's wearing a shimmering sea-green dress that Annie instantly wants to alter, cut out strategically placed rectangles and back them with fishnet the same colour as the dress. Add a heavy bracelet of knotted rope.

"I'm fine," says Jill. "Annie, where's your hair?"

"My hair?" She gropes her head as if in a panic, then laughs. "Just wanted to know how Les feels. I'm donating it to Wigs for Cancer. Do I look seriously disproportioned? I've got a little Chihuahua head, don't I?" She takes a step back to give Jill a better view but Jill is looking past her. "*You've* still got a waist," says Annie, knowing she's being a faucet mouth but unable to turn it off. "And you've had two kids. How do you do it? I'm inflating from the neck down."

"Did Kenneth lock my mother in the car?"

"He did but he left a window cracked for air. I tried to get her to open the door but I don't think she remembers me."

"He thinks it's funny. Kenneth, give me the keys." she yells over her shoulder.

He appears in the hall behind her, a glass of wine in hand. "Full-bodied," he says with a little up-nod to Annie and for a moment she thinks he's referring to her figure.

"We don't have all day," says Jill.

He tosses the keys and Jill, clearly not amused, snatches them out of the air and strides away.

"You *are* siblings," says Annie, envious, believing she and Les, not having grown up together, missed out on a primal level of bickering nastiness.

"Pour you a glass?" offers Kenneth.

"Thank you. Yes. Sure. But I've got some more things to bring in from the car." She pauses to see if he might offer to help, but he disappears down the hall. "I'll just get those things," she says to no one in particular and then Beau materializes beside her, glowing like some Greek god.

"Beau. Beau. Beau." Hugging his warm, loaded muscles is like hugging life itself. "Look at you. You're massive. You're a wall. And you have hips like a girl!"

"And you are one hairless auntie."

"Sibling solidarity." She raises a fist. "Turns out I've got a teeny head on a growing body." She forces a laugh, waits for him to contradict her, but he laughs too.

"You need a hand with something?" he asks.

"I've got gifts for the likes of you, but shit, I hope I made yours big enough. You should tell me whenever you moult and move up a size."

"Is something in the oven?" Kenneth calls.

A shiny black bird, or bat, streaks down the front hall towards her. She ducks and it flies out the front door.

"Beau, tell me, did a bird just fly out of the house?"

"Did a bird what?"

"Here we go," says Jill, helping Nancy out of the car, relieved to see that her mother's clothes are clean, her hair tastefully cut and styled. She's wearing the lavender blouse Jill brought her on her last visit and the colour looks great on her. And is that a hint of perfume? She kisses her mom's cheek which is floury soft to the touch.

"I've been here," says Nancy, taking Jill's arm. "Jiggity jig."

"Yes, you have." Jill shuts the car door and reminds herself to bunch the wine bottles on the back counter by the fridge and the non-alcoholic drinks on the island, in clear view for Quinn.

"I don't trust that man who brought me here," says Nancy.

"Of course not." She should put on some background music, something cheerful but not too cheerful.

"He has long hair."

"Isn't that silly."

"Silly," says Nancy, then stops and with an alert yet gentle smile looks right at her before saying, "Jilly."

The recognition causes Jill to lean against the car for support.

"Hi, Mom." Her mother's hazel eyes are pouched in wrinkles, the left one a cloudier shade of green. She squeezes Nancy's hand and Nancy squeezes back. Maybe upping her coffee intake *has* made a difference, thinks Jill, and she can't resist giving her mother another kiss.

Leaning on her cane for support, a trusty purse — whosever

it is — dangling from her other hand, Nancy speed walks compared to Les.

"I have a green tree outside my room that I like," says Nancy, stopping to lift her eyes to the oak.

Jill had specifically asked the facility for that room and is thrilled to hear Nancy speak positively about her living situation. She tells her mother, "Your tree's called an arbutus."

"Arbutus," repeats Nancy, then points at the flower box under the dining-room window.

"Geraniums," says Jill.

"Geraniums."

The moment whisks her back to those timeless afternoon walks with Quinn as a toddler and feeding him the precise terms for flora, never generics like flower or tree, and even the Latin when she could recall them. How she was convinced he was gifted if not a genius.

"I was on that big thing today," says Nancy.

"The ferry?"

"The ferry."

"Did you sit by the window?"

Inside the house the smoke detector lets loose its high-pitched scream and Nancy does a sharp U-turn back to the car.

The smoke has cleared, the burnt quiches sizzle in the garbage and Nancy, lured by Jill's promise of coffee, has finally come inside where Jill gets her settled in the recliner beside Les's. Trusting her mother will stay put for a while, Jill watches Nancy take a puckered sip of coffee then reach over and pat Les's hand at rest on his armrest. "It's good you could come," Nancy says.

"You too, Nance," says Les.

"The coffee here is very good."

"Hope you like baked brie," calls Annie from the kitchen. "With slivered almonds."

"I do," says Beau. He's brought out his laptop to show Les and Kenneth online footage of some of his best tackles and tries. Explains his modest salary again, how it's tied into team performance bonuses.

The candles, Jill thinks and hurries to position eight white candles along the mantel. She steps back to look at them, thinking Vivaldi's *Four Seasons*. Or would that be too much? She puts on Charlie Parker instead.

"Kenneth, after you guys are done there, I need you to scrape the barbeque for me please."

"Put all your guests to work?" he says.

"You're family. Families pitch in." She's gratified to see him flinch.

The phone rings and Annie, being quickest, picks up.

"It's Pema!" she practically screams.

Les gives a wave.

"Where is she?" asks Jill, her stomach gone fluttery. She wishes she'd answered the phone.

"She's stopping at Katie's for a shower and to get changed."

"We do have running water here," says Les.

"Why not come -? She just is," says Annie. "But will be right over. He can't wait to see you, too."

Beau stares at the phone in his aunt's hand then roughs up the front of his just-washed hair.

"Your dad and I finally look like siblings," Annie says into the phone. "You'll see. Hey, Grammy's here, your uncle Kenneth. Hi everyone from Pema." She squints into the yard but whatever creature it was or wasn't, is gone.

"Hiiiii," calls Jill, signalling she wants to talk to Pema

but Annie doesn't catch it, says, "See you soon, Doll," and hangs up.

"I had a cat named Henna," Nancy announces to the room. "She got run over." She slides her hand across the air. "Vroom." Wearing a mock-sad face, she pats Les's hand again. "You don't like cats, do you, dear?"

Les stares at her and Nancy stares back. Then, perhaps to mirror his oxygen tubes, she make the peace symbol and lays the tips of two fingers against her nostrils.

"Something to snack on," Jill says and places a platter of veggies and bowl of pistachios on the coffee table. "I want to see those videos later," she tells Beau as he shuts down the computer.

"Me too," says Annie who has a camera that she holds out to Kenneth. "Will you do the honours, please? I want a picture of the skinheads. Oh yeah. We should be wearing biker jackets with silver-studded collars, leather chaps." Pursing her lips, she pumps devil-horned hands in the air.

"What happens if you push that button?" says Beau as he reaches towards the mole on the side of her head.

She swipes his hand away and thrusts her face in his, making him laugh aloud. "You don't want to know, Cheeks."

Jill can't help but feel a little outdone by her sister-in-law's ease around the kids, and her vivacity, however screwball.

Kenneth puts on his glasses to aim the camera. "Let's see here," he says, his voice sounding so much like their father's.

He sure has aged, thinks Jill, taking in the half glasses riding his nose, the crow's feet, the deep vertical furrow dissecting his eyebrows. Their father had the same dark furrow and when she and Kenneth were kids, he called it his change purse and magically made pennies and dimes appear and disappear from it.

"Okay, you two," says Kenneth. "Cheese time." He points the camera.

Perched awkwardly on the arm of Les's chair, Annie touches her bald head to his, then jerks away as something streaks past Les's feet.

"Something wrong?" asks Les.

"Nada, nothing, no thing," she says, resuming the pose and sprouting tears at his concern. No one cares about her as much as he does. No one. She reminds herself of her promise to Jill not to lose it and gives Les's head a kiss, his skin startlingly cool against her lips.

Like a slow-falling tree, Nancy leans sideways in her chair until her disembodied head is in the picture.

"Show me your teeth," says Kenneth.

Nancy opens her mouth, Annie's smile trembles as she holds back from crying, Les sticks out the very tip of his tongue trying for a laugh from Beau but Beau's looking elsewhere. Kenneth takes the picture and then another.

"Okay, the barbeque, Kenneth. Please?" Jill says.

"Jill," says Annie, "do you have a pair of sunglasses I can borrow? Just for tonight?"

Jill knows better than to ask why. "Sure."

Voices recede and fade as Beau slips away and up the stairs, unconsciously counting the number of steps as he goes. "Lucky thirteen," he mumbles before he recalls his old childhood habit, then wonders why he never counts the stairs on his way down.

The upstairs hall smells musty and unlived in. He walks towards the teak laundry hamper against the far wall that divides the doors to their two rooms, his and Pema's. The hamper was a prime hide-and-seek spot back in the day; he remembers burrowing beneath the dirty clothes, their tangy smell like moist dirt. He lifts the lid and lets it drop with a smack, the favourite old sound of a bullet in his back which he grabs as he stumbles —"Got me" — into Pema's room. He drops, theatrically, into her old desk chair which continues to spin in a circle. Stops himself to face the window that overlooks their cul-de-sac, imagines her pulling up on the street below. Takes a big breath in and blows it out.

Unlike his old room, which has been converted into the guest room, Pema's is exactly as it was: the same fake leather beanbag chair, same quilted duvet cover and lace curtains, same pictures and mementos covering the lilac walls like one giant collage. Every school picture, every vacation, every birthday and Christmas is recorded on her walls, and to wander through Pema's room is to cocoon oneself in the past. Pema's Facebook page had become the grown-up equivalent of the same, and sometimes he thinks she needs concrete proof she didn't dream up the events of her life.

He pulls open the top drawer just to feel the roll, hear the familiar wood on wood. Peers in and sees a notepad, her collection of animal erasers, cute pens and pencils. He'd like to see her at a distance first, in order to gauge his feelings. She'll have changed, no doubt, and reality is rarely as good as one's memory. Might not even look like her. Might have shaved her fucking head for all he knows, gone all Buddhist nun.

He picks up a single stubby purple pencil and writes on the pad: "I love you and want you more than you can know, Beau." He shuts the drawer. She probably has a boyfriend. There was some Tibetan guy in her Facebook pictures, his arm around her waist in a possessive sort of hold. Opens it again and tears off the note, crumples it into his pocket.

He's had his share of girlfriends. Most recently Kendra, whom he dated for over a year. More like seven months, if you count being on tour. Kendra was South African, from Capetown, though her mother was Filipina. And like all the women he's attracted to, she looked more Asian than anything else. Black hair, dark eyes, caramel skin.

Sexy, funny, even athletic if dressage counts, Kendra came from money and was studying to be a horse veterinarian. His teammates were jealous as hell and always teasing him. *How much you paying her? Can't be the size of your pipe.* After the relationship broke up, two months ago now, the guys oozed sympathy. When he told them that he was the one who'd broken it off, they assumed he was lying and were even more sympathetic. He earned a lot of free beers that week.

He liked her. A lot. And she was totally into him. Women didn't get much better than Kendra, and he was starting to believe something was seriously wrong with him. A part of him felt that he wasn't good enough for her and he had too much pride to wait until she figured that out. A day after the breakup, he called his friend Satomi and told her his latest sad story. Satomi was studying art in Japan. She'd fallen in love with her calligraphy teacher, a woman ten years "wiser", and they had moved in together, were contemplating having a baby. Satomi had, at least for now, found happiness. She was already making a name for herself. After the tsunami and nuclear disaster, surrealism was making a comeback, and Beau fully expected the painting he had of hers from high school, of a fat goldfish busting the buttons of its school uniform while swimming alongside a pale pod of naked humans, would be worth millions some day. Should ask Uncle Kenneth if he's heard of her work.

Beau told Satomi all about Kendra, how perfect she was and that as far as he could tell, she loved him unconditionally. "What's wrong with me?" he demanded.

"Nothing, Beau. Nothing's wrong with you. Maybe that's the problem," she said. "Be more wrong. More of a fuck-up. Get foolish."

With his foot, he pushes off the edge of the desk and spins in his chair. This is stupid. He's being stupid. Gets up to return to the party downstairs and as he reaches the door there's the sound of a car outside. He trips over himself rushing back to the window, leans over the desk, heart thudding in his ears. A rusted Honda Civic is in the cul-de-sac. It swings around and, though the oak's in the way, he can tell it's parking in front of the house. He breathes in through his nose then exhales hard enough to rattle his lips. Did he just sound like a goddamn horse?

A woman whose shoulders fill out her red leather jacket has stepped into the driveway. She wears brown cowboy boots and from up here he can see the dark roots of her straight blonde hair. His first thought is she's a friend of Auntie Annie's until his brother appears by the woman's side, puts an arm around her neck and kisses her on the cheek. So this is the older woman.

As lean and pale as ever, thinks Beau. Definitely needs a workout routine. And some sun. And a haircut.

Under his shaggy hair, Quinn glances up at the house. Beau gives a quick, embarrassed wave but Quinn, now checking his pockets, didn't see him after all.

Hesitant to walk in unannounced, Quinn knocks on the front door. A large man with a goatee opens it and stands there blocking the doorway, his legs apart and hands behind his back, frowning at them. For a confounded second, Quinn wonders why Mom's hired a bouncer.

"Uh…" starts Quinn, mind racing to remember if Auntie Annie has a new man, if his parents' friends were invited. The man looks somehow familiar. "You must be…"

Leaving his eyes on Quinn, the man turns his head in profile as if to encourage a guess. Quinn decides he's trying to be funny.

"Let them in, Kenneth," calls Jill.

"Uncle Kenneth, I'm so sorry I didn't recognize you," says Quinn, though the last time they met Quinn was probably eight. "Great to see you."

They shake hands and Quinn introduces Holly.

"Advance," says his uncle, stepping aside. "You are welcome here."

As soon as Jill comes around the corner, her eyes fix on Holly. "Kenneth, can you see if Mom needs to use the facilities?"

"Facilities. Such as the lavatory?"

She ignores him and hugs Quinn. "Hi Sweetheart. You're looking great. I do appreciate the tie, thanks."

"Mom," he says, about to introduce Holly, but Jill speaks first.

"This must be Holly. Very pleased to meet you."

She's overenunciating, like a snob.

"Nice to meet you, Mrs. Wright," says Holly in her too-raspy voice.

"Please," Jill says with a small snort as if she's about to correct Holly's formal address but then continues with, "do come in and I'll take your jackets."

Each crisp, defined word, thinks Quinn, is a brick being placed in a wall.

"Such a gorrrgeous dress," coos Holly. "That kinda green's my favourite."

Uneducated, he can hear his mom say to herself as she takes Holly's jacket which will smell of the cigarette she smoked in the car. He deliberately takes Holly's hand and kisses it.

"You can put your gift on the hearth in the family room," instructs Jill, pointing to the package under his arm.

"Hey," says Beau, walking heavy-footed down the stairs and looking bigger and more muscular than ever.

Quinn readies himself. Why isn't Beau dressed up?

"Bro," says Beau before he chest-bumps him and Quinn has to let go of Holly to keep from falling over. "A tie?" Beau reaches for it and Quinn eases his hand away.

"You're the rugby player," says Holly. "That's so awesome."

"Awesome me."

"Beau, Holly," says Quinn.

"Gawd, I'd never guess you were brothers." She looks from one to the other. "You don't look anything alike."

"You should see our sister," says Beau.

"She's, like, from Tibet, eh?"

"Just like from Tibet," says Beau, and Quinn gives him a look.

"How do they say rugby in French?" asks Jill, sounding even more pretentious.

"Rrrugabee?" says Beau, rolling his R.

Jill's laugh is too loud. "It is funny how the French, who appear so certain in their thinking, make questions out of statements," she says.

Holly gives her an uncertain smile and Jill gestures towards the kitchen. "Help yourselves to...refreshments." She turns and fusses with the flower arrangement. Shutting him out, thinks Quinn, for not meeting her standards.

Quinn takes Holly's hand again. "Thirsty?"

"And oh, did you bring the slide show?" asks Jill.

"Yes." He pats the USB key in his shirt pocket.

"I've got my laptop hooked up to the TV like you told me," she says, "and I'll let you know when that's going to happen."

"And what do you do, Holly?" asks Beau as they move towards the kitchen.

"I work in an old folks' home. Some people love kids, I love oldies. Not that I don't like kids."

"Somebody's got to love 'em." Beau nudges Quinn. "Game of ping pong later?"

Ping pong was the one physical game at which Quinn consistently beat his brother.

"Holly can beat me. Killer overhand spin." They played a lot in rehab, he doesn't say, and finds it both typical and funny how his competitive brother looks anew at Holly.

"I'd love to play," says Holly.

"Soon," says Quinn and gently guides her away. "I want you to meet my dad."

The sight of the shrunken bald man napping in his father's chair and attached to tubes makes Quinn feel weak. Sleeping upright, Les's chin recedes into his neck and the corners of his opened mouth drag down in a sad grimace. There's truly no such thing as a happy ending, thinks Quinn, and tries not to linger on the thought or the sight, guiding Holly over to the kitchen where the "refreshments" are front and centre on the kitchen counter.

Beside the mock champagne bottle of sparkling apple juice is a full glass of red wine. A merlot, he guesses by its colour. The tangy scent claws awake a familiar blind hunger and he instantly locates the wine bottles beside the fridge, the box of beer in the corner, the accessibility of the liquor cabinet. *His* refreshments include pomegranate juice, an easy camouflage for wine of either colour and he reaches for it before realizing there's another bald person on the other side of the counter, wearing oversized sunglasses, her nose against the oven window. It takes another couple of seconds before he recognizes her.

"Auntie Annie?"

"*Quinnnnn,*" she yells without looking up. "I'm smothering you with kisses but my brie's under the broiler so wait, don't move and that must be your new friend, wait, wait... four, three, two, one."

She lifts out the bubbling cheese and sets it on the counter. "Okay, okay, come here. Damn you skinny people," she says hugging him. "You need to eat some of my cheese. And I've got presents," she sings, "but let's wait 'til Pema's here. So this is..."

"Holly."

"Holly." Annie gives her a hug too, for which he's grateful.

"You're the designer," says Holly. "That's so cool. And so is your buzz. Can I touch it?"

Annie offers her head and Holly strokes it. "I love that feeling."

"Against the nap," says Annie.

"Exactly." Holly takes Quinn's hand. "Feel."

"I'm going to start rubbing up against your legs in a minute," says Annie.

He's never touched his auntie's head before. Its random moles and freckles make curious patterns. He makes out a parallelogram, an obtuse triangle, and his hand twitches, longing to connect them with a pen. In rehab he learned the term OCD as it applied to him and, taking a deep breath, forces his gaze elsewhere.

He wants to ask why the sunglasses when Annie says, apropos of nothing, "Don't you wonder, sometimes, if the world isn't thinking you, and not the other way around?"

"I kinda know what you mean," Holly says, never one to disagree with people.

It's the type of question with no answer, and he won't think about it. "Holly, what would you like to drink?"

"Is that Quinn?" Les's voice is a hoarse gurgle.

"Here." Quinn lifts his hand and forces a grin.

It takes several long seconds for Les to clear his throat. "Come introduce me to your prickly Christmas plant."

Without waiting for Quinn, Holly strides over and takes Les's offered hand in both of hers. "Its leaves are almost as poisonous as its berries," she says, "but they won't kill ya. Just make ya drowsy and give ya the runs."

"I could use some then," says Les, and Holly throws back her head and laughs her free-throated laugh.

Like an alerted dog, Jill, now standing stiffly in the doorway, looks up at the sound and Quinn scans the labels of the wine then the yard for a secluded spot he and Holly might escape to. Just beyond the patio a mallard lands in a patch of sun, his head a brassy green. Quinn twists the cap off the pomegranate juice.

As the family gathers around the appetizers on the coffee table, Jill slips over to the kitchen to take a mug from the cupboard, thinking that, for Quinn's sake, she'll be discreet about having some wine. Between her mom, Kenneth and this Holly person, she needs it. It's a large mug and she fills it up to avoid having to refill it. She takes a sip and then another, watches Holly beside Quinn on the couch, her shoulders hunched, one red bra strap showing. Holly's not drinking? What do you bet they met in rehab? She takes a long drink. What is the attraction? She would be hard-pressed to believe the woman has ever seen the inside of a college classroom and she looks ten years older than him. Quinn is unaware that he's dripped some vegetable dip onto the table and Jill's about to say something when Holly wipes it carefully away with her napkin.

Is it a mother issue? Is it her fault?

"I read in the *Globe*," says Kenneth to whoever's listening, "that the World Bank president announced to the press he was thinking of buying gold."

Les nods, takes a deep breath as if working up a comment.

"Meaning?" asks Jill.

"Meaning," says Kenneth, "to quote Ian Brown in the *Globe*, that's like some staid old dad arriving home from work to announce, 'You know kids, I think I'd like to try some of that crystal meth everyone's talking about.'"

"Don't ever try crystal meth." Annie shakes her head.

"One in twenty Tea Partiers" — Les pauses for a breath — "bought gold in the past year."

"I like coffee," says Nancy, rattling her cup.

"Would you like some more, Mom?" says Jill.

"What do you make of the Tea Partiers?" asks Quinn, sipping his juice, the smell from the open wine bottle on the table a cartoon waft curling into his nostrils.

"God, Guns and Gold," says Kenneth.

"If God would only speak up and tell us what *he* believes," says Jill as she takes Nancy's cup.

"Would people even listen?" Holly says.

Clever comment, thinks Jill.

"Only if he had the gold and guns." Kenneth laughs. "So, the World Bank guy. If people think money is going to become worthless, like it did in the Depression, they'll cash out their retirement funds into gold and the panic becomes —"

"A self-fulfilling prophecy," says Les.

Quinn leans into Holly to sing her a line from a song but can't recall it exactly, something about a guy owing money to money he owes.

Nancy spits her piece of bread and brie out into her napkin.

"I don't like this."

"Don't eat it then, Mom," says Jill.

"I know this Columbian shaman?" says Annie. "Beautiful man, wow. His ancestors, the Makuna, believed gold contained the light of the stars and sun. They called gold the stars of the earth."

"Neat," says Holly.

"Even crows collect the bright and shinies," Kenneth says.

Les struggles to clear his throat and everyone waits to see if he'll speak.

"It's animal instinct to be attracted to light," says Beau and tosses a baby carrot in the air but fails to catch it in his mouth.

"Not if you're a bat," says Quinn.

"Beau, don't," says Jill, returning with Nancy's refilled cup. "You can choke."

"Darkness has its charms too," Annie says from behind her glasses.

"If you're a bat hunting bugs," says Les. The room hangs on his words in case there might be more.

"Hunt," says Jill. "From the Old English word hentan meaning seize or try to seize."

"Carpe diem," says Nancy and everyone looks at her.

Jill hiccups with pride as, all eyes on her, Nancy gives a queenly wave.

"On that note I'll have some more wine," says Kenneth with a laugh.

Jill sees Holly whisper the question to Quinn who translates the Latin for her. Quinn catches Jill looking at him and she looks away, but not in time.

Pema asks Katie not to pull into the cul-de-sac but to let her off at the corner so she can sneak up on the house and not the other way around. After Katie drives away, she stands there for a minute, feeling out of place in her chuba and seeing her old world with new eyes: the colossal size of the trees, the curious fact of lawns, each home as big as Jampaling's carpet factory, magnolia blossoms the size of her head. Houses in Canada are very big. This was one of the simple English sentences she used to teach her students but she'd forgotten how true it was.

She starts up the street, rolling her suitcase behind her. Despite the weather no one is out except for a tortoiseshell cat in the yard to her right, toying with something unseen in the grass. Pema veers away. Cats have always made her uneasy and her feelings were justified in cat-free Jampaling. Cats get no love from Tibetans. They were the only animal that didn't cry when the Buddha died, she was told, and are considered to be the sociopaths of the animal realm. Mice, on the other hand, were a daily sight.

She realizes that with the exception of Darwin and his sister, Hailey, whom she used to babysit, she can't recall the names of any of her former neighbours. In Jampaling she not only knew her neighbours' names but their family histories, their jobs, their eating and bathing habits.

Half-hidden by the friendly giant, as she always called the oak, her old house looks exactly the same. Closer now, she sees that the white clapboard is streaked grey with water stains and the yellow flower boxes are also in need of paint, but the bright red spill of geraniums makes up for it, she thinks, knowing that painting the house had been Les's job.

She parks her suitcase and backpack by the front door and glimpses Jill through the dining-room window, wearing what Pema used to think of as her *Little Mermaid* dress. A familiar shyness shrinks her stomach. How she used to be embarrassed to open her mouth around Jill who constantly corrected her

English or pointed out yet another stupid mistake in her homework. She's grateful now, but it was mortifying then. She wonders if Jill's still upset with her for not finishing high school? At the time it seemed that bothered Jill even more than Pema's leaving home.

A ladybug lands on her sleeve and she urges it away with her finger. She hears the familiar song of a bird – a robin? – and then the clicking sounds of a ping pong game. Sounds like Beau's losing to Quinn she thinks as she hears a gruff shout. She used to refuse to play with Beau because of that smirk of his whenever he was winning.

Holding onto her noisy silver bangles, she picks her quiet way along the patio stones down the side of the house to spy through the fence. The silver Roman sandals she'd borrowed from Katie – her one salute to fashion and Auntie Annie – are rubbing a heel wrong.

She hears swearing. Definitely Beau's voice.

For the past three years she's been surrounded by the alert touch and windy talk of sisters. Hearing her brothers causes her muscles to twitch, and she wants to run and leap on Beau's back. Smack him around the head for not keeping in touch.

She sneaks up to the fence, peers through the slats. Is that really him? This guy is the bulked-up version of the Beau she knew. He has tight lines like parentheses around his smile, his blond hair is now a woody brown. He misses the next point and hisses under his breath. Is he wearing the Coldplay T-shirt she gave him for Christmas back in grade ten? It was way too big for him then, and now the sleeves cut into his biceps. God, she is seriously overdressed.

"I'm out of practice," says Beau. "Let's call this a warm-up game."

Pema rolls her eyes.

An unfamiliar female laugh is followed by, "Sure."

He brought a girl. Isn't this a family event?

She retraces her steps to the front door, finds it unlocked and manoeuvres her bags inside. Sticks her nose into the flowers on the hall table and inhales. She can hear Auntie Annie say something about osteoporosis and Japanese green tea and pictures Datso's husband showing off his braided red and brown leather belt with the snakehead buckle. "Designer snake belt," he boasts to everyone he meets, then holds up a finger. "One of a kind." His brother grew so jealous that Datso had to make sure the belt was shared between them.

She slips down the hall, still unnoticed, and stops before entering the doorway into the family room and kitchen. Smiles to see the same yellow kitchen counters with the blackened half circle next to the stove. She'd set down a pot of melted marshmallows while making Rice Krispy squares for some event at school. What was she, eleven? She was so afraid of what Jill might say that she let Beau take the blame with some of his mute macho shrugs, and he lost his computer privileges for a week. She felt badly about that.

She peeks around the corner into the family room. Looking just like herself only with whiter hair, Grammy sits in a chair by the windows spreading something on a piece of bread. Pema pokes her head in a little further. In the chair beside her grandmother sits what looks like an old man, but she knows it's Les, turned to the window and watching the ping pong game. He's gaunt as an Indian aesthete, nothing but skin stretched over bone, and every breath looks like a tragic effort. Her hand moves unconsciously to her heart and at the jingle of her bracelets he turns his head. His eyes are a more eager blue-grey than she remembers, but the person behind them is the very same, and she shrugs hello, smiles while biting her lip to keep from crying. His head lifts off the back of his chair and her name comes out as a pinched squeak. She walks straight over and hugs him, apologizes for her clumsiness as one of her arms gets tangled in his tubing.

"Never apologize," he whispers and holds her face in his hands.

With those two words, her worries about this homecoming are much relieved. "Thank you," she manages to whisper back.

They hold each other's teary gaze for a moment longer until Auntie Annie screeches, "It's Pema! Pema! She's here!"

And then she's hugging Auntie Annie, who's also bald for some reason, and then Jill, whose surprisingly fierce embrace squeezes the breath out her. Then sincere, sombre Quinn's brief hug and "Welcome home," before Pema's mysterious uncle and virtual stranger is also hugging her. And then she's shaking hands with Holly, Quinn's and not Beau's girlfriend, and finally there's Beau, his muscled legs in torn jeans. After such a transfusion of love, it takes all her willpower not to look up at him. She pauses and goes still to give him a few seconds to say something, to speak first or step forward and initiate a hug. But being that he's a let-people-come-to-me sort of guy, she knows he won't. She pretends she hasn't seen him and turns to Jill. "Nice to be home. Could I possibly have some water? Planes make me so thirsty."

Jill stands in the kitchen looking around without seeing. She has barely eaten today and the wine has gone straight to her head. What time is it? She'd like to get this ceremony started but an overexcited Annie is herding everyone into the family room so she can give her gifts to the kids.

"We're saving Les's gifts for later," calls Jill.

Annie ducks as if Jill's words were solid objects flung at her.

"Just the kids, just the kids," she says.

Jill surreptitiously refills her mug. Leaning on the kitchen counter, she watches Pema settle on the floor beside Les's chair, reach up and take his hand. Les's mouth doesn't actually move but Jill can tell by the tilt of his eyes that he's smiling. His eyes have grown strangely bright of late, an eerie silver, as though the lens of his eye has grown thinner too, or some tremendous light inside him is pushing its way out.

Beau is on the couch with his arms crossed, staring dagger-eyed at Pema. What is going on with those two? They used to get on like a house on fire. Holly shares the ottoman with Quinn and as he opens his gift she drapes her arms around his neck, slides her face alongside his. A public display, thinks Jill, sipping her wine.

"I'm hungry," announces Nancy as she spreads brie on another round of bread.

"Mom, you don't like that cheese, remember?" says Jill, frustrated all over again about the burnt quiches, knowing Nancy would have devoured them. "Have some veggies and dip. The nuts."

Nancy taps her teeth in response.

"Just plain bread then," says Jill as Nancy continues to stab a knife at the cheese. On the table beside her sits a pile of napkins filled with half-chewed pieces of bread and brie.

Holly gently takes the knife from Nancy and moves the cheese to the far end of the table. At least someone's listening, thinks Jill, unable to bring herself to say thanks.

She preheats the oven for the potatoes. What else does she need to do?

"Thanks, Auntie Annie," says Quinn over Pema's oohing. "Black and blue. My colours," he says.

The vest is black cotton in front and royal-blue satin in

back, but Jill worries he's being metaphorical, that already, at twenty-five, he feels beaten up by life. Did she push him too hard? She takes a long drink.

As if *she's* his mother, Holly helps Quinn off with the vest he's wearing then helps him on with the new one.

"Cool," says Holly as Quinn turns to show Les the back of it.

"Cool," says Jill under her breath.

"Holly has a kid, you know," whispers Kenneth, suddenly behind her. "Four years old. Owen. I've always wanted to name a son Owen." He refills his glass.

"It's a purse, a bag," says Annie, handing a box to Pema. "Just so you know."

"It's a box," corrects Nancy, and Beau barks out a laugh.

Jill takes Kenneth by the arm and pulls him through the swinging door into the dining room. "How do you know she has a kid?"

"Because I'm not avoiding her like you are. She's not so fresh-faced but seems decent and sweet."

Jill sighs. "I'm sure she is. I just had a different vision of things is all." Hit with a wave of fatigue, she pulls out a dining-room chair. "Feels like I don't even know my own kid any more."

"How well can we know anyone?"

Not helpful, thinks Jill.

"He seems like a bright kid," says Kenneth as if catching her thought. "Thoughtful. A little nerdy. He'll do fine."

"A little nerdy." Jill hadn't bothered to confide in her brother about Quinn's drinking, the blackouts, arrests, a stint in rehab. Can all that fit with nerdy?

He sits down too, turns his chair in order to face her. "Can I talk to you about something, Jill?" He runs a hand over his head and winces as he tugs on his ponytail.

The defenseless look on her brother's face whisks her back thirty-plus years to Kenneth knocking on her bedroom door for advice about a girl he liked or a coach he wasn't getting on with, and how proud she was that it was her, not Mom, he'd sought out.

"Is this a good time?"

What time is it? "Sure. Is this about Kimmie?"

"Yes."

"Kimmie and Kenny." She smiles and drinks from her mug.

Like he always did when he was embarrassed and about to spill his guts, Kenneth scratches inside his ear and focuses on the floor. The wine floods her body like warm syrup and she feels more relaxed than she has all year, since the news of Les's cancer having spread. A sudden rush of sisterly love and she's saying, "Have I told you, Kenneth, that it really is very nice to see you. You who've been gone forever."

He looks up. "No, you haven't. You've just put me to work."

She huffs a laugh, gives his hand a stroke.

"Nice to see you too," he says, "and your brood. You've done a great job, you know that?"

"Thank you." She hooks her thumb over her shoulder. "That guy in there helped. A lot."

"I'm so sorry about Les," he says, and she's tearing up before she's even aware enough to stop it.

"Ohhhh," she breathes. "Yeahhhh." It's as though she'd forgotten what this evening was about. She yanks at the nearest cloth napkin, sending a fork flying, and wipes her eyes.

"How're you holding up?" he asks.

It takes another minute before her voice is hers again.

"I'm always holding up." She bites on a smile. "That's what I do."

He takes her hand and she revels in its warmth. "I want to thank you for being there for Mom," he says. "I know it was a hard choice to make, moving her out of the house."

She points at him. "And I hated you for not being here. I did. I do. I hate you." She gives his leg a whack.

He nods. "I'm not as brave as you."

"Brave." She drinks her wine. "I don't know about that. I still think of you as Mom's hero."

Kenneth gives a humble snort and she can't help but love him for it.

"And mine," she adds, because that's how she'd felt. "Yes, mine too."

It was Nancy's birthday. Kenneth was recently sixteen and overnight, so it seemed, he'd grown to be as big and heavy-shouldered as their father. Drunk even before dinner got started, Dad had Nancy pinned against the kitchen counter as he insisted on giving "the birthday gal" forty-six kisses. Nancy's laugh was forced, nervous, as she told him that he was hurting her back and the roast was ready. Jill angrily ripped lettuce for salad, ignoring them as best she could, when, in his newfound baritone, Kenneth said, "Get off her." He didn't say it loudly but the words rocketed around that room.

When Dad didn't move, Kenneth took hold of the back of his white shirt — the one Nancy would have ironed on a Thursday — and wrenched him off.

Their father's signature passive-aggressive attitude suddenly lost all its passive part as he whipped around and shoved Kenneth in the chest. Jill held her breath, expecting Kenneth to go flying, but he only took a step sideways, his arm swiping the butter dish to the floor where, miraculously, it didn't break. Despite the spine of butter along his arm, Kenneth looked like he'd just hit a moon shot, then stepped up to the plate and shoved back, sent Dad crashing between two chairs and nearly to the floor. To Jill's horror, Kenneth took another step towards him. "Don't ever hurt her again," he said in the saddest of tones, as if he'd just lost and not won the brief battle. To Jill's knowledge, Dad never bothered Nancy after that.

"So, wha's going on, Kenneth?" Did she just slur? "You all right?"

"Kimmie's pregnant," he says.

Jill sits up in her chair so quickly it teeters to one side. A cascade of laughter is heard from the other room. "That's wonderful. I'm so —"

He holds up his hand like a stop sign. "It is wonderful. We didn't think we could have kids. I'd really given up."

"I'm positively giddy." She dabs at her eyes again. "Crybaby here. Mascara." She checks the napkin for black. "But wow, congratulations."

"What with Fukushima and the radiation scare, Kimmie would like to have the baby here. She wants to move here."

Jill coughs, choking on tears. "Sorry, but that makes me stupid happy. You know, you can stay here until you get settled. I mean that. We've got plenty of room. Heck, we have an entire master bedroom suite we're not using."

"I appreciate the offer and may just take you up on it, but there's a problem." He hangs his head again.

"Is something wrong with the baby?" Please no.

"No, baby seems fine." He smiles weakly. "They say it's a girl."

"Ohhh, don't start me crying again."

"But why I need to talk to you" — he pauses, shakes his head — "I've been seeing someone else."

"What?"

"I've been seeing someone else."

"Really?" She slaps his leg hard this time and reaches for her mug. "How long has that been going on, you..?" Pig-slut, she finishes in her head.

"Three years."

"Three years? Sounds like bigamy." And then she just can't stop herself. "Or is it pigamy?" She covers her smile with a hand. Not a smiling matter.

"I'm in love with them both. Kimmie and Junko."

An image of a porcelain doll and the canary Kenneth had as a pet when he was a boy comes to mind. Kenneth was inconsolable the day the canary escaped its cage, flew into the picture window and died. It was their first experience of death and Nancy orchestrated an elaborate burial ceremony in the backyard.

"They're both intelligent, good-hearted women," he says. "And *you* know I always wanted kids."

"A baseball team. A midget team." This isn't the least bit funny yet she can't seem to stop.

"And it wasn't ever going to happen with Kimmie. Or so I thought. And..." His eyes close. "The universe being a black comedy with impeccable timing, they're both pregnant."

"The canary is pregnant too?"

He looks confused then says, "Junko's carrying my son." Then it's his turn to tear up. "And I haven't had the guts to tell Kimmie."

"Oh, Kenneth, I...overstand," she says and laughs, unable to contain herself any more. "I'm sorry," she says. "I'm just so —" Another wave of laughter bends her in half and a warm wetness spreads between her legs. "Oh gawd!" She groans and laughs harder.

"I need to go for a drive," she hears Kenneth say and she

gropes blindly for his hand but he's already up and moving away. By the time she stops laughing, his rental car is pulling out of the driveway.

"A baby." She'll be an auntie. Auntie Jill. She reaches for her wine. She will call this Junko person, get a translator if need be, tell her she made a mistake sleeping with a married man and so sorry but Kenneth is moving here with his wife. Kenneth will have to give her up. No choice. But a son, she thinks, tears sprouting. Pure heartbreak. She takes a long drink. Poly gamy. Many gametes. Many games. Such slippery phonemes... polygamy...sounds rolling under and over each other.

She dries her eyes, replaces the used napkin with the one at her place setting and resets the fork at a crooked angle. Heads back into the family room where Beau is trying on a belt made of chain mail and leather, while Annie gathers up a pile of wrapping from the floor. The candles on the mantel glow with light. All eight of them. Who lit them without asking?

Les is wholly relieved when Jill finally appears in the doorway. Where has she been? He's had to pee for the last twenty minutes. He waves her over but she's not looking his way. Frowning, she walks towards the mantel, tripping slightly on the edge of the rug before continuing. Pema stops her with, "Look at the purse Auntie Annie made me."

"So beautiful." Jill grabs it, turns it over. "All those pretty patches. What kind of material is this lining?"

"Jill," Les says, his voice cracking.

Jill looks at him and then at Pema. "You're such a wonder." She draws a finger down Pema's cheek which elicits a blush.

"If I can help you with dinner or anything," Holly offers.

Jill stares dumbly at Holly's wide-open expression, then claps her hands. "We need to get this wake thing started."

"Jill," Les tries with more urgency and she finally comes over. "Bathroom," he whispers. "I don't want the kids watching me. Can you get them to, maybe, set the table?"

"That's done," she says and stands there as if awaiting further suggestions.

"Jill," he pleads.

"Okay. Kids, go...to your rooms."

Quinn and Pema gawk at her, ready to laugh at her joke.

"We have to get some things organized here," Jill says, her eyes glancing off Les.

They understand just enough and slowly stand.

"I don't have a room, any more," says Quinn.

"Poor you," says Beau.

"I want to see mine," says Pema.

"Go. Skedaddle," adds Nancy. "Now," she shouts, startling everyone into motion.

"Mommm," moans Jill.

Pema disappears down the hall to the stairs and Beau follows.

"Come see the mallard," says Quinn leading Holly outside to the patio.

"Thank you, Nancy," says Les. He reaches to steady himself on Jill's arm.

"You too, young man. Go." Nancy points at Annie who hasn't moved.

Annie makes a comical about-face. "Does she not see the earrings?" she says and follows Quinn and Holly outside.

Holly lights a cigarette, apologizing to Annie. "Stupid habit. Let me know if it's blowing your way."

Standing between Holly and the patio door to block any sightlines, Quinn checks over his shoulder to see if Jill's watching Holly light up. Notes the open bottle of wine beside the fridge.

"Stupid habits are my forte," says Annie.

He couldn't believe his mother didn't have the decency to respond to Holly's offer to help. Just stared at her like she was some sort of freak. Jesus. He'd leave right now if it wasn't for Dad.

"I used to smoke clove cigarettes when I was young," says Annie, "and thin."

"I've never heard of clove cigarettes," says Holly.

"You could only get them in smoke shops. They're from India? Delicious, really. I thought that they were herbal, that I was doing my smoking self a favour. Only to find out they were equivalent to smoking Camel Straights."

"How did you quit?"

"I forgot I smoked. Was on some meds that messed with my memory."

Nobody except Grammy is in the family room. Just one glass is all he needs.

"I like your gecko tattoo." Holly points to Annie's ankle.

"A guy named Jesus did that. On the beach in Puerto Vallarta. Sounds like there's a story in there but there isn't."

Holly laughs and Quinn smiles along.

Annie removes her sunglasses, breathes hotly on the lenses before cleaning them with an end of her shirt.

Not like one glass is going to send him off the rails. Although his rehab counsellor said there was no such thing as one drink, he believes he can limit himself. And unlike most of the folks in there, he was a high-functioning drinker – finished his goddamn degree after all – and really only let it loose on the weekends. And hell, it's a weekend.

"Okay, tell me you guys see a duck over there." Annie points to the shaded corner of the yard.

A couple of shots of vodka in pomegranate juice would taste a lot better than wine in it.

"Is that the duck you mentioned?" Holly asks Quinn.

He has to do it now, before Mom comes back.

"Wonder where his mate got to?" says Annie. "Maybe he's guarding the nest."

"It's a mallard," says Quinn, believing he was just asked about the duck. *"Anas platyrhynchos."*

"What?" says Holly, laughing.

"It's the species name. Latin."

"Quinn's the family genius," says Annie.

He smiles weakly. Genius. Don't think so.

Holly blows a smoke ring that sails past Annie who slashes it open with her finger.

If I can't drink while watching my father turn into a living skeleton, thinks Quinn, when can I? Should do wine, though. Gentler than hard booze. One glass.

"Boy, Nancy's gotten feisty," says Annie. "Used to be the most soft-spoken thing."

"Personalities can change pretty radically with Alzheimer's," says Holly. "I have one lady, an absolute angel, whose daughter says she used to be super frosty. Was never one to hug or touch or anything. Now she's super touchy and it's sweetheart this and darling that."

"I'll make us another drink?" Quinn says quickly and avoids Holly's eye as he takes her glass.

"Sure," she says, "but just one shot of vodka this time, please, not two."

Quinn's eyes jerk up. Holly laughs to tell Annie she was joking but the pinch of worry in her smile is enough to bring the outside world back into focus and he counts three deep breaths like they were taught.

Holly kisses him softly beside his ear. "You're lucky," she whispers. "Nice people."

"Mom?" he whispers back, making a face.

"She's got a lot on her mind," says Holly. "I mean, God."

He kisses her back. Wishes they could go upstairs and get naked. Clean, sober and naked. Let the buildings of our selves come crashing down.

Beau waits at the bottom of the stairs, working up the courage to follow Pema. He can't blame her for snubbing him. He deserves it. But shit, he's tired of pretending, of keeping up this front. Out of sight hasn't meant out of mind. In fact, denying his feelings for her, he realizes now, might have even turned up the heat. She's prettier than Kendra, if that's possible, and her coolness, now that she's no longer needy, at least no longer needing him, makes her all the more attractive. It's time to come clean with the reason he's kept his distance. It's not fair to her and it's fucking killing him. For all he knows she has the same feelings for him. It's not out of the question. Those long letters she wrote to him, signing off *with love, Pema*. And if she doesn't feel the same way, what's the worst that can happen?

He starts up the stairs, takes them two at a time as if momentum might be the same as courage. Once he hits the landing, he finds himself stepping quietly down the hall then pretending to turn into his room and slowly turning back to stand just outside Pema's open door. She's sitting on the end of her bed, angled away from him, thumbing through what looks like a high school yearbook.

She must know he's standing here, because she always knows where he is in relation to her. Just like when she arrived and saw him standing right there and deliberately ignored him. Playing him as she's always done and is doing again right now. Fine, he can wait, is content simply to look at her, elegantly foreign in her navy silk chuba embroidered with silver dragons. Those come-undress-me sandals. A stillness about her that he doesn't recognize.

Illuminated by the sun through the window, her hair races down her back to brush her waist. There are no streaks of blue or green, no glitter or beaded braids, just a clean beautiful black. How he loves her hair. He's allowed to love her hair.

She flips the page of the yearbook with a casual whip of one finger. He doesn't buy her cool for a minute, senses the space between them loud with anticipation and is convinced she feels the same about him as he does about her and that girls are simply better at hiding their desire, usually even from themselves.

Another flip of her finger, a tilt of her face, and he's convinced otherwise. It's just him who's the pervert here. Pema is his sister. No, biologically she's not. He'd looked online to see how common or uncommon it was to have the hots for an adopted sibling. It was common enough if a child was adopted when the child and siblings were older but rare if they grew up together from an early age like him and Pema. Which only made him feel worse, rare being another word for deviant pervert.

Oh shut up and get it done already. Wuss. He inhales deeply and breathes out her name. "Pema."

She whips around as if startled — did she really not know he was here?

"Hi." He waves. "Remember me? Beau?"

She snorts, tucks her hair behind one ear and turns back to her book. "I did recall a Beau somewhere in the distant past. We were close in fact. But after he went off to some fancy school, he forgot I existed." The resigned weight of her shoulders makes him instantly lonely. "Then I went away, tried writing him long, wonderful letters and never heard from the shithead."

"I am a shithead, and I'm sorry."

She flips the page.

"Thanks for those letters," he says, nodding though she can't see him. "They were great."

"Yeah, they were."

"I'd like to meet your other family. Maitri sounds almost as much fun as you were as a kid."

No response.

"She looks a lot like you. Saw your photos on Facebook."

"But you're not even on Facebook."

"I have my ways," he says trying for humour.

She sighs into a full-body clench, as if holding back from yelling at him.

"Pema, I had my reasons for keeping my distance. And they weren't because I didn't want to see you."

"Well, that certainly makes sense." She tosses the book aside and swings her legs around the corner of the bed to give him her full attention which, he can't help thinking, is all he's ever wanted. Hit with unbearable shyness about what he's about to confess, he looks out the window. "I don't know if I can explain it." His intention is to move towards her, but his feet aren't budging. What he used to consider his safe place is now a minefield.

He feels her waiting, maybe starting to give up on him all over again. He focuses on her knees, exactly as if he were going in for a tackle, which enables him to move across the threshold of her doorway. Once in the room, he keeps going. The bed dips as he sits beside her and his eyes fix on the line where her chuba just barely touches the knee of his unwashed jeans. She doesn't move away; he prays this is a good sign.

When he dares look up, her lips are firmly closed and her eyes cynical. He smiles and her eyebrows rise, expectant.

No, fuck, he can't. He'll challenge her to a game of ping pong instead.

"So, hey," he says.

"What?" Pema says. She scratches at the back of her head then checks her fingernails.

Be more wrong, Satomi told him. *Be more of a fuck-up.* At this moment he can't think of anyone he hates more in the world than Satomi. Except maybe himself.

His heart whooshes in his ears. "What I want to say is," he begins then, knowing words won't cut it, tentatively reaches out a hand and scoops Pema's surprisingly heavy hair up and away from her neck with the intention of planting a kiss. He leans over and she jerks back.

"Are you checking my hair for lice?" she says.

"I...I...I..."

Their eyes lock and he lets himself be seen. She blinks as the idea of what else he might have been doing dawns, and he sees it's not a rose-coloured dawn but more of a pornographic flip book of their childhood years. In an instant he understands he's grossly wrong about his desire being mutual. And before the idea of him being "in love" with her imprints in her brain, and every future time together is spent in hateful embarrassment, he abruptly drops her hair and screws up his face. "That's your parting gift to Dad? Lice?"

"I do not have lice, Beau."

"I was sure I saw a pod —"

She hits his shoulder with the butt of her palm, just like old times, and he scrambles to the door and yells out, "Pema's got lice!" And he's running away from her smacks — "Nepali lice, extra large, Himalayan" — trips on the hamper and stumbles to the floor. Pema laughs her bleating laugh and he's a kid again, sitting on the floor and she's just his attractive older sister.

That's all. Because that's the way it has to be.

As soon as Jill returns from the bathroom with Les and gets him settled back in his chair, Nancy wants help out of hers.

"Can you tell me, please, where is the teachers' bathroom?" says Nancy elegantly and with a gracious smile.

As Jill points her mother in the right direction, she hears scuffling upstairs followed by Pema's inimitable laughter and her heart melts with nostalgia.

"I'm starved," says Les.

She turns to him. "Really?" For weeks Les has claimed to have lost his appetite.

"Can we save the shenanigans for after the meal?"

"I guess so." She wonders if he's delaying facing the ceremony and only hopes the professional celebrant was right when she said this passage was even more important for the person dying than for those left behind.

Annie's bald head peeks in at the patio doors. "Am I allowed in?"

"Yes," croaks Les.

"Did you know," she says, stepping inside, "that Einstein was epileptic?"

"Is the oven on?" Jill wonders aloud.

Annie peers over her sunglasses at the stove. "Yes it is. And Plato too."

"I can't seem to find the teachers' bathroom," calls Nancy.

"Einstein, what?" Les asks.

"To your right, Mom."

"Holly was just telling me about her mother, who's epileptic."

"Beau?" calls Jill. She needs him to start the barbeque.

"You sent him to his room, I think," says Les.

"She says swallowing one's tongue during a fit is an urban myth," continues Annie. "That it's not humanly possible."

"Can you put in the potatoes for me, please?" Jill asks Annie. "I need to find Beau."

"Sure, Jill. Is that something on the back of your dress?" Annie points. "Or am I just seeing things?" She barks out a laugh.

Hell, she forgot about changing her dress. "Yes, I, I sat in something. I'm going to change."

Down the hall Nancy is struggling with the locks on the front door. "That's not the bathroom, Mom," says Jill and guides Nancy to the right door, waits until she's safely inside and is about to say don't lock it *because sometimes the lock sticks* when she hears the doorknob turn and click. She goes to find Beau when he comes barrelling down the stairs.

"Whoa!" Jill takes an unsteady step backwards and thumps against the wall.

"I can't run in this chuba," complains Pema as she trots down after him.

"I need Beau on the barbeque. Barbeque Beau," Jill calls after him. "On the bob bob kabobs."

Pema laughs and so does Jill. "I'll tell him," says Pema, going after him.

Jill retraces her steps to the kitchen, needing to put the timer on for those potatoes. Reclined in his chair, Les's eyes are closed though she can't imagine he's really asleep, what with all this commotion. This locomotion. Loco, motion.

"What should I put the timer on for?" says Annie, standing at the stove.

"Thirty-five."

"Shall I get out the kabobs?"

"Yes, Beau's going to cook them." Jill absently picks up

and drinks from someone's wineglass, realizes what it is she's doing and puts it down. She heads to the bedroom to change and once there, tired and, she has to admit, more than a bit drunk, she eyes the bed longingly before steering herself to the closet. What to wear now? Loose beige silk pants and top; dressy looking but as comfortable as pajamas. Same shoes. So things aren't going quite as planned, are a little out of order, but that's all right. After dinner, with some food in her stomach to counter the wine, she'll get things back on track. Yes, she will. Will it so. There is no will, once dead. Despite the paperwork.

Dressed, she's making her way back to the kitchen when she hears a doorknob rattling.

"Hello? This door won't open." It's Nancy in the bathroom.

Jill lays her forehead against the door. "Where oh where are you, Kenneth? Mom was your job."

"Kenneth?" says Nancy.

Some minutes of poking the opened end of a paper clip into the doorknob and Jill gets the lock mechanism to release. She finds Nancy sitting primly on the closed toilet seat, her purse on her lap. She's wearing her skirt and slip, her shoes are off and her lavender-coloured blouse hangs from the hook on the back of the door. On the floor at her feet is a silver scatter of hundreds of paper clips. Jill looks at the bent paper clip in her hand and back to the floor, wonders what it all means.

"I tried to use my tickets to get out of here," says Nancy, with a defeated glance at her shoes.

Jill retrieves the blouse and asks her mom to put her arm into the sleeve.

"Use your tickets, he said," mumbles Nancy. Never one to cry or make a scene, Nancy breathes hard through her nose, clearly upset but trying not to show it.

Jill steers her mother's other hand into the other sleeve, eases the shirt up over her shoulders. "I'm sorry, Mom. Wish I knew what you're talking —" Jill's hand flies to her mouth. "Dad," she says and Nancy nods, her eyes filming over with what looks like relief and gratitude.

Jill's father, in his crudely funny way, referred to breasts as tickets. "Use your tickets," he used to joke when Nancy was on her way to buy a new appliance, tires for the car, insurance. That's why she undoes her shirt in front of the male nurses at the care facility, thinks Jill, her stomach dropping. Because she's so desperate to get out.

Jill feels her own tears rise and sniffs them back. Now's not the time, she reprimands herself and finishes buttoning Nancy's shirt. She has an impossibly sentimental moment of imagining them all under one roof again, she, Nancy and Kenneth with his new baby, sharing chores and taking care of each other. Their lives gone backwards. Or come full circle. The next second she realizes the idea's mental and that once again she's trying to save everyone.

"There's no need to use your tickets for anything," she says, feeling the need to address it. "Nobody takes those tickets any more." That doesn't sound right.

"Oh, I see," says Nancy as if she actually understands.

"I'm going to get you closer by, Mom," she says. "I promise." Even if I have to use my own damn tickets.

Nancy seems visibly to relax so Jill does too.

Jill helps her on with her shoes then starts to sweep up the paper clips. "What would you think about you, me and Kenneth living in the same city again. All close by. Wouldn't that be nice?"

"Who's Kenneth?" demands Nancy.

Since Jill seems to have disappeared, Annie has taken over dinner preparations. Nothing makes her more crazy-happy than being useful to this family of hers. She discovers tomatoes in the fridge beside the Greek salad, takes them out and starts chopping. Having a task to focus on helps to settle down the flying animals, the sunglasses only a partial deterrent. She puts the covered tray of naan bread in the oven with the potatoes, and when Pema offers to help, puts her in charge of hunting down Les's recipe for the salad dressing. She can't figure out what the bowls of chopped mango and scallion in the fridge could be for, nor the toasted pine nuts on the counter, and leaves those to Jill, wherever she is, then realizes she hasn't seen Kenneth in a long time. Maybe the two of them are off somewhere having a sister-brother spat, she thinks enviously.

Holly appears, stinking of cigarettes, and offers her services.

"Everybody's getting hungry," says Annie, thinking aloud. "Is that it?"

She gives her the bowl of tzatziki to take to the dining room along with a bottle of red wine. "Opener's over there." She points. "It should breathe, though I must admit I have no clue why."

"Oxygen neutralizes the acids and tannins, makes it smoother," says Holly, expertly screwing in the opener.

"You're a bucket of information, girl, are you not?" Annie says before realizing she's speaking to an alcoholic.

Holly giggles, expertly extracts the cork and exits to the dining room.

Was that wrong, to give an alcoholic a bottle of wine and an opener?

Quinn is leaning over the sideboard studying his grade nine science project when Holly swings into the room. "Hey."

"Did you make whatever that is?" she asks.

"Seismograph. Grade nine science fair. It worked too." He's startled to see the opened wine in her hand and can't not watch as the bottle is placed on the table.

She slips her hands onto his shoulders, gently kneads the muscles as she looks over his shoulder. "What's a seismograph again?"

"Measures earthquake activity."

"Right. How does it work?"

Jill arrives steering Nancy towards a seat, and his train of thought derails. Holly massages a little harder, asks her question again.

"This delicate arm," he says in a quiet voice, pointing and tapping, "suspended over this rotating paper, moves with any of the earth's movements."

"Cool. Owen would love it."

"Do you think?" says Quinn, not sure Owen wouldn't break it.

"Sit here, Mom, okay?" says Jill. "And just stay put. Dinner is about to be served."

"It's about time," mutters Nancy and places her purse in the centre of her plate.

"Mom, your purse," Jill says. "Not on the table."

Quinn catches Jill's eye but she seems to look right through him. Is he invisible to her now?

Nancy waves at Holly as if she's a waitress. "I'd like some coffee please," she says. "Black."

"Coming right up," says Holly with a laugh. She kisses Quinn's neck and goes out, just as Beau comes in with a platter of sizzling kabobs. The air fills with citrus and pepper.

"Ohhh," groans Jill. "I forgot to make the rice. Beau, bring that meat into the kitchen." She pulls him by the sleeve back through the swinging door and Quinn is left alone with Nancy.

"Hi Grammy," he says and can't stop himself from grabbing the bottle of wine by its neck and topping up his half-empty glass of pomegranate juice. Before he has a chance to put the bottle back down, Annie's bringing in a basket covered with a dishcloth.

"Sure, Grammy," says Quinn, too loudly, and pours wine into her wine glass.

Nancy narrows her eyes at him. "I ordered coffee."

"And Holly's getting you some of that too." He puts down the bottle and turns back to the sideboard and his seismograph, his face flushing with shame. Is his auntie looking at him? He waits for her to say something. Wants her to say something he can deny.

When Annie disappears back though the door, Quinn holds the glass under his nose, his heart racing with the excitement of a horse at the gate about to be thrown open, his thoughts obliterated, words standing no chance.

"I have a son," says Nancy, amiably. "He teaches baseball in China."

He'd forgotten she was here and smiles at her, but now she's looking out the window. He holds his glass to his mouth, tips it to wet his lips when she asks with an earnest smile, "Do you have children?"

He stops. This time she's looking right at him, expecting an answer. "I, well, Holly, my girlfriend, has a son."

"What's the boy's name?" asks Grammy, leaning towards him, all ears, her smile real.

"Owen."

"Owen."

And he thinks of picking up Owen tomorrow night from Holly's mom's place. How once they get home, Owen will pretend to be asleep so that Quinn will be forced to carry him from the car and up into his bed. The boy's resolute arms will wrap Quinn's neck, his head burrowed under Quinn's chin and he'll smell clean in the way dirt smells clean. Quinn will smell a child's hair, as all parents have, for millennia, the smell of bringing your child home to your cave. Imagine if your home was a hole in the side of a mountain. A building shaped by tectonic plates to keep us safe.

Quinn sets his glass on the table beside his place card. He'll have it there, just in case. Then pictures Holly seeing it, knowing it, the silent burst of fear in her eyes before that shared moment of complicity. And then her hapless willingness to follow him into sweet, dim oblivion. A warm double suicide. Which leaves Owen where? They'd talked about this. Maybe some of the first honest words of his life were some of the words he'd spoken to Holly.

"Excuse me, Grammy," he says and picks up his glass again. Forcing his attention on each foot as it contacts the floor, he makes his way to the front door and, after one last inhale, dumps the mixture outside in the hedge. Feels like he's pouring his own blood out and thinks he might faint.

Jill pulls from the fridge the chopped mango and scallion intended for the rice and dumps them over Beau's platter of meat. "Garnish. Voila," she says and spins on her heel to take the bowl to the sink.

"I was wondering what those were for," says Annie.

"Actually, they were for the rice, which I forgot to make." Jill throws up her hands.

"And these pine nuts?" asks Annie.

"Also for the nonexistent rice." She picks up the bowl and stands there, unable to think.

"How about in the salad?" Annie points.

"Why not?" Jill dumps them unceremoniously in the salad Pema's about to take out. Then Jill grabs Pema's arm. What else has she forgotten? She should put on some more music but that's not it.

"Pema dressed it," says Annie. "Les's recipe."

"That's what I was groping for." Jill shapes her hand like a gun, rolls her eyes up to heaven and shoots herself in the head.

Jill sure seems more relaxed than when I left, thinks Pema taking the salad to the dining room. Could she possibly live in this house again and go to school? Would Jill even want her here?

Quinn and Beau are standing together in front of the sideboard. Brain and Brawn, she thinks, smiling. God, Beau pisses her off, yet still she can't help adoring the selfish imp. Whatever goes on in Quinn's head is still a mystery, and she suspects it always will be. Holly, who doesn't seem to have a secretive bone in her body, is probably good for him. Out on the patio, she was telling Pema, a virtual stranger, about the time she got so drunk she passed out in the bathtub and came to underwater. And the naked way she talks, unblinking, looking straight at you, arms loose by her sides, makes you want to wrap a blanket around her. And yourself. Some people live more life than others do.

If she came back here to stay, would she keep living life?

Pema sets the salad on the table and sees the place cards. "I made these," she says in surprise.

"But do you remember this brilliant moveable staircase?" Beau steps back to reveal their Hogwarts diorama.

"Of course I remember." She comes and stands shoulder to shoulder with him and feels him stiffen. Really she can't blame him for wanting to keep his distance considering how she used to boss him when they were young in order to get what she wanted. She was a bit of a puppet master and could get him to do anything for her. Was trying to show him in her letters that she'd changed, but he probably saw them as more of the same.

"I think these paper fastener things, that made the stairs swivel, were my idea," she says.

"What?" says Beau. "I thought of those."

"Did not." She elbows him in the ribs and he grabs her, wrestles her back against his chest, his breath a little off and too close to her ear. "Let me go," she laughs.

"Excuse me?" says Quinn. "The brass clips were my idea."

"Oh yeah," they say together and Beau lets her go.

Jill swings in for a last-minute check of the table and is about to go and wake Les, tell him it's dinnertime, when he's suddenly standing in the doorway steadied on Holly's arm. Holly manoeuvres him and his tubing with seeming ease into the seat at the head of the table and adjusts the chair's pillow for his back. The tubing, Jill knows, isn't long enough to reach from the oxygen tank in the bedroom all the way to the dining room. Which means Holly must have gone in and moved that unwieldy tank into the hall.

"Hired," mumbles Jill and sits down heavily in her chair at the other end of the table. "And thank you," she says to her marvel of a chair. "So nice to sit down. Chair is such a perfect sound, don't you think?" she says to no one in particular. "That thanks you feel when you sit in one. Chair."

"Did you say something, Mom?" asks Quinn, and she dismisses the question with a flip of her hand.

"Is it someone's birthday?" says Nancy as the rest of the family hunt for their designated seats.

"It's someone's Living Wake day," says Jill. "Liv-ing Wake.

Blunt assertive phenomes. Life Celebration. Nicer. A gentle downhill rhythm." She raises her hand and dives it downward towards the open bottle of wine. Fills her glass first then holds the bottle over Pema's.

"Sure. Thanks," says Pema, taking her customary seat beside Beau and across from Quinn. Jill fills Pema's glass nearly to the brim.

"Oops," says Jill and Pema wonders if her adoptive mother has actually changed or is just sauced.

"You made these place cards for my ninth birthday," says Beau.

"Your tenth," says Pema.

Beau reads his acrostic poem aloud, "Best Boy, Eats a lot, Awesome, Ugly not."

"It was your birthday," says Pema. "I had to lie."

"Please pass the shish kabob," says Nancy.

"Artistic," reads Annie, blinking in the light, having slipped her sunglasses to the top of her bald head. "Neat, as in cool, Never lies, Ingenious, Energetic. You're too kind,"

"Yours is true," says Pema.

A group of tiny, sleek black birds appear to jet over Annie's plate and disappear into the kitchen. "Whoopee," she says and lowers the glasses back into place.

"Quinn, this is such a cute Father's Day card you made," says Holly. "With all the pockets?"

"There's a message in each pocket," says Quinn. "Or there used to be."

She fishes in a pocket, brings out a tiny paper package and begins to unfold it.

"That's insane how much you folded that paper," says Beau as the process goes on and on.

As the plate of shish kabob is passed to Nancy, she takes one in two hands and begins to eat it like it's corn on the cob.

"Mom," whispers Jill. "Wait, please."

Nancy intentionally ignores her and Jill decides she must be awfully hungry and lets it go.

"I love my dad because he makes the best French toast," Holly reads.

"The others don't get any more profound," says Quinn. Holly's eyes widen and she whispers to him that she forgot to call Owen as she'd promised.

"That card was my favourite," Les says and Holly passes it to him before excusing herself. He is beyond caring if he is allowed to say such a thing, with other cards, and other kids, gathered so close.

"You did make the best French toast," says Pema.

He winks at her. He always hated winkers but talking is now difficult. "Vanilla, pinch of nutmeg, cream not milk." Maybe tomorrow he'll have the energy to make some. The batter at least.

Beau points at the empty place. "Where's Uncle Kenneth?"

"Your uncle," says Jill and sips her wine, "had the urge to go for a scenic drive and should be back soon."

Les watches his family pass dishes, read place cards and birthday coupons in a fuzzy overlap of conversation. These faces, as familiar to him as his own, at this table, in these seats, with the evening sun throwing its airy pink light against the walls, feels oddly like permanence. And, at the same time, as temporary as a breeze. Interesting that it can be both.

Beau holds the wine bottle over Quinn's glass. "Wine?"

"Beau," scolds Pema.

"Just kidding," says Beau, though his instinct, as always, is that Quinn needs toughening up. "Thought I'd go to the gym tomorrow. You want to come?"

Quinn can't tell if he's still kidding, gives him a quizzical look and doesn't respond.

"Pass the pita or whatever it's called," says Jill, pointing to the basket of bread.

"Naan bread," says Pema, surprised to be correcting this mother's English.

When Holly returns and everyone has food on their plate, Les clears his throat. "I'd like to say grace."

"What?" Beau and Pema say in unison, look at each other and smirk.

"You never once said grace in our entire lives," says Quinn.

"Getting closer to grace every day. Hedging my bets."

"God is great, God is neat, Good God let's eat," says Nancy as bits of meat spray between mouth and plate.

Jill sputters with laughter and Nancy beams proudly at her.

"Someone once said," continues Les, "that love only exists when it is given."

As Quinn listens to his father, he imagines him being strong and healthy, at home in his body again.

"Because of all of you" – Les pauses to take a breath in – "I've had the unbelievable gift of being able truly to love. Therefore," he says and his voice slides up an octave, "my life feels complete." He taps his heart and swallows hard and Quinn receives his small, wounded smile.

As Les raises his glass, Quinn gropes for Holly's hand under the table and Beau realizes he has no clue what love is.

Overcome with a love for everyone here and not here, Pema suddenly misses her other family so much it's as though she's being ripped in half.

"Here's to love," says Annie, tears streaming behind her sunglasses. She leans so far to one side to clink her glass with Beau's that she smacks her ear hard against his shoulder.

"Ow," she says half laughing, half crying.

"My bad shoulder apologizes," Beau whispers, clinks his glass to hers.

As the sound of crystal rings through the air, Jill catches Les's eye.

"We did this," she calls out, looking from one side of the table to the other to indicate these kids, this family, this moment. When Jill and Les raise their glasses to each other, the rest of the family are unsure if they should join the toast. "Where did the time go?" Jill says, though she didn't mean to speak her thought aloud. Les snaps his fingers, a single loud snap. Thank you he mouths, though she thinks he's merely licked his lips and doesn't catch it.

"Uncle Kenneth," says Pema.

Through the dining-room window, Kenneth's car can be seen pulling up in the driveway.

"Good timing," says Holly returning to her seat.

"Ohhh," sighs Jill, shaking her head.

"Nice job on the meat," Les compliments Beau, though he can tell by the crimped edges that it's overcooked.

Pema slides her lamb chunks from the skewer and sneaks one onto Beau's plate, not wanting to explain the karmic logic of why she'll eat cow or yak meat but no longer eats small animals. Four more pieces to go.

Rubbing his hands together, a sheepish Kenneth comes into the dining room. "Smells good. Sorry. Got a little lost."

"And we're going to help you find your way back," says Jill. "Come sit, you poor man." She points at his forehead. "You got any change in there?"

Pema whispers to Beau. "Is she drunk?"

"Magic pennies," says Nancy with a satisfied nod.

Jill laughs a sloppy laugh. "Yes. You remember that, Kenneth?"

"I do." Kenneth doesn't smile. Food is passed his way and Jill wants to remind him about their father calling breasts tickets before her thoughts veer elsewhere. "I'd like to makeanannouncement," says Jill, words running together.

"She drunk?" Holly whispers to Quinn who's staring at his mother as if he's never seen her before. He shrugs, unsure.

"My big baby brother," says Jill, "my personal hero, Kenneth, is going to be a daddy."

Congratulations erupt quietly around the table. Kenneth nods his thanks and looks sideways at Jill. "Yes, Kimmie is four months pregnant," he says, sliding potatoes onto his plate. "I'll be mistaken for the kid's granddad, but better late than never."

"And I'm sorry for not being sympathetic about your dilemma with the bird." Jill waggles her fingers in the air.

Kenneth keeps his eyes on his plate.

"It's a messy-mess but I'm going to help you do whatever it takes to —"

"Jillian!" Nancy scolds in her teacher's voice. "That boy's lost his bird. Now leave him be."

Jill dips and shudders with laughter and Kenneth looks at Nancy surprised and pleased that she remembers.

Les laughs dryly, which starts him coughing, and Holly quickly passes him his water.

"Anyway, I wanna thank y'all for coming," Jill continues despite Nancy's shushing beside her. "So far away. This is our dear dear family and oh, I want you, Pema, to know that I 'clude your other mom and all Tibetan peoples in that family." Jill reaches for her glass and knocks it flat, wine staining the white tablecloth an alarming red. "Fffuck."

There's an audible inhale of disbelief.

"Too much wine," says Les, and asks a grinning Quinn to pass Jill's glass down to him.

Doing his best not to laugh, Quinn hands his mother's glass down the table as Nancy picks up the shish kabob on Jill's plate and holds it to Jill's mouth. "Open your mouth, little bird," she sings, "your food wants in, wants in, wants in."

Quinn smothers a fresh wave of laugher in his napkin and a moment later is bent clear over the table to hide his streaming eyes. Holly smiles and shrugs as she rubs his jumping back.

"Quinn's lost it," says Beau.

"Best keep it lost," says Annie.

Quinn pops upright, startling Holly, and his laughter bursts out, uncontrollable and loud, a cascade of obscenely merry notes. He laughs like a stranger, like a different species, capable of anything. Everyone can't help but join in except for Nancy and Jill as Nancy concentrates on coaxing food into her daughter's resistant mouth.

The rest of the meal is eaten in near silence. Quinn helps Les cut his meat into smaller pieces. A quiet conversation passes between Annie and Kenneth about Japanese food and another between Pema and Beau when he realizes she's been slipping meat from her plate onto his. Without a word, Jill gets up and weaves her way into the family room to lie down.

"I don't think I've ever seen her drunk before," says Beau.

"It's been about twenty years for me," says Les. "Taking care of this" – he lays his palms on his chest – "must finally be getting to her."

"She needs more help," says Annie as if it's a no-brainer. "I'm coming every day."

"She'll need help." Les nods weakly and takes Annie's hand as she starts to cry behind her glasses.

Everyone clears the table. Holly and Pema put away the leftover food but the washing of dishes is abandoned with the promise that Quinn and Beau will do them later. Without being told, people migrate into the family room where Jill is crashed out cold in the recliner beside Les's.

Pema points to the mismatched packages on the hearth and reminds Les that he hasn't yet opened his gifts.

"Okay," says Les, trying to sound enthusiastic despite a sudden crushing fatigue. What he'd prefer is to recline in his chair and join Jill in dreamland.

Beau offers his gifts first. "They're not exactly wrapped," he says, handing over the bag that bears the logo of the de Gaulle airport.

"A waste of trees, wrapping," says Les, his voice gone scratchy, and reaches into the bag to pull out a bottle of champagne. "The real deal," says Les, reading the label and guessing that Beau, who never was good at gift buying, would have settled for expensive.

"From Champagne."

Les looks to Jill beside him, expecting her to retell the story about the time they had real champagne at an inn in Toulon. It was at that same meal that, having misunderstood the waiter's explanation, she'd ordered the house special and ended up with a steaming plate of pig intestines. Her eyes, however, remain closed.

Quinn raises his phone and takes his parents' picture, more as an excuse to record the event of his mother being drunk and passed out. Seeing her drunk has completely cured him of needing a drink, for tonight at least, and the picture might be a handy deterrent in the future, you never know. He does know exactly how she's going to feel tomorrow. Wants to slip her some aspirin and a couple of glasses of water.

"I'll share," says Les and holds up a box of hand-dipped chocolates which Pema offers to pass around. The last of Beau's gifts is a tin of duck pâté.

"Some give credit to Italy for teaching the French how to cook," says Kenneth.

Les nods. "Italians taught them sauces. But instead of olive oil, the French have a secret weapon."

"Duck fat," says Beau.

"Duck fat," says Les.

"When I was in Paris even the most tawdry of restaurants had better grub than most of the fancy restaurants here," says Kenneth. "Or maybe it's the wine that makes everything taste so good."

"Duck fat," repeats Les.

The pâté is also passed around and when it reaches Nancy, she slips the tin into her purse. Kenneth, beside her on the couch, leans over and whispers, "Mom, did you just steal Les's pâté?"

Nancy brushes the air around her ear as if at an annoying bug, and he decides to leave it until later.

Les opens Pema's gift next: an amulet made from silver and lapis lazuli.

"The stone's supposed to have healing properties," she says, hoping she doesn't sound too trippy or like she's offering some kind of miracle cure. "Lapis lazuli means azure or blue and translates as heaven." She tells them she had it blessed by the Dalai Lama. "When I went through the blessing line, I lifted my head, which you're not supposed to do, and asked him, I mean I told him about your illness. He touched the stone to his forehead then his lips then his throat while repeating, "May all beings be at ease, may all beings feel safe."

"That's my favourite prayer," says Les. "And it's not just

because I don't know any others."

"Beautiful," says Annie, teary again. "I love that man."

"Can you say that prayer in Tibetan?" asks Quinn.

"Nge rewa la drowa minam dechi dang kar serme peigui dedrup part shok."

"Jesus, I could hear caves in that," says Kenneth.

Trusting no one will know if his French is exactly right, Beau says, "Que tout etre soil a l'aise, que tout etre se sente end securite."

"It's not a competition," says Quinn.

Beau doesn't look at his brother but thinks he hears a hint of jealousy.

The next gift is from Quinn. It's the size of a shoebox and wrapped meticulously in plaid paper and green ribbon. When Les picks it up, it makes a sloshing sound. "More fish for my tank?" he says, tearing off the paper.

"Mom said symbolic." Quinn's cheeks redden as he bites on his lip.

Les opens the box and lifts out a half-drunk bottle of Canadian Club. The room goes quiet.

Les holds the bottle in front of his face, as if waiting for the sloshing to stop completely. "Couldn't be more proud of you," he says.

"Here, here." Annie has to remove her glasses this time, in order to wipe her eyes which are now unattractively red and swollen.

"I'll drink to that," says Beau, lifting his beer, and Pema gives him a shove.

"I'll have some, please." Nancy extends her coffee cup towards the bottle.

There's scattered laughter as Les unscrews the top and tips a little into her coffee cup. "Strong, Nance."

She sips and makes a pained face before looking incredulously at Les.

"You were warned, Mom," says Kenneth taking the cup away.

"I think it's music time," announces Annie with forced cheer and, hands dancing, she jumps up from her seat. "Quinn, is the computer hooked up to the TV?"

"Auntie Annie, why *are* you wearing sunglasses inside?" asks Beau.

"'Cause I can't stop fucking crying, alright?"

Jill sleeps through the viewing of Les's frowning baby pictures, the gap-toothed five-year-old with a bullfrog balanced on his head, the giddy eight-year-old squeezing a just-caught salmon to his chest. All of which are accompanied by the Chordettes' "Mister Sandman," a song nobody recognizes except Nancy who hums and sings, "Hmm...hmm...Poliatschi...hmm... hmm...Liberace."

"God, memory's a strange animal," mutters Kenneth.

"Funny what sticks," says Annie.

"I think," says Beau and glances at Quinn daring him to contradict, "our brain contains everything that's ever happened to us and it only takes the right trigger or code to unlock any memory."

"Smell is supposed to be a stronger trigger than sight even," says Quinn and Beau's shoulders relax.

Language is a huge trigger, thinks Pema, remembering that day during the first monsoon when she suddenly understood everything people were saying and how her senses of smell, sight, sound and touch blossomed outward as if the sensory memories of herself as a three-year-old came rushing back. How even her posture seemed to make a shift. She looks at Jill who's probably read about such things and wants to tell her about it.

The high school basketball pictures with the short shorts and the shaggy-haired prom pictures of Les in a white tuxedo are set to the Temptations' "Pappa was a Rollin' Stone." When Pema turns the music up, Nancy rips up a napkin and sticks it into her ears while Jill sleeps on and Annie and Holly rise to dance with Pema. Pema tries not to look too closely at Holly as she makes these goofy little sideways hops while circling her bum in the air.

Debby Boone sings "You Light up My Life" alongside the picture of the college dropout mugging in front of a cooking school in Turin, while Annie tells them this was the year she and Les met. Though everyone but Holly has heard the story more than once, she goes on to describe their first encounter in the airport.

Jill snores softly throughout the photos of her and Les's wedding and Wham!'s "Wake Me up Before You Go-Go." Kenneth points ironically at his sleeping sister while Pema and Holly get up to dance again, pulling a reluctant Quinn off the arm of the couch. He takes Holly around the waist and dances holding on because no way is he going to let Beau watch him dance.

"Mom looks so pretty," says Pema, wistful. "I want a veil when I get married."

"If you get married," says Beau, earning another slug.

"I made her veil and that dress," says Annie. "Pieced together from two wedding gowns I bargained for at the Salvation Army. Your mom wanted a short skirt so I attached a train to the waist and let it just sweep the floor."

"Her tail," says Les.

"That's what you kept calling it," laughs Annie, swatting at a shimmery half moon in front of her right eye. Migraine aura? "There were some really bad jokes going around."

"When I get married," Pema says pointedly while looking at Beau, "I'd like to mix a classic wedding dress with a chuba." She turns to Annie. "Could you make something like that?"

"Do birds shit while they fly?"

Nancy frowns at the language and opens her purse to peer inside.

"Separate Lives" by Phil Collins and Marilyn Martin accompanies Quinn's baby pictures.

"Kid was born with a perfect mohawk," croaks Les and can't help wonder what portentously silly song will top the charts on the day he dies.

The slide show over, Holly heads outside for a smoke and Beau follows, challenging Quinn to a game of ping pong. "You enjoy humiliating yourself, don't you?" says Quinn.

"I'm watching this," Pema says.

With what's left of his voice, Les tells Annie that there's a cake in the freezer looking for meringue. "We were doing an Alaska bombe. With triple sec. My cooking partner has skipped out on me." He reaches over to stroke Jill's arm.

"Oh, so that's what the eggs on the counter are for. Don't worry," Annie says, "I've whipped up many a meringue in my day."

"I know everything about meringue," says a defiant Nancy.

"Thank God, 'cause I was lying through my teeth," says Annie and she offers Nancy a hand up off the couch.

Les reclines the chair, shuts his eyes, only half listens to Kenneth talk about an American conspiracy behind the Toyota recall scandal. "It was just a pack of lies to help Detroit back on its feet. Poor Japanese had no choice but to apologize and pump zillions into ads."

Nancy insists on wearing an apron — a thing she expertly

mimes tying behind her waist — and Annie finds the one she once made for Les that incorporates old plasticized menus. Suited up and with her purse over her arm, Nancy instructs Annie how to crack the eggs on the counter and not against the side of the bowl. When the whites and yolks are separated, Nancy mysteriously places the bowl of yolks on the floor.

"Kenneth," Annie calls over to the family room, "when you were growing up did you have a dog or cat?"

"Nope and nope."

Annie beats the whites with the electric mixer while Nancy slowly adds the sugar and cream of tartar stopping Annie every ten seconds to have a look and a touch before gesturing with a karate chop to begin again. When the eggs are ready to Nancy's specifications, Annie lets her do the honours of spreading the meringue over the cake-encased ice cream. The cake is only half covered when Nancy licks the knife, places it in her purse and returns to the family room.

"Your mother just put a knife in her purse," Annie says to Kenneth.

"It's for the pâté," he calls back.

Annie finishes up and puts the cake in the oven. She watches it through the oven window and gives Nancy, who's sitting back in the family room, a continuous report on the colour of the peaks. When she says, "Starting to brown," Nancy calls out, "Now!"

"Les asks are the tips toasted," calls Kenneth.

"Just toasted," says Annie, carefully setting the masterpiece on the counter.

"Dusting of dirt on the snowy mountain asks Les," Kennth adds.

"We did it," says Nancy.

Pema enters from the back yard.

"I bet you've always been a good cook, Nancy," says Annie. "Very good."

"She makes the best gingerbread in the world," says Pema.

"In the world," says Nancy.

The sun has gone down when the Alaska bombe is positioned on a TV tray in front of Les, along with a demitasse, a bottle of triple sec and the tall box of fireplace matches. The picture windows now reflect the objects and people and light inside as though all that exists in the world is contained in this small heartfelt space.

"A lady's in my chair," says Nancy from her seat on the couch.

"The lady's not feeling well," says Quinn as they both look at Jill, whose arms are crossed over her chest and whose mouth hangs open to the point where her tongue shows. He takes another picture, feels badly about this and deletes it.

Nancy huffs. "I want to sit in front of the birthday cake."

"The wake cake," whispers Les, and Holly hears him and laughs. "Nancy can sit on my walker," he says to Holly. "It has a seat."

As Nancy is settled in front of the Alaska bombe, the others gather on either side of her to form a half-circle in front of Les and Jill.

"We have to turn off the lights," says Beau.

"Wait," whispers Les. He wedges the demitasse into the top of the cake, removes the top from the bottle. His hand shaking, he pours booze into the cup until it overflows its rim and meanders in rivulets down the cake's sides, pooling around the rim of the plate.

"More," urges Beau and Les gives the cake another dowsing.

"I love the smell of booze," says Quinn with a fat sigh and

Pema smiles sadly at the floor.

This evening could have been grim, thinks Les, screwing the top back on, but it isn't. It's good. He'll remember to thank Jill later. He'll thank her slowly and he'll thank her twice. "The lights now," he says, pointing with his chin.

"What's the difference between this and baked Alaska?" asks Kenneth.

"Not much," says Quinn.

"How it burns," says Les. He slides a match from the box.

Beau switches off the overhead light in the kitchen and Annie turns off the lamp behind Les's chair. Only six of the eight candles still burn on the mantel.

"Shouldn't we wake Mom?" Beau says. Everyone looks at Jill.

Les gives her arm a few pats. "Jill?" He tries again. "Here in spirit. She worked hard to make this day happen and deserves her sleep."

"Let's make it all dark," says Pema.

Holly helps her blow out the candles. When a street light becomes apparent, Kenneth draws the shade. The room goes black and slowly their eyes adjust to the meagre light that sifts through the windows from vague sources.

A wave of vertigo shifts the ground under Les's chair and he rides out the accompanying nausea.

Annie can't see a thing and removes her glasses.

"Good night," says Nancy.

"Huddle," says Beau, stepping in closer to the cake. He puts his arm around Pema's shoulder, because he can, and everyone follows suit.

"Drum roll," says Kenneth. He stamps his feet, running in place.

They follow his lead and the low rumbles fill the room.

Nancy looks at Annie then lifts a foot, shakes it in the air while Jill groans and rolls over to face Les but doesn't open her eyes.

Les strikes the long match, once, twice and feeling the room's concern, gives a push of effort for a third time and it sizzles into being. A single transfixing light that shifts to a gentle quality as it begins to burn wood. Raising the match reveals his family, a ring of bright spirits looming over, surrounding him here in the valley of his life. A fine valley it is. He draws down a slow line of flame and whispers, "Three, two, one."

"Happy birthday to you," Nancy begins to sing in a small, clear voice.

A single whoosh and the liquor in the cup erupts with fire. Nancy's singing stops.

"Whoa," says Annie in a low voice.

Les secures his hand over Jill's.

In the hushed quiet, Jill opens her eyes in time to see the blue-and gold-tipped flames roil and rise from the peak of the cake and cascade down its sides like clear and weightless lava. A ragged flame races around the rim of the plate, chasing the circle closed. For a long moment, the tiny mountain dances with light.

Acknowledgements

....

I'm extremely indebted to my early readers – Joan McLeod, Bill Gaston, LFC's Eve Joseph, Janice McCachen, Jennifer Frazer, Carol Matthews, Lucy Bashford and Patricia Young. I'd like to extend a special thanks to Jampa Gyaltsen for sharing his stories of escaping Tibet and of being a refugee.

Thanks to everyone at Coteau for making this book happen, especially Nik Burton for his sustaining influence and his Nik Burtoness, and my editor Sandra Birdsell for her keen insight, her frankness and all-round brilliance.

The writing of this book was made possible by a B.C. Arts Grant. The first and third chapters of the book were first published in slightly altered forms in the *Malahat Review* and the *Fiddlehead* respectively.

About the Author

Every Happy Family is Dede's second publication with Coteau Books, following the acclaimed short story collection *The Cult of Quick Repair* in 2008. A two-time finalist for the city of Victoria's Butler Book Prize, Dede is the author of the novel *Sympathy* and two YA novels, and was a co-editor of the collection *Great Expectations: Twenty Four True Stories about Childbirth*. Her first published story was short-listed for the CBC Literary Awards; her stories have been published in numerous literary journals.

A former professional ballet dancer and choreographer, Dede Crane has studied Buddhist psychology and psychokinetics at Naropa Institute in Colorado and the Body-Mind Institute in Amherst, Massachusetts, respectively. She currently calls Victoria, B.C., home.